"… a thriller that opens along the lines of Robin Cook; but with more social and psychological issues, which are explored in greater, more satisfying detail.

…. a strong, compelling, multifaceted read that's perfect for those who like their stories unpredictable and thoroughly engrossing. In the End, what matters isn't an individual life alone, but the entwined lives of millions and how they lived, loved, and finally, let go."

—D. Donovan,
Senior Reviewer, Midwest Book Review

"Against a backdrop of an impending catastrophe, five individuals of varying backgrounds, faiths, ethnicities and financial means come together during a complex and difficult medical procedure.

All five have experienced setback, tragedy, accomplishment during their lives.

All are challenged with the meanings of their lives. Is religion the answer? Is there an afterlife? Why are we even here?

Transcending faith and human frailty, In the End offers a message of hope and unification in an era of despair and divisiveness.

This novel will keep you thinking for days after you finish it. And that is the mark of a memorable and worthy read."

—Doug Ross, author
of *Hard-Boiled*

"All writers write from what they know. Even science fiction writers are no different. Instead of writing only about what they know for certain, they take what they know today and project where this knowledge might put them tomorrow—even into 2,000 years of tomorrows. Weisberg takes a daring leap here, and invites you to take it with him. Accept that invitation, read the final chapters of this book with the wide-open eyes of imagination, and perhaps you'll agree that this could be one answer to defining the meaning of life."

—Harriet Gross,
Columnist, *Texas Jewish Post*

IN THE END

A MODERN NOVEL OF FINDING THE MEANING TO LIFE

A NOVEL BY
MICHAEL F. WEISBERG, M.D.

gatekeeper press
Where Authors are Family

This book is a work of fiction. The names, characters and events in this book are the products of the author's imagination or are used fictitiously. Any similarity to real persons living or dead is coincidental and not intended by the author.

In the End

Published by Gatekeeper Press
2167 Stringtown Rd, Suite 109
Columbus, OH 43123-2989
www.GatekeeperPress.com

ISBN (hardcover): 9781642374544
ISBN (paperback): 9781642374537
eISBN: 9781642374520

Printed in the United States of America

This book is dedicated to my cousin, Seth Weisberg, in appreciation for his meticulous yet gentle editing of the book. I also want to thank Seth for teaching me how to ride a bicycle when we were children. Seth, your intelligence and wit have made the journey through life much more enjoyable and rewarding for me.

BOOK ONE
IN THE BEGINNING

IN THE BEGINNING GOD CREATED THE HEAVEN AND THE EARTH. AND THE EARTH WAS WITHOUT FORM AND VOID, AND DARKNESS WAS UPON THE FACE OF THE DEEP; AND THE SPIRIT OF GOD WAS WAVING OVER THE FACE OF THE WATERS.

AND GOD SAID, LET THERE BE LIGHT; AND THERE WAS LIGHT. AND GOD SAW THE LIGHT THAT IT WAS GOOD; AND GOD DIVIDED BETWEEN THE LIGHT AND THE DARKNESS. AND GOD CALLED THE LIGHT DAY AND THE DARKNESS HE CALLED NIGHT. AND IT WAS EVENING, AND IT WAS MORNING, THE FIRST DAY...

AND GOD MADE THE BEASTS OF THE EARTH AFTER THEIR KIND, AND EVERY THING THAT CREEPETH UPON THE EARTH AFTER ITS KIND: AND GOD SAW THAT IT WAS GOOD...

AND GOD SAID, LET US MAKE MAN IN OUR IMAGE, AFTER OUR LIKENESS; AND THEY SHALL HAVE DOMINION OVER THE FISH OF THE SEA, AND OVER THE FOWL OF THE HEAVEN, AND OVER THE CATTLE AND OVER ALL THE EARTH, AND OVER EVERY CREEPING THING THAT CREEPETH UPON THE EARTH. AND GOD CREATED MAN IN HIS IMAGE, IN THE IMAGE OF GOD CREATED HE HIM; MALE AND FEMALE CREATED HE THEM. AND GOD BLESSED THEM, AND GOD SAID UNTO THEM, BE FRUITFUL AND MULTIPLY AND FILL THE EARTH, AND SUBDUE IT; AND HAVE DOMINION OVER THE FISH OF THE SEA, AND OVER THE FOWL OF THE HEAVEN, AND OVER EVERY LIVING THING THAT MOVETH UPON THE EARTH...

AND GOD SAW EVERY THING THAT HE HAD MADE, AND BEHOLD, IT WAS VERY GOOD.

EXCERPTED FROM THE FIVE BOOKS OF MOSES

PRESENTED BY THE NEW HEBREW
SCHOOL OF BROOKLYN

TO FRED WEISBERG AT HIS BAR MITZVAH
NOVEMBER 5, 1938

"I CALL HEAVEN AND EARTH TO WITNESS YOU TODAY; I HAVE PUT BEFORE YOU LIFE AND DEATH, BLESSING AND CURSE—THEREFORE CHOOSE LIFE!

—(Deuteronomy 30:19)

CHAPTER ONE

The dream was all too familiar and all too real. Gabriel's deep subconscious was signaling that it wasn't real, it couldn't be happening again. But yes, yes it was; though terrifying and troubling and anxiety-provoking it was too good not to be real. It was Ray and he was alive again. The setting: the monstrous downstairs family room of their house. The floors laid with antique wood imported from France covered by an enormous plush rug of yellow, red, and lilac roses. The drapes, adorned with white lilies floating in a sea of mauve, were closed, with the sunlight blocked out, rendering the room almost dark.

When he tried to speak, Gabriel could only stammer. "What about your future, Ray? Why take time off now? If you're going to medical school, go! Why wait?"

The sides of Ray's mouth curled upwards and dimples settled into both cheeks. He spoke calmly. "Dad, there's plenty of time for medical school, for being a doctor like you, for life. Please don't rush me." He smiled confidently and showed dazzling white teeth.

Suddenly Gabriel felt despair; he was keenly aware of the sweat covering his face. He fought the urge to end the dream and glanced wildly around the family room. The door to the patio was open, and the sounds of splashing in the pool drifted in. Their white Havanese dog, Ricky, lay by the door, sleeping motionless in the sun. A paw wavered upward without direction and fell silently to cover his face. The oversized couches on the porch seemed tired and worn by the sun.

Gabriel shouted, "But Ray, don't leave. Don't go to New York for that girl!"

"Dad, I'll work in New York for a couple of years and then maybe apply to medical school. We'll see how things go. Carol is a wonderful, wonderful woman and I want to be with her. And besides, I'm twenty-two. I just graduated from Harvard, the greatest college known to man. It's my time, Dad."

Ray rose from his seat on the couch and walked over to the tall armoire at one end of the room. The armoire was made from dark pine with delicate inlays of a dense forest scene in which the trees were devoid of leaves and appeared to be dying. The door on the right had a keyhole with an antique key twisted in place. In the muted morning light, the entire piece of furniture appeared darker, almost black. Gabriel looked again; the armoire had turned over on its side and was now a rectangular box of pine wood—a coffin.

"No, no, no, not now," Gabriel screamed as Ray opened the coffin lid and placed one leg inside.

Ray smiled. "It's time, Dad, it's my time."

"Dallas, Texas, it's five thirty and it's time—time to get up. It's another hot September day with highs expected into the nineties."

Gabriel rolled over in the king-sized bed and turned off the radio. He wiped the sweat off his face with his pillow. He glanced around the bedroom, his eyes adjusting to the darkness. No, no Ray and no wife. Sarah was in New York spending Rosh Hashanah, the Jewish New Year, with her family. Gabriel had been invited, but he'd decided to work on Rosh Hashanah and Yom Kippur rather than observing them in synagogue. Since Ray's death he'd been angry at God and questioning God's existence. Therefore, rather than celebrating the Jewish high holidays, he would work.

Gabriel showered quickly and then shaved. He examined his fifty-eight-year old face in the mirror. The beard stubble was more parts gray than black, as were the remnants of hair on his scalp. Two years before, when Ray went bald from chemotherapy, he'd shaved his head and the hair came back in haphazardly. There was a tuft of black hair flecked with gray in the front, an area of baldness for two to three inches behind it, and then thin, graying hair applied unevenly to the rest of the head. On the crown of his head, he was bald. Sarah had suggested hair implants to even out the look, but Gabriel refused. The hair made him look older and he certainly felt older. He felt no need to improve his appearance.

He dressed in a pair of dark blue scrubs and tennis shoes and stumbled down the long hallway separating the upstairs bedrooms. He and Ray had nicknamed the hall "Ray's Gallery" because it contained gold-framed photographs of Ray from birth until age twenty-two. Here the boy was in a white sailor suit with a blue anchor adorning the chest, holding a tiny sailboat; there he was with a quarter-sized violin held close against his tiny chin with the bow at ready. At the end of the hallway was a picture of Ray in his Harvard football uniform, a football tucked securely against his body by his powerful right arm, eyes locked to the left looking for an opening to run.

Ricky barked his welcome as Gabriel turned on the kitchen lights. Gabriel opened the door and Ricky ran outside. Gabriel opened the cabinet containing his medication box. He hadn't thrown any medications out, and still had the bottles of Paxil, the anti-depressant, and Xanax, the anti-anxiety medication, neither of which he had taken in over six months.

When Ray was diagnosed with colon cancer, Gabriel fell into a deep depression. He wanted to be strong for

Ray and comforting to his wife but looking back he knew he'd been neither. The time between Ray's diagnosis and death had been almost a year, a time clouded in darkness in Gabriel's memory. He remembered crying and crying when left alone while Sarah took Ray for his chemotherapy. He remembered the long weekends when he lay awake in bed until two or three in the afternoon until Sarah insisted he get dressed and join them. Then Gabriel would sit around the house, trying to engage his wife and son in conversation. No motivation, no energy, no purpose. He had to be an actor; he wanted to do nothing and be nothing. After Ray moved back into the house three months before his death, Gabriel had to take on the persona of a living human being. To do so, he needed Paxil and Xanax.

How could your only son die before you? How could a wonderful, brave young man die at age twenty-four? Gabriel would never accept that Ray was gone and couldn't understand why Ray had to die from a disease so central to Gabriel's field of Gastroenterology. As a gastroenterologist most of Gabriel's practice was devoted to performing colonoscopies to prevent colon cancer, or to detect it at a curable stage. How could his own son be diagnosed with stage four colon cancer at age twenty-three and die from it at age twenty-four? When Gabriel was forced to think about, read articles about, diagnose or treat colon cancer, he always thought about

Ray and his own failure to diagnose Ray's cancer. He couldn't forgive himself, even though he'd been given no clues to Ray's disease prior to the diagnosis. Yet through the year of Ray's illness, Gabriel had not missed one day of work or one day of call.

Paxil took away a little of the dark gloom which surrounded Gabriel. Before he started taking the anti-depressant, he couldn't think like he had before Ray's diagnosis. He constantly had the sensation of a word, phrase, or thought hidden somewhere in his brain that he couldn't capture. It was frustrating; one day to be sharp and articulate and then, a curtain closing in his mind. Paxil had been intolerable at first. He'd started it on a weekend and slept the entire weekend. He'd have a meal with Ray and Sarah and then excuse himself to go lie down. But as his body adjusted, he increased the dosage, and slowly the curtains rose. The ideas he wanted to convey and the answers to patients' questions were now within his reach. He knew he'd never be happy in his life again, so he kept the full bottles of Paxil and Xanax handy, in case he felt he couldn't go on.

Gabriel backed his Mercedes out of the garage of their Mediterranean-styled Highland Park home and stopped the car in the middle of the driveway to pick up the newspaper. He tore off the plastic covering and looked at the headlines:

FEAR GROWS THAT TERRORISTS HAVE ACCESS TO NUKES

Gabriel threw the newspaper into the backseat and began the drive to work. The headline didn't faze him. The concern over nuclear weapons in the wrong hands had been in the news for the last few years and had dominated the news in the last month or so. When Ray was dying, Gabriel would hear the news and secretly hope that a nuclear holocaust would occur, and the world would end. *If my son must die, why shouldn't the whole world be destroyed? Why should other parents be able to love and care for their offspring when my only child is taken away? Yes, the world should end so that my grief will end. No one will know of light, beauty, love.* Even the Paxil couldn't rid Gabriel of the desire to see the world end. But now, a year after Ray's death and six months off Paxil and Xanax, he felt more resigned. If the world ended it wasn't that big of a deal, but if it continued, he'd go on living and working to save the lives of others.

As he got on the Dallas Tollway, he turned on the radio. The newscaster was giving the top stories of the day. A spokesman for a radical terrorist group had just issued a statement saying that they now had within their means the capacity to destroy the world with nuclear and chemical weapons. The commentator droned on, and Gabriel was about to switch channels when the commentator finished the news with, "And to all of our Jewish listeners, Happy New Year. Happy Rosh Hashanah."

Rosh Hashanah. Gabriel's mind drifted back to his childhood. He remembered going to High Holiday services with his father in the small town he'd grown up in. The services lasted from morning until evening and were physically and mentally exhausting for a little boy. In the middle of the day, the Rabbi would take a break, and Gabriel and his father would walk around the block holding hands. His father talked and philosophized, so Gabriel would remain silent and listen. Then they'd return to daven, praying in the traditional Jewish fashion with Hebrew words and choreographed movements. His father was one of the leaders of the Jewish community of their town and had served as president of the synagogue many times. Gabriel had been bar mitzvahed and confirmed, but his Jewish identity was shaped more by growing up in a small town than it was by what took place in the synagogue. He saw being Jewish as being an outsider, someone different who never totally fit in. He saw being a Jew as being someone who must always work harder to be good than his Christian neighbors, since he didn't have Jesus on his side to forgive his sins and misdeeds.

Gabriel lit a Yahrzeit candle every year on the anniversary of his father's death, and in a few weeks, he'd light the first one for Ray. His wife had already bought Ray's candle and had hidden it in one of the kitchen cabinets. Gabriel had accidentally come across it a month ago, and this was a paralyzing moment. It was a round white candle with a long white wick surrounded by a light blue glass. There was Hebrew lettering in gold on the glass container which Gabriel looked at but refused to read. That was the day that Gabriel decided for the first time in his life that he would work on the Jewish High Holidays.

Gabriel didn't think about work until he got to his office and read the schedule on his desk. Today was a clinic day so he was seeing patients in the office in the morning. There was only one procedure today, a colonoscopy on Charlotte Traylor scheduled for ninety minutes at one o'clock. On the computer-generated schedule there were separate columns for the type of procedure, the patient's name, and the indications for the procedure. Charlotte Traylor's indication was listed as anemia.

Charlotte Traylor. Gabriel remembered her well and had been dreading this day. Charlotte Traylor was the sixty-one -year-old wife of an oil tycoon. Her husband, a former Dallas mayor, was now running for governor of Texas. She'd come from a wealthy coal mining family in West Virginia and was considered one of Dallas's premiere socialites. She and her husband lived in a twenty-five thousand square foot Highland Park mansion on ten acres that was frequently used for major social events.

Charlotte Traylor. Gabriel had first seen her eleven years ago at age fifty, for a screening colonoscopy. She'd had a previous hysterectomy and the adhesions from the surgery had made her colon extraordinarily difficult to traverse. The colon itself appeared normal, so Gabriel told her to come back in ten years for another colonoscopy.

She'd returned last year as instructed after having bladder-suspension surgery six months before. This made her colonoscopy even harder to perform. Twice Gabriel had to ask Cindy, the nurse in the room, to turn the air conditioning down because he was sweating profusely. Finally, Gabriel saw the ileocecal valve and appendiceal orifice which signaled the end of the colon and silently whispered a prayer of thanks. He glanced at the room's clock; it had been just over an hour from when they started. He slowly pulled the scope back out of the colon, trying to carefully observe every twist and turn. The colon was poorly prepped, making his job more difficult. The sigmoid colon was packed with diverticula, the partial holes in the colon where the wall was weaker and pooched out. The sigmoid colon was bruised from where the elbow of the scope had beaten it, but there was no perforation. As Gabriel finished the procedure he remembered thinking how thankful he was that Mrs. Traylor had no polyps and wouldn't need to return for another colonoscopy for at least five to ten years.

Gabriel sat down at his desk and looked again at Charlotte Traylor's name on the schedule. One week ago, he'd received a frantic phone call from Mrs. Traylor's internist, Theo Thomas. Theo had seen Mrs. Traylor in the office three days before complaining of fatigue, weakness, a change in her bowel habits, and pain on the right side of her abdomen. He'd ordered labs which showed iron deficiency anemia with a hemoglobin three points below normal. With her symptoms and her anemia, the internist had ordered a STAT cat scan of the abdomen and pelvis, and he'd just received a call from the radiologist who reported uneven thickening of the right side of the colon, which was worrisome for a mass. There were also prominent lymph nodes around this area of wall thickening, and multiple lesions in the liver which were read as possible metastases. The radiologist was concerned that there could be a malignancy in this area of the colon and advised that she undergo a colonoscopy. Gabriel had seen Mrs. Traylor later that afternoon and explained to her that she'd need to have another colonoscopy now instead of waiting at least four years. He tried to sound confident and sure of himself, but several times his mouth felt dry and he had trouble talking.

"Why do I need another colonoscopy?" she asked. "If there was something there it would have been there last year, right? And you would have seen it, right? How could something have grown so quickly in my colon?'

"No test in medicine is one hundred percent accurate. We now know that people can grow large, very flat, and difficult to see polyps on the right side of the colon. These polyps may be faster-growing than the usual colon polyps and may turn into cancer more quickly. These polyps are called sessile serrated polyps, and they were first discovered in Japan. We never knew until their research was published that these polyps can turn into cancer. Until then, we treated them as benign growths not worth the risk of taking out."

"You think I have cancer? Aren't I too young to have cancer? I thought colon cancer was a disease of the elderly."

"I don't know at this point if you have colon cancer or not. You could have lost blood from somewhere else. The radiologists are notorious for over-reading CT scans. All I'm saying is we need to look at your colon. We'll schedule you for this week."

Gabriel wanted it to be done as soon as possible to know for certain what was going on. He knew that he'd obsess about it daily until he had an answer.

"No, no, no, I've got the Diamond Charity Ball at my house this weekend. If I need to suffer through the colonoscopy again, I'll do it next week. The procedure itself isn't so bad since I'm asleep, but that damn prep. Have they come out with anything new to clean yourself out with?"

"They're always coming out with new preps and I'm sure we'll find one you like better. I'll let you talk with my medical assistant about your choices. I'll work you in whenever you want. We'll book the procedure for ninety minutes to give me plenty of time to examine the colon."

Thinking about their encounter last week made Gabriel sweat. At one o'clock today he'd tackle Mrs. Traylor's colon. What if he'd missed a cancer a year ago? The nightmare of the gastroenterologist—a missed lesion in the colon-might be realized today. *What if Gabriel's ineptness was to be the cause of the premature demise of Charlotte Traylor?* He felt nauseated and dizzy as he got out of his chair and walked to the exam room to see his first clinic patient. She was a ninety-two-year-old white female who had never had a colonoscopy but had been referred by her internist to Gabriel because her stool contained microscopic blood. He walked into the room and immediately saw that she was sitting in a wheelchair and wearing dark glasses because she was blind. She was accompanied by her daughter. He introduced himself but received no response from the patient. The daughter spoke up and told him that her mother was severely demented and deaf and that even getting her dressed and to this appointment had been a major undertaking.

Gabriel sat down and spoke to the daughter. "We usually don't do colonoscopies on ninety-two-year-old patients. The risk of prepping and going through the procedure far outweighs any benefit. Your mother's condition makes it even more dangerous."

The patient didn't move or acknowledge Gabriel.

"I agree with you," answered her daughter. "I don't want to put my mother through a colonoscopy. She's deaf, blind, and not in her right mind. She just sits in a chair all day in the nursing home. She's incontinent and must be constantly changed. I don't want anything more done to her."

Gabriel nodded his head slowly in agreement. "I'll send a letter to Dr. Thomas that I've seen your mother and spoken to you and that we both agree the best thing to do is to do nothing. If you change your mind or your mother has any gastrointestinal issues, I'm always here to help."

Gabriel typed a quick note on the computer and then rolled the patient in her wheelchair out to his medical assistant's desk.

CHAPTER TWO

Adonis Gonzalez heard the two-toned siren over and over, the classic sound of the French police car as it barreled down Rue de Rivoli in Paris. He was safe inside his luxurious room in Hotel Le Meurice, sipping champagne in bed with his lover, Jean-Baptiste. They had come to Paris separately one week before with Adonis flying in from Dallas and Jean-Baptiste from San Francisco. Adonis had just finished a grueling stretch of three nights and five days on first call in his job as an anesthesiologist. Jean-Baptiste was taking his first full week off from his hair salon in months. They hadn't been together in a month and the week had gone by so quickly. But why wouldn't the police siren go away? Suddenly Adonis woke up and realized that it was his alarm clock beeping and it was time to get up. He turned off the alarm and walked to the bedroom window.

Adonis had a condominium in Turtle Creek, in one of the most exclusive buildings in Highland Park. He lived on the eighteenth floor with breathtaking views of downtown Dallas. The smattering of city lights made downtown look dark and tired. Nothing at all like the "City of Light," Paris, which he'd left the day before. He compared his view of Dallas with the view he'd had from their sofa table at the Jules Verne restaurant over four hundred feet above the ground in the Eiffel Tower. The view now was like watching black and white TV, while the view from the Eiffel Tower had been high definition color. He felt the coldness of the black leather curtain as he closed it, and then he walked into the bathroom.

He showered with the steam turned on and used the new shampoo and conditioner that Jean-Baptiste had purchased for him in a quaint shop near the Champs de Elysees. He dried off and then applied the body lotion he'd purchased at the same shop; it was a thick white cream that smelled like vanilla. He looked at himself in the mirror. Not bad for fifty-eight, he thought. He still had a full head of dark luxuriant hair which had been supplemented a few years before by hair plugs. His face appeared much younger thanks to regular Botox injections. He'd had a nose job at age forty to correct a deviated septum, or so the report to his insurance company said, which gave him a striking profile. It was competitive in the gay community and Adonis knew he still had the looks to stay in the game.

✦ ✦ ✦ ✦ ✦

Adonis's kitchen had been featured in an architectural magazine. It was black and white, with chrome instead of glass on the cabinets. On the large white marble island in the center of the kitchen stood abstract sculptures of pieces of fruit. A brilliant yellow banana, grotesquely fat in the center, with long, tapering ends, lounged next to a fire-engine-red apple which looked like stretched toffee with a series of waves in the middle. Finally, there was an orange carrot chopped into ten pieces with a thin green stem at the end. Adonis sat at his chrome-and-smoked-glass breakfast table and read the *Dallas Morning News* while he drank his espresso and ate a bowl of high fiber cereal.

FEAR GROWS THAT TERRORISTS HAVE ACCESS TO NUKES

Adonis glanced at the headlines. In Paris, this had been the topic of conversation from the gelato shops in Saint Germain to the cafes lining the Marais district. The terrorists were now issuing statements that they had the means to destroy the world in a nuclear holocaust and would only refrain from doing so if the United States immediately surrendered to their rule. They also demanded that the state of Israel cease to exist, and that all the Jews in Israel and throughout the world immediately convert to Islam. Their stated goal was to establish a Muslim Caliphate to rule the world.

Adonis grunted a "huh" as he read the article. He knew that the United States and Israel would never agree to these outrageous demands. Somewhere in the world he was sure there were spies or military operatives working for the United States who would find the terrorists, recover their nuclear weapons, and destroy them—just like in the James Bond movies.

What if the world ended today? What would be the meaning of his life? He'd lived a lie, Adonis thought. He'd lived two lives: here in Dallas he was an in-demand single heterosexual who had an active social life. Hell, he even screwed the women he dated on occasion. He ran marathons and triathlons and worked out with a trainer three days a week. People may have suspected he was gay—fifty-eight and not married and living in an immaculate high-rise in Turtle Creek—but no one knew for sure.

His second life, though, was the true Adonis: gay. He'd known for sure since he was in medical school. In college it was confusing. He spent so much time studying to get into medical school that he didn't give his sexuality much thought. With his good looks and engaging personality, he'd always had dates when he wanted them, but something didn't feel right.

In medical school, Adonis met an openly gay black medical student named Rashard. Adonis was grouped with Rashard and two other students in an anatomy lab to dissect a cadaver. After their anatomy practical exam, Rashard invited Adonis to go for dinner. They went to a pizza place in the gay section of the city.

After they sat down, Rashard asked Adonis, "You know you're gay, don't you?"

"I'm not gay. You're gay," Adonis replied angrily.

"Don't get all huffy with me. I know I'm gay and I have known since I was five. I look gay and I dress gay. I'm wearing a pink shirt open to my belly button and white pants with no underwear. I'm gay. I'm effeminate. You're not effeminate, but I can tell you're gay. You look at me differently. You don't flirt with any of the girls in the class."

"We're anatomy partners so I have to work with you and it's better if we get along," Adonis retorted. "I've always been a neat freak. I've dated girls in high school and college; medical school has been too busy for a social life. I'm straight. I am. Don't laugh at me, and don't stereotype me!"

"Well, just be careful. You've heard about this new disease that's starting to pop up in homosexual men? HIV is what they call it. Spread from one gay to another. No one knows how yet, but probably through screwing guys. Be careful if you start to experiment... it could be deadly."

While he was eating breakfast, Adonis thought about his father's friend who had died, not from being gay but from making fun of someone else who was gay. Adonis had grown up in Miami Beach in the nineteen sixties, and his father was Adonis Gonzalez Senior, the famous Cuban middleweight boxer. Donnie, as he was known then, had grown up in the boxing gym; his father had insisted he learn to box at the age of four and it was something little Donnie was good at. He enjoyed training and punching the heavy bag, but never liked strapping on the headgear and fighting other boys his age or a year or two older. He preferred shadow boxing, with his father calling out the combinations of punches.

Adonis Senior was best friends with the world welterweight champion who was from Cuba, Benny "Kid" Paret. The two of them had trained together and sparred together in Cuba. Then they had moved to America together and lived in the same apartment for a while. Even though Benny lived in New York and Adonis lived in Miami Beach, they never missed each other's fights. Benny was defending his welterweight title against Emile Griffith, and he had invited Adonis to come watch the fight in Madison Square Garden with his wife and Adonis Junior. The fight would be on national television, but Adonis wanted to be there for his friend rather than watching it on television from over a thousand miles away.

Adonis was four at the time, and the fight was the earliest thing in his life that he could still remember. They squeezed into their front-row seats right behind one of the corners of the ring. Adonis sat on his mother's lap, and he was proud of how well-received his father was. All the men seemed to know him from his boxing career and from living in Cuba, and they all came over to wish him good luck in his upcoming fight.

Adonis leaned over to whisper in his wife's ear. "Benny has a strategy for this fight. He found out Griffith is queer, so he patted him on the butt at the weigh-in and called him a "maricon," a faggot. There were newspaper reporters there who heard it and will probably write about it. He thinks that by getting Griffith angry the guy won't be able to concentrate and will make mistakes that Benny can capitalize on."

Donnie didn't know what a "maricon" or a "faggot" was, but he didn't have time to think about it. Cuban music started playing, Cuban flags were waved all over the Garden. Finally, "Uncle" Benny came out of his dressing room and walked up the aisle. He stopped to slap his glove against Adonis Senior's hand and then hugged Adonis' wife and son. His manager carried his world championship belt high above his head. It was gold and red and inlaid with shining jewels.

"Buena suerte, Kid," shouted Adonis Senior.

"I don't need luck with this faggot. He'll be back home crying to his mommy when I finish with him." It was well-known at the time that Griffith lived with his mother.

Benny climbed through the ropes into the ring and danced around, waving to the crowd. He took off his robe and was wearing white boxing trunks with a black line on each side. All the lights in Madison Square Garden went out except those directly over the boxing ring. The ring appeared bright as daylight, while the surrounding arena was dark, with cigarette smoke drifting up to the ceiling. Adonis stood with his mother and father and applauded when "Uncle Benny" was introduced. "Uncle" Benny winked at Adonis' father and then threw a series of punches into the air before going back to his corner to wait for the bell to ring. The bell rang, and both fighters rushed out of their corners to the center of the ring, eager to start the fight.

The fight seemed to be going according to "Uncle" Benny's plan, as Griffith was angry and leaving himself open for punches. In the sixth round, "Uncle" Benny came close to ending the fight, with one punch landing after another, but the bell sounded before the fight could be stopped. Adonis' father hugged his mother after that round and gave his son a playful tap on the cheek.

The fight continued, and little Donnie sat in his mother's lap throwing his own punches in the air as he watched the action in the ring. The twelfth round began, and it seemed both men were tired. Then, suddenly, Griffith backed "Uncle" Benny into the corner directly above their seats and began pummeling Benny in the head. After four or five punches it became obvious that Benny was no longer able to defend himself, and Adonis Senior jumped to his feet and yelled for the referee to stop the fight. He jumped up and down and waved his arms frantically. The entire fight seemed to slow down, and the crowd quieted as the thud of Griffith's gloves accurately connecting with Benny's head continued.

Little Adonis began crying uncontrollably and buried his head in his mother's chest as Benny sank further and further into the ropes. Still, the punching continued. Finally, after what seemed like an eternity, the referee stepped in and stopped the fight. Uncle Benny slid further down the ropes to the canvas, never to wake up again. He died ten days later. Adonis and his family stayed in New York with Benny's pregnant wife and small son until after the funeral.

Later, the news came out in the sportswriters' columns about Benny calling Emile Griffin a faggot and people sensed that this was why Emile continued to pound him even after he was obviously unconscious. Emile denied this vehemently. Donnie's father cancelled his next fight and quit boxing at the urging of his wife. He went back to school and got his teaching degree and became a high school history teacher and coach. He still took Adonis to the boxing gym in Miami Beach two or three times a week so they could work out together, but he discouraged his son from pursuing this as a career and told him repeatedly to make something of himself with his mind, not his fists. He did, however, teach his son how to box in the Cuban method to defend himself.

Donnie had last laced on the gloves at age twelve and was enjoying the work-out in the gym with his father. A boy from school who was known as the playground bully and always looking for fights came over to him and called him a faggot. He said Adonis always ran away from him on the playground because he was scared. It was true that Adonis always avoided fights at school because he felt he was there to learn, and most of the boys who wanted to fight had been held back a year or two and were bigger and stronger. He'd been able to avoid fighting until now.

Adonis Senior looked at his son. "I don't want you to be a boxer, but you have to defend yourself, Adonis."

"Your son is a pussy and a fucking faggot and if he stepped in the boxing ring with me right now I'd knock the faggotry out of him."

"Let's go," said Adonis Junior.

There was no one using the ring in the middle of the gym, so the two boys climbed through the ropes. The challenger, whose name was Felipe, was joined by his older brother who was a Golden Gloves champion in Florida and training for the National Golden Gloves Tournament.

"What about head-gear?" asked Adonis Senior. "I don't want either of you to get hurt."

"Head-gear is for queers," replied Felipe. "Men fight like men."

"Fight for three, three-minute rounds," said Hector, Felipe's older brother. "Santiago, you referee this fight?"

Santiago was a middle-aged trainer who had been sitting in a corner of the gym smoking a cigarette waiting for a boxer who needed a trainer. He sported a well-worn white baseball cap and white shirt and pants. He threw the cigarette to the floor, crushed it with his toe and yelled, "Sure, don't have nuthin' better to do."

Adonis Senior said to his son, "Remember what I taught you. Footwork is everything in boxing. He's older and bigger than you so he'll have a reach advantage. Work your way inside with your left jab and then throw the left hook to the body. If you have an opening, go left hook and then right cross. Remember to keep that right hand up all the time and no stupid right uppercuts unless he drops his left hand low. Here's your mouth-piece." Adonis opened his mouth and his father put the mouth-piece in place.

Hector rang the bell under the ring and the two boys met in the middle. Adonis put out his glove to show good sportsmanship, but Felipe punched it away. Felipe was strong and aggressive, but he hadn't developed the footwork needed to be in position to throw a punch with the body torqued for maximal explosion. He was used to intimidating his playground opponents, wrestling them to the ground, and then pummeling them.

Adonis easily avoided Felipe's wild haymakers and began to land his left jab with accuracy right under Felipe's right eye. When Felipe moved his right glove up to protect his face, Adonis feinted the left jab, then violently torqued his body back and landed a left hook to Felipe's liver. Felipe gasped and used both his arms to hold Adonis and keep him from punching further.

"Okay, clean break," said Santiago, "let go of him, Felipe."

Adonis moved back as the referee instructed, but on the break, Felipe stepped forward and hit Adonis with a hard right cross to the nose that immediately drew blood. Most of the boxers working out in the gym had stopped what they were doing and were now gathered in the center of the gym at ringside. A few of them booed the illegal punch.

Adonis' father shouted out, "He hit him on the break. That's illegal. Stop the fight."

"I see the little homo needs his famous father to stand up for him. Can't take a little blood from your fucking nose? You're going to quit, aren't you?" sneered Felipe.

"Do you want to quit?" asked Santiago. "Since you were fouled I'd give you five minutes to get that bleeding controlled."

"Don't stop the fight, Padre," said Adonis as he carefully backed away from Felipe and spoke without looking back at his father. "I'm going to teach this bully a lesson. And, thanks for the offer, ref, but I'm ready to fight now. Only a faggot would take time off to recover, and I'm not a faggot."

The blood flowing from his nose made it a little harder to breathe, but otherwise Adonis felt fine. He went back to his strategy, peppering Felipe with jabs and then following up with hooks to the body.

Hector shouted, "Don't just let him hit you and get out of range, Felipe. Move your body and throw combinations."

This was what Adonis had been waiting for. Felipe threw a left jab followed by a straight right and Adonis stepped under Felipe's right hand and landed a vicious uppercut to Felipe's chin. Adonis saw the life go out of Felipe's body as his hands slowly fell to his sides. As Felipe's left hand went down, Adonis took a step back and then stepped in and landed a right uppercut to the other side of Felipe's jaw with all his power. Adonis could see Felipe's eyes roll back in his head as he fell face-first and landed on the canvas in front of Adonis.

"This fight is over," the referee needlessly announced. He raised Adonis's right hand straight up. "The winner by knockout in round number one is Adonis Gonzalez, Junior. Do you have the time of the knock-out, Hector?"

"Fuck the time of the knockout," said Hector coming through the ropes, "how is my little brother?"

Adonis' father came into the ring and lifted his son high into the air. Hector turned his brother over onto his back; he was just regaining consciousness and began throwing combinations into the air from his back. Adonis told his father to put him down, and he went over to see how Felipe was doing. Then he ran out of the ring and got some ice in a towel to put on Felipe's chin.

"Are you okay?" asked Adonis. "You're a good fighter but just a little wild. You should train more here in the gym with your brother instead of picking fights on the playground."

Felipe was too dazed to reply. He looked at Adonis with a combination of confusion and anger.

Adonis and his father stepped under the ropes and out of the ring.

"I never wanted you to become a boxer like me, but you sure have talent," his father said.

"I like helping people more than hurting them. And I'll never forget what happened to Uncle Benny. He called Mr. Griffith a faggot, too. I think my boxing career is over."

That was the last time Adonis or his father ever went into a boxing gym. They concentrated on soccer and track and field and other sports. It was also the last time that Felipe talked to Adonis, much less called him a faggot.

Adonis began to "experiment" discretely in medical school when on vacation and away from those who knew him. At first, he decided he was bisexual and just liked sex with men and women. He dated women in medical school and found one that he liked enough to consider marrying. Laura was her name, and she was a beautiful blonde nurse on the cardiology floor whom Adonis met while doing his cardiology rotation. Many of the other students had their eyes on her and asked her out, but she only had time for Adonis. They dated for six months and had sex once or twice a week. She was smart and witty and considerate and reminded Adonis a lot of his own mother. Adonis went shopping for engagement rings and planned on popping the question.

He'd gone on a trip to Cancun, Mexico with some gay friends during a break between clinical rotations. The four of them would wake up late each morning and then eat brunch at the hotel's incredible buffet. After eating they would lie by the enormous swimming pool after sensuously applying suntan lotion to each other. After tanning for hours, drinking margaritas, and occasionally going for a swim, the four headed back to their room. They undressed and had sex while they showered. They taxied to one of Cancun's top restaurants and then a gay nightclub. There they danced until the wee hours of the morning. When they got back to their hotel room they blindly picked underwear out of a suitcase to determine who would sleep with whom.

While on vacation Adonis realized that being married to Laura would be a farce. He didn't love her, would never love her, and didn't want to live with her and have sex only with her. He still didn't want people, including his own family, to know that he was gay, so he decided to continue living a double life. He broke up with Laura by telling her he still wanted to date other women and wasn't ready to make a commitment. She'd been crushed, and soon moved away and Adonis never saw her again. Since then, he'd dated women in the city in which he lived but lived his true life on the frequent vacations he took with male lovers.

Anesthesiology had turned out to be a perfect field for Adonis. Patients never got to know him and couldn't care less if he was gay or straight if he kept them safely asleep during their procedures. Besides, there were quite a few gay residents in anesthesia at his training program, some of whom he travelled with. They all agreed that anesthesia was the right profession for them since they could easily keep their private lives private because their interactions with patients were limited. For Adonis it was also important to be in a medical field in which he could set his own hours and make plenty of time to travel with his lovers.

What if the world ended today? On the one hand, Adonis thought, it would be somewhat of a relief. No more living a lie. Maybe in the afterlife there was a place you went where everyone was accepted. Maybe in the afterlife gay wasn't a dirty word. Maybe in the afterlife calling someone a faggot didn't lead to them beating you to death while the world watched. On the other hand, his life could be beautiful, particularly in a place like Paris with a lover like Jean-Baptiste. He thought of the elegance of Versailles with its hall of mirrors and magnificent gardens, the beautiful art inside the Louvre, the romantic waters of the Seine. There was so much in life that was enjoyable and good. Life is still worthwhile, he decided.

Adonis waited for the steel parking gates to separate, and then he drove his Porsche 911 out of the condominium's parking garage. When he got to the Tollway he dialed his office. The secretary answered. "Hello, Mabelle, it's Doctor Gonzalez."

"Welcome back, Doctor Gonzalez. How was your vacation to Paris?"

"Paris was… is wonderful. Just called to see if there were any changes to my schedule today. Do I still finish at eleven thirty?"

"Let me check. No, while you were gone we added on a one o'clock case with Dr. Gold at his endoscopy center. A colonoscopy booked for ninety minutes. Sixty-one-year-old woman named Charlotte Traylor."

"*The* Charlotte Traylor? The socialite and soon to be governor's wife?"

"I assume so."

"Why ninety minutes? He usually books his colonoscopies for forty-five minutes. Must be something unusual. Okay, is that my last case of the day?"

"That's your last case. Have a good day."

Adonis hung up and thought about Charlotte Traylor. He had been to a few fund-raisers at her house with some of the elite divorced women in Dallas, but he'd never gone up to her and introduced himself. He was drawn to her husband, Blaze, who Adonis felt was one of the more attractive men his age around. He hoped Blaze would be there to pick up his wife after the colonoscopy, so they could talk again. He turned on the Bluetooth in his car and began listening to his Pandora shuffle. Steppenwolf's "Born to Be Wild" blasted through his speakers.

CHAPTER THREE

RC's body tensed as she moved her head on the pillow. She felt throbbing just below her right eye, but it wasn't intense enough to wake her. Suddenly her mind veered into a dream. She was smoking on the porch outside their apartment and she could see her boyfriend, Randy, through the glass door. Her back felt heavy and she had problems getting air into her lungs. Joshua, her eight-year-old son was piggy-backed on her, clutching his tiny arms tightly around her neck. She sensed Randy advancing towards her even though she could no longer see him. Suddenly, Randy exploded through the front door.

"I'm leaving you, Randy!" she gasped. "This is it! I'm leaving you." She tried to get up, but the weight on her back was too much.

Randy laughed. "You'll never leave me. We've been together for four years now. No one else will take you or that half-wit son of yours. You may screw your occasional doctor who's hard up for sex, but none of them wants you and him for long. You're stuck with me, bitch."

Randy grabbed RC by the hair and pulled her to her feet. "I'll mess up that pretty face of yours if you fuck with me."

"I'm calling the police. Help!"

RC heard the police sirens. "They're coming for you, Randy. They're going to take you away."

Relieved, RC breathed deeply and turned her head to the other side. She opened one eye and realized her alarm clock was going off. She turned off the alarm and looked over at Randy. He didn't move when the alarm sounded, and he was snoring loudly. Still in a drunken stupor, RC thought. RC put her feet on the floor and felt a sharp ache under her right eye which shot like a bullet to the back of her head. Fucking hangover, she thought. How much did I drink last night? They'd started a bottle of wine with dinner and then drank a second bottle watching some stupid reality show on TV. Standing up, she felt dizzy and nauseated. *I may just have to call in to work*, she thought. *Tell them I'm sick with the flu.*

The nausea increased as RC stumbled to the bathroom. She knelt in front of the toilet and lifted the lid. She vomited twice. First up came chicken and rice from last night's TV dinner, and next came more partially digested food stained with green bile. She thought that was all, but when she struggled to get up she became more nauseated and vomited up coffee grounds-old blood. She knew that she had probably vomited last night and torn herself internally, resulting in the old blood. She was sweating profusely so the cold tile floor felt good. After a few minutes lying on the floor, she decided to wash herself off and crawled over to the sink to pull herself up. She looked in the mirror and noticed that underneath her right eye was a huge fresh bruise. Blotches of old blood mixed with food speckled her lower face, and the top of her over-sized white T-shirt looked like a Jackson Pollack painting.

That bastard hit me again, she thought. Last night was a total blur, but somehow, she knew Randy had beaten her again. *That bastard, that mother-fucking prick*, she thought. Her indignation gave her strength and she stood up straight. She looked awful. She was only twenty-seven, but without make-up and with a bruised face now punctuated by a fresh black eye, she looked ten years older. *I need a shower*, she decided, so she pulled off the T-shirt and her panties and climbed into the shower.

The warm water felt good as it pelted her body. *What happened last night and what did we fight about?* It couldn't have been her son, Joshua, since he was spending the week with his father in Houston. Joshua's autism had been the source of many of their fights, especially when Randy got drunk and made fun of Joshua's peculiar behavior. But he hadn't been around for a week, so it wasn't him.

RC got out of the shower and toweled herself off. She sat down on the commode and lit a joint while she peed. The pain under her eye was still there, but not as sharp. After finishing the joint, the nausea left. She wiped herself and flushed the stub down the commode with the toilet paper.

Although she didn't feel one hundred percent, she decided that she was going to her job as a nurse in the endoscopy center. Even with her problems with Joshua, the fights with Randy, and her drinking problems, she'd rarely called in sick. Besides, she didn't want to spend the day in the apartment around Randy.

Rachel Carly, known as RC, had been the homecoming queen at her high school in a suburb of Houston. With long flaming red hair and magnificent green-eyes, she made boys melt. She could get whatever she wanted and what she wanted most was attention. She dated the top athletes and fell in love with a football star her senior year. They did everything together, and all the other students worshipped them. RC lived with her alcoholic father who worked as a grave-digger and who smoked and got drunk nightly and beat RC the nights she mistakenly returned home early. Her mother had left them years before and hadn't communicated with RC in over a decade.

RC had started smoking when she was in the eighth grade, when she was dating Ron, a junior in high school. She smiled when she remembered Ron. "You sure look good with that cigarette in your mouth," she remembered telling him. "It makes you look—what's the word—sophisticated."

He blew smoke at her. "Try one, RC?"

"Why not. I like the way it smells."

She began bumming cigarettes off him and only smoked a cigarette or two when they were together. But she craved them more and more and by her junior year she smoked at least a pack a day.

Ron also introduced RC to alcohol and sex. They drank beer or wine to excess every Friday and Saturday night. They'd have sex in Ron's car and then pass out for a few hours. When RC got home in the early morning hours, her dad would be passed out on the couch and he never woke when she came in, so he couldn't hit her.

One woman with two lives, that's what she was. A high school cheerleader, homecoming queen, outstanding beauty attracting offers to model on one side. An alcoholic smoker brought up by a drunken, uncaring, abusive father and no mother on the other. How would it play out?

RC's future was decided towards the end of her senior year of high school. Her boyfriend now was Chip, the high school hunk and quarterback on the football team. Chip was an outstanding athlete, captain of the football and basketball teams his senior year. But he was also a heavy drinker and was one of the few boys who could keep up with RC when it came to partying.

On their way home from partying late one night, Chip swerved his pick-up off the road while RC was giving him a blow job and hit a tree. RC hit the dashboard and suffered a concussion and a broken arm. Chip went through the windshield and among other injuries, severed his spinal cord and became paraplegic. While she was in the hospital recuperating they did a pelvic ultrasound and told RC she was three months pregnant.

When she was well enough, RC was discharged with only bandages on her face and a cast on her arm. She was still quite pretty, but the dazzling beauty never returned. She would visit Chip in the intensive care unit every day. One day she told him she was pregnant, and he began to cry. Before she had the chance to tell him she was getting an abortion, he spoke to her.

"A baby, my baby," he choked out.

She reached out and wiped his face. He took her hand and looked in her eyes. "Marry me, RC. Let's take care of our baby together. We'll be a family and build a life together. My folks will help and I'm still a hero to everyone in the town from playing sports, so everyone will chip in. Please marry me. I promise to be good to you and the baby and to take care of both of you. With all the new discoveries in medicine, maybe someday I'll be able to walk again. Please, please marry me! You won't regret it."

There wasn't a day in her life since then that RC hadn't regretted her response. She couldn't say no, not to a boy she'd known all her life and who was the father of her child. She wondered if other men would want her with her altered looks. She'd thought about getting an abortion before their encounter, but in the intensive care unit that day she decided to keep the baby and marry Chip. They kissed and hugged, and the intensive care unit nurses brought her an engagement ring made from suction tubing which Chip placed on her finger.

The marriage was a disaster from the start. RC's pregnancy progressed normally although she still smoked a pack a day and the occasional joint. The baby was born, but once Chip was released from the reha- bilitation hospital in Houston, she became his full-time nurse as well as taking care of her newborn son. She helped Chip in and out of bed and pushed him in his wheelchair. She learned to catheterize his bladder four times a day to keep him from getting bladder infections. When he developed a large bed sore on his sacrum she learned how to clean and pack it. After two years she couldn't take it anymore, so she divorced Chip and moved with Joshua to Dallas to get away from Chip and the demands of being his wife and caregiver.

RC worked as a waitress for six months in Dallas, and saw her life going nowhere. She continued to find refuge in alcohol and cigarettes, although she cut back somewhat to be able to take care of Joshua, who wasn't developing mentally and emotionally as a child of his age should. She took him to a pediatrician who referred her to a specialist. The specialist told her Joshua was autistic. RC began reading books on autism and did everything possible to help her son. She changed their diets, she put him on probiotics. Anything that a study said might be helpful, she did for her Joshua. One day she woke up and realized that from her experiences with Chip and Joshua she wanted to be a nurse, and that day she applied to nursing school. She completed an associate degree in nursing in two years and took her first job working in an emergency room.

RC met Randy during one of her shifts in the emergency room. He came in with an ankle sprain and RC was the nurse assigned to him. He'd been out drinking with a few buddies, and when he went to the restroom he slipped and sprained his ankle. He was tall and rugged-looking and RC liked him immediately. He had a roughness about him that she was sure hid a heart of gold. He asked for her number and they went out drinking the next night and had sex at his apartment. Two weeks later she and Joshua left their tiny apartment and moved in with Randy.

During her four years with Randy, RC had had affairs with two of the doctors she'd met at the hospital. The first one was a young emergency room doctor, Matt, who was a locum tenens doctor for six months in the emergency room. He was cute and kind and represented a better life for RC and Joshua. Things progressed well, with dates for drinks, then dinners.

Then Matt started talking about settling down with the right woman and working at one hospital rather than traveling around the country as a locum tenens doctor. One day he showed up unexpectedly at her apartment in his shiny black Corvette.

The doorbell rang, and RC answered. Matt was standing there with a bouquet of red roses. "Happy birthday, love. These are for you, the most beautiful woman in the world who I love with all of my heart."

"Why Matt, thanks I love you, too. How did you find out where I lived? We always met at restaurants or bars for our dates."

"I got your address from administration. I've become friends with the Nursing Administrator and she gave it to me. Now the mystery is gone, and I know where you live so we can be together more."

Suddenly Randy appeared ominously next to RC in the doorway.

"Well, well, what do we have here? Some little twerp bringing roses to my wife. You'd better be the flower delivery boy or you're about to get seriously hurt."

Matt took two steps back. "You nnnever told me you were mmmarried," he stammered. "I wouldn't have dated you if I'd known you were married. You said you had a son…"

"I'm not married. Randy and I live together. I was going to tell you about our relationship. Please don't leave."

"You've got three seconds to get in your little Corvette Stingray and drive off or I will tear you apart," Randy snarled. Randy moved in front of RC, so she could no longer see Matt. He put one finger up in the air to begin his count.

Matt dropped the roses on the cement step and ran to his car. The engine roared as he drove away as fast as he could. Two days later, he moved on to another hospital and RC never heard from him again. That night Randy burned the roses, beat RC, and blackened both of her eyes.

The second affair was a short-lived escapade with one of the heart surgeons at the hospital. He'd had affairs with other nurses there even though he was married with children. Right from the start, he told RC that they were only having sex and that she could expect nothing more from him. He never even brought her flowers or a present. The sex wasn't that great; he was only interested in his own pleasure, so RC broke off the affair after two months and he moved on to another nurse in the intensive care unit.

Eventually, though, in addition to taking care of Joshua and the difficult relationship with Randy, the emergency room proved to be too exhausting for RC. She saw an advertisement for an opening in an endoscopy center and she applied and got the job. Now she worked four, ten-hour days and had all nights and weekends off. The pay was less than what she made in the emergency room, but living with Randy, their costs were much less. Since Randy worked from four until midnight as a security guard, he watched Joshua during the day until she got home. The days that Joshua went to his special school, Randy would drop him off and pick him up.

RC drove her battered red Ford 150 pickup truck off the apartment parking lot and headed to work. She turned on the truck's radio to her country-western station. On the radio, she heard, "Terrorist groups are now claiming they have the means to destroy the world in a nuclear attack. Ultimatums have been delivered to the president of the United States and to the prime minister of Israel. The president has scheduled a news conference for this afternoon to outline his plan for dealing with the terrorists' demands. No word yet from Israel's prime minister, but Israel's policy in the past has been absolutely no negotiations with terrorist groups. Keep your radio tuned to ninety-seven point eight FM, the leader in country music, for more details."

The music came on and RC half-listened. She thought about the state of the world. Normally it wasn't something that concerned her too much since she was so caught up in her own life. But what if the world ended today? What would happen? She was a Christian simply because her parents were Christian, but she could count on one hand the number of times she'd gone to church. She thought about Jesus and salvation. Whatever the afterlife was, it had to be better than this. At least it would get her away from Randy and give her and Joshua a new life together. But if there was no alcohol in Heaven or pot or cigarettes, what would be the point? Just to sit around all day thinking holy thoughts, what kind of a life would that be? She stopped at a red light, rolled down the window, lit a cigarette and began blowing smoke out of the car.

CHAPTER FOUR

ester felt the familiarity of the dream surge through his body. He shrugged. It was inevitable, this dream was going to happen no matter what he did. Yet, he had to hold out hope; maybe this time it would be different. The view was telescopic: the football field went in and out of focus, always black and white. He'd read that some people's dreams always lacked color, and his dreams were so cursed. He saw himself in his black Saint Mark's high school football uniform, number twenty-two, in the middle of the huddle.

The Southwest Preparatory Conference championship game, played on their home field. The stadium lights blinked on with more intensity; on the field it was bright as daylight. Somewhere in the back of his mind he was preparing himself for the darkness. The Greenhill Hornets across the line, had dazzling white uniforms showing no dirt or stain after four quarters of grueling football. They stood there forming a formidable white wall. Ray Gold was calling the play.

"This is it guys, the game-winning play: twenty-two draw on three. Ready!"

Twenty white hands and Lester's black hands came together and clapped as they broke the huddle. Twenty-two draw was Lester's play, here on the five-yard line, fourth down and goal to go with twenty seconds left in the game. It all came down to one snap, one play, and it was his. He'd take the hand-off and follow Luke Jackson, their mammoth left tackle, and somehow find his way into the end zone. It was perfect. Everyone would be expecting a pass on fourth down and the blocking would set up like a pass until the instant Ray tucked the football into Lester's gut.

Lester pulled his telescope back from the field and surveyed the stands. Big crowd for a private school game, at least three thousand people on their feet screaming at the tops of their lungs. In the front row at mid-field was his mother, Henrietta. This was the first game she'd been to. She had just finished detox from drugs and finally felt well enough to attend his final game. She looked so proud and wore a large button picturing Lester in his football uniform on her only dress which he'd bought her from the Army-Navy Store the week before. Just yesterday she'd shown Lester a magazine picture of the dream house she wanted when he became a professional football player.

Back to the field. In his three-point stance, Lester could feel the army of black around him and the blockade of white on the other side of the line of scrimmage.

"Hut! Hut! Hut!"

The ball was snapped, and Ray faded back in slow motion. The receivers ran down the field and started to make their cuts in the end zone. Lester elevated from his three-point stance and stared ahead. All he saw was Luke's enormous butt and one linebacker parked in the middle of the field. The ball was firmly placed in between Lester's arms and he began to accelerate. Here's where the dream broke down; sometimes he felt like he was running in sand with leg irons, and other times he wouldn't run at all but would just stand there in fright. This dream, though, was true to life, just how it had gone down six years before. Lester followed Luke, saw him level the linebacker and then, just when he was sure he was going to score, he felt a terrible pain tearing apart his left knee. He hit the ground and bounced off his right shoulder pad and then hit the ground again. The pain was so excruciating he didn't care if he'd scored, but he knew from the joyous rising waves of white uniforms around him that he had not. The safety had come in from the blind side unblocked and had leveled Lester at the two-yard line. Lester heard the horn go off and knew the game was lost. The horn kept going off as his teammates gathered around him on their knees.

The coaches came out and cried, "Lester, are you all right?" but they knew he wasn't when they saw the team doctor's face lose color.

"I'll be okay," Lester gritted through clenched teeth as he removed his helmet. "Just turn off the horn and let me rest in peace."

Lester opened one eye and knew it was his alarm clock going off, so he climbed down from his top bunk and turned it off. He looked around the little efficiency apartment he shared with his mother. She wasn't there now; since they had reunited in the past year she spent most of her life as a patient at Medical City Plano Hospital. She was only forty-two, but she had lupus and hypertension and was on dialysis for kidney failure. She'd once confided to Lester that she now enjoyed life more in than out of the hospital.

He'd had high hopes six years ago when his mother had re-entered his life. After a decade away, she'd heard that her son was a football star. After Lester's injury she had returned to life as a junkie and living on the streets. Lester's childhood had been spent living with aunts, uncles, and a grandfather who shuttled him from one home to another. He'd shown talent as a football player as well as a student, so in tenth grade an uncle had directed him to meet the Saint Mark's football coach. Lester was convinced that graduating from such a prestigious private school would take his life where he wanted, so he enrolled as a sophomore. He excelled in football, starting at running back all three years, and did well enough in academics to attract the attention of several Ivy League schools. His small stature, five feet eight inches and one hundred and sixty pounds, made major college football impossible. However, for a school like Harvard, which began recruiting Lester in his junior year, his size and skill level were a perfect fit.

Until the injury. Ligaments that had obeyed his every twist and turn were now torn from their moorings and thrashed around like unsecured sails in a storm. Two surgeries had given him back the ability to almost walk properly, but he would never again play football. Harvard's coach called him one more time after the injury to tell him that they were withdrawing their scholarship offer and to have a good life.

Lester walked over to the white Ikea dresser across from the bed and opened the drawer containing his scrubs and pulled out a pair. He'd found the dresser dumped upside down in a garbage bin, and a lot of the white paint was chipped off. But he needed someplace in the tiny efficiency apartment to store their few clothes, so with the help of a friend he carried it three miles back to their apartment. The dresser stood straight without rocking and still had drawers that opened, making it the most well-put-together piece of furniture in the apartment. The bunk bed had two thick yellow-page phone books under one chopped off leg, but still swayed a little when Lester climbed up and down. The bed had been purchased by Lester for twenty-five dollars from the crack house next door to their apartment building.

The apartment consisted of a bedroom, a tiny kitchenette, a small walk-in closet, and a bathroom that contained a shower, a toilet, and a sink. Above the sink was a cracked mirror, the result of his mother fainting once while washing her face and smacking her head against it before she fell to the ground. Lester now looked in the mirror whose cracks divided his face into pieces like a jigsaw puzzle and spread shaving cream across his face. He shaved and brushed his teeth and then gargled with Listerine. Going to Saint Mark's had taught him the importance of making a good outward appearance no matter how much turmoil lurked inside. After he dried off his face and applied deodorant, he walked back to the closet and set up an ironing board and plugged in the iron.

He pressed his scrubs until their creases were perfect and thought of his mother. The ironing board and iron were her only contributions to the apartment and she had inherited them from *her* mother. Everything else in the apartment had been earned by six years of Lester's sweat. Once he realized he wasn't going to Harvard or any college to play football, he looked for a way to support himself. The community college offered a six-month course on becoming a surgical tech which he thought he'd use as a springboard to go on to nursing school, and then to medical school. Instead, he'd worked as a surgical tech for three years, then left for a higher paying job as a gastrointestinal tech at an endoscopy center in Plano. He worked forty hours a week at fifteen dollars an hour and kept alive the dream of returning to school someday to become a nurse and then a doctor. But fate intervened in the form of his homeless mother who he hadn't seen since his last, fateful football game. He'd taken care of his sick, stubborn grandfather until he had died, and now he felt an obligation to help restore his mother's life.

This time he had found her in downtown Dallas, living on the street under a scraggly brown blanket. One of his uncles had told him her whereabouts, and he took the bus downtown to get her. Though ready for the worst, he was still shocked when he saw her. She was pale, with a wad of uncombed, unwashed hair covering her head and forehead, and had lost most of her teeth. She struggled to move and couldn't muster a smile when her only son, the one person in this world who cared about her, came to rescue her.

Lester had carried his mother to the bus stop and took her back to his apartment in Garland, Texas. They had to change buses twice, and each time he gathered her in his arms like a stack of logs and carried her to the next bus. After washing off her face and feeding her, he took her to the hospital. She stayed in the hospital for over three months. Diabetes, lupus, kidney failure requiring dialysis, all were diagnoses made during that stay. The doctors told him that if he'd waited another week to bring her in, she would have died. Chronic pain syndrome was soon added as a diagnosis, and like many chronic pain patients, his mother quickly became addicted to narcotics. Vicodin was okay, but the real treat was the Dilaudid which streamed through her veins directly to her brain and gave her that joyful, peaceful sleep. She'd go to the emergency room weekly seeking Dilaudid and admission, and when she was refused admission she'd let her blood sugar get so out of control they had to admit her. Once she was a patient, she'd call for the Dilaudid every two hours, complaining of back pain from her arthritic spine, or abdominal pain from no one knew where.

Doctor Gabriel Gold had been consulted multiple times when she was admitted to Medical City Plano for abdominal pain and he put her through a battery of tests. He'd done an upper endoscopy, colonoscopy, CT scan of the abdomen and pelvis, small bowel series, duplex doppler of the mesenteric vessels, sonogram of the gallbladder, gastric emptying study. Nothing showed up, but since she had lupus, there was always the possibility of vasculitis. Vasculitis was an inflammation of the blood vessels, including those supplying blood to the intestinal tract, which caused a reduced blood flow. The decreased blood flow caused abdominal pain which mimicked heart attack pain. After Dr. Gold discussed this possibility with her, she was sure this was what she had. Lester's mother would be dialyzed in the hospital, and on the rare occasions when she was home she'd be picked up at their apartment every Monday, Wednesday, and Friday by a specially equipped van staffed by two men who carried her down on a stretcher. Lester made sure to give them each a Christmas card stuffed with a twenty-dollar bill for taking such good care of his mother.

She was an inpatient now at Medical City of Plano, which was attached to the endoscopy center where Lester worked. He'd see her that afternoon on his lunch break. He took a rotting banana from on top of the refrigerator, peeled back the brown skin and ate it. He opened the refrigerator and took out the carton of milk he'd bought at half-price since it had expired two days before, then poured himself a glass. Also, in the refrigerator was a piece of chocolate cake which Lester had brought home for his mother from an endoscopy center birthday party a week before. It was hard when Lester picked it up, but he put it into his mouth and washed it down with the milk. He tore off a piece of paper towel and wiped his face and then left the apartment.

As Lester walked to the bus stop, he noticed a news-paper stand. He usually looked at the headlines to see what the Dallas Cowboys or Texas Rangers were up to, but today the headline caught his eye even though it had nothing to do with sports:

FEAR GROWS THAT TERRORISTS HAVE ACCESS TO NUKES

Lester boarded his first bus on the hour trip north to Plano. He thought about the headline. What would happen if the United States was nuked? Lester was twenty-five; he was too young to die. He thought for a moment about Doctor Gold's son, Ray, who had been his teammate and friend at Saint Mark's School and who had died last year. Ray had accomplished something; he was a star college football player. His death was a tragedy, but at least he'd done the one thing Lester had always aspired to.

The entire football team from Saint Mark's had come to Ray's funeral, and Lester saw how successful some of them had already become. Some were getting MBA's at the big-name schools like Wharton and Stanford, others were finishing law school and interning with fabulous law firms in New York, Los Angeles, and Dallas. Several were in medical school and told Lester how tough it was, but how much they loved it. Each of them shoveled dirt onto Ray's casket at the bottom of the cold grave and then handed the shovel to the next in line.

Lester was the last to shovel dirt and he looked down into the hole where his teammate's plain pine coffin with an engraved Star of David lay. On the bus ride home, he reflected on the symbolism of his being the last in line to shovel dirt. He was so far behind his former classmates in accomplishments that it bothered him almost as much as Ray's funeral. He burned with a desire to relive the success he'd had in those three short years at Saint Mark's. Over the past few months he'd finally made plans to move on with his life in a positive direction. Small steps, yes, but improvement. He was applying to nursing school and would start night classes there in four months if accepted. After graduating and working for a few years to save money, he'd apply to medical school. His goal now was to be a doctor in ten years, but he'd mentioned it to only the few people he trusted, including his occasional lower bunk-mate mother.

What if the world is destroyed before I accomplish my goals? The grim thought tugged at Lester's brain. *The world can't come to an end yet. I've got too much to do, too many bridges to cross, too many dragons to conquer.* Lester closed his eyes and pictured himself as an orthopedic surgeon going on rounds in the hospital and seeing his mother as he passed by her room. She'd be proud of him, he knew, even if her mind was clouded by the Dilaudid she craved. More importantly, he'd be proud of himself. One of his teachers at Saint Mark's had once told him that every human being has a flame inside that can either be fanned to a fire and lead to great success and accomplishment or allowed to slowly die out and lead to a life without meaning and hope. Lester's flame had flickered and almost gone out for six years, but as he boarded the next bus on the route to Plano he resolved to stoke that fire and to become the man he wanted to be.

CHAPTER FIVE

Charlotte looked at the gallon container and then at the glass in front of her. Over the past three hours she'd drunk glass after glass from the container, and the only bowel prep solution left was in the glass on the marble table. She picked it up and began drinking, but almost immediately had to set it down and scramble to the bathroom.

"This bowel prep is hell!" she shouted to her husband who was in the closet adjacent to the bathroom, packing for his trip to Austin. The yellow liquid poured out of her, as clear as the liquid in the glass she was drinking.

"You've done a great job, honey," came her husband, Blaze's, reply. "You get clear, so Doctor Gold will get a good look and find out why you're so anemic. I'll get you a towel to wipe your forehead."

Charlotte could feel a cramp in her lower abdomen, and then more clear, yellow fluid filled the commode and splashed onto her buttocks. "My butt is so red and sore, it looks like an orangutan's butt. What a pain! I just wish I could go to Austin with you for this campaign trip."

Blaze brought Charlotte a towel to wipe off with while she was sitting on the commode. "There will be plenty of trips for you to go on. Let's just find out what's wrong with you and get you better. I love you and I need you."

Charlotte glanced at Blaze. He had a full head of gray hair, but otherwise he'd changed remarkably little since their marriage forty years before. Of course, he'd had a face lift, but what candidate for higher office didn't do everything to improve their looks? He was handsome and in top physical condition. His plan was to win the governorship, run the state for four years, and then run for president of the United States. She sometimes felt embarrassed given the hundred pounds she'd put on over their forty years of marriage but Blaze always reassured her by telling her how beautiful she was. She still had her sparkling blue eyes and the gorgeous face that made her one of the most photographed people in the city and which had won Blaze's heart. On numerous occasions she told herself she could and would lose the weight, but the willpower wasn't there. Charlotte loved eating rich food, never skipped a dessert, and she never exercised. There was a twenty-five-hundred-square-foot exercise room on the third floor of their mansion which Blaze had outfitted with the latest weight machines, stationary bikes, ellipticals, and stair-steppers for the two of them. Blaze worked out daily with a trainer and maintained his one hundred and ninety pounds on his six-foot three-inch frame. But Charlotte only saw the exercise room when she was giving someone a tour of Dallas's premier home.

She used the baby wipes to clean herself off, flushed the commode and then got into bed. "I've had enough of the prep and I'm clear, so I'm leaving this last glass. If I'm not clear enough, it's Dr. Gold's fault, not mine. I followed the instructions to the letter."

"Sure honey," Blaze said as he came into the bedroom. "I'm done packing. Let's go to sleep; we've both got big days tomorrow."

Blaze turned off the lights and lay down on his side of their super king-size bed. He rolled over three times until he was next to Charlotte and then he kissed her on the lips. "Tastes like lemonade. Sweet dreams my love. Everything is going to be okay, you'll see."

"Everyone thinks I have cancer. What if I do? What will happen to me and to you?"

"You don't have cancer. It's something completely benign. You'll see. You're going to be fine. You'll be joining me on the campaign trail in two days."

Blaze rolled back over to his side and almost immediately fell asleep. Charlotte stared into the dark space for a few minutes, and then fell into a deep sleep herself.

Almost immediately Charlotte began dreaming. The dream started off in the living room of her parents' house on McCoy Road in Huntington, West Virginia. Her father, Ray Jones, was the largest coal mine operator in West Virginia and her mother and father were world travelers. They always brought back gifts for Charlotte, their only child, but what she enjoyed most were the slide shows they presented on their projector, filled with pictures of the exotic places they'd been. Each carousel contained space for sixty slides and a typical trip could fill five or six carousels. That night, they were watching a trip taken to Spain, and eight-year-old Charlotte sat in a trance as her father narrated the slide show and puffed on his cigar. She'd sit on her mother's lap, and her mother would add a word or two, or a gesture or cough to show that she, too, had been there and experienced that. Her mother smoked Tarleton cigarettes, and was careful not to get ashes on Charlotte. Charlotte marveled at the grand style of the bull -fight and clapped her hands as the paintings of the Spanish master, El Greco, came to life on the screen, appearing just as they looked in the Prado. She envisioned her future while watching those slides and vowed to get out of that small town and see the world.

The slide changed and there was a picture of her boyfriend, Tom Patterson, taken from the passenger side as he was driving her in his new Corvette. Tom was a senior at Harvard. He'd picked her up from the University of Virginia and drove her back to Huntington for their engagement party. She'd known Tom since grade school, and his father was the second largest coal operator in West Virginia. It was said that anything the Patterson and Jones families didn't own in West Virginia wasn't worth having. Their two families were the richest in the state, but that wasn't what attracted her to Tom. He was adventurous and cool. He wore his aviator sunglasses as he drove, the same ones he wore to pilot the American Champion Citabria Single Engine plane he'd bought two years before and flew everywhere. He had a confident look that made others feel he was in command of the situation. His blond hair was cut short and he wore a crimson Harvard shirt with the buttons undone. He'd look at her sitting next to him and then back to the road; sometimes she'd be there as an eight-year-old watching a slide show, and other times she'd be the graduating college senior admired for her beauty and charm.

She looked out the window as they passed through Virginia. She'd been all around the United States, but still felt that Virginia and West Virginia were the most picturesque places she'd seen. The highway was framed by hills and small mountains covered with lush green grass and trees. Occasionally, the view was broken by a nondescript stone building which Tom said was a historic inn and which was dwarfed by the mountains behind it.

Then suddenly the sign:

WELCOME TO
(written in white)

WEST VIRGINIA

WILD AND WONDERFUL
(written in warm red) stretching completely
across the two lanes of the highway.

Now they were in West Virginia and some farms
could be seen. Charlotte saw a magnificent white horse
galloping around a fenced-in pasture looking for a way
out. The large red barn behind the horse contained more
horses looking outward. The horse reminded her of
Tom, beautiful to look at but with a defiant wild streak,
always willing to push the limits. The horse paused
for a moment to return her stare and then returned to
galloping.

They reached a section of highway where they
could see the two lanes going in the opposite direction.
Charlotte reached across and put her hand on Tom's
head and began playing with his hair. "I can't wait for
you to see my new dress at our engagement party. Then,
only three short months until our wedding. Mom and I

still have so much planning to do. It will all be worth it. We've got so much to look forward to ahead of us."

Tom took his eyes off the road for a second and looked at Charlotte. "I'm the luckiest guy in the world. I'm marrying the prettiest, smartest, nicest woman around. They've already broken ground on our big, beautiful house in Huntington. It should be finished in six months. I'm looking forward to having children. I'll teach the boys how to run the family businesses and you'll teach the girls how to be gorgeous and elegant. Oh, by the way, Blaze is coming in for the engagement party and bringing some new Radcliffe girl he claims is the one. He collects girls like I collect speeding tickets."

Blaze was Tom's best friend from Harvard and was very handsome and sweet. They had met as freshman roommates and continued their close friendship all four years. Charlotte liked being around Blaze; he talked about politics and the Kennedys and LBJ and how his father, who was an oil baron, had helped bankroll LBJ's successful campaign for president. He knew the whole Johnson family, LBJ, Lady Bird, Luci Baines, and Lynda Bird, and spoke of them like family. His father had known President Kennedy and had been in Dallas at a reception for him the day he was shot. Blaze said he was going into politics and hoped one day to be president of the United States. At a party at a restaurant in Boston, Blaze had once pulled her aside and told her that he had everything it took to be a successful politician, looks, money, contacts, but he needed to find the perfect wife. None of the women he knew fit the bill. They had the pedigrees to be first lady, but none had the combination of beauty, poise and charm that she did.

Tom was across the room talking to friends when Blaze confided in her, but still she blushed. "I'm sure you'll find just the woman you're looking for," was all she could reply.

She was taken aback by Blaze's lack of discretion and the way he objectified women. He knew she was Tom's girlfriend, but he was blatantly making a pass at her. She walked away from Blaze and joined Tom. She wondered how much of what she'd just heard was Blaze, and how much was the alcohol talking.

Looking out the car window again she could see where the mountain had been blasted away to make room for the highway. The first eight to ten feet of the mountain was formed by naked rough boulders with no covering, but higher up the trees still grew undisturbed.

They went up a high incline and then came down into a spectacular valley with rolling fields of trees and grass framed by mountains. Since it was summer the scenery was monochromatic, but the greens showed variety based on how the sunlight hit that stretch and whether it was covered by trees or only grass. It looks like Ireland, Charlotte thought, remembering her family trip to that gorgeous, scenic country where everything was some shade of green.

Charlotte looked up at the blue sky and the few wisps of scattered white clouds which dipped under the blue sky to touch the mountains in the distance. The scenery was so beautiful that she smiled and felt her face glow. They passed by a small town nestled on a mountainside with white clapboard houses dotted among trees. She thought of the happy husbands and wives living in those homes, surrounded by their loving children and pictured a future when she would join their ranks as a wife and mother.

A yellow diamond-shaped sign with a picture of a deer prancing and below it a square sign saying

NEXT ONE MILE

was now outside Charlotte's window. ***What a gorgeous day and what an incredibly lucky woman I am***, Charlotte thought.

Then the dream changed abruptly. She was at the Guyan Country Club, the only country club in Huntington, in the beautiful purple dress she had bought while shopping with her mother in Paris. She was waiting for Tom to arrive for the engagement party. Tom had gone out earlier that morning to fly his Champion plane with his boyhood friend Chris, and they weren't at the party yet. Suddenly Charlotte felt uneasy and then scared.

Blaze walked up to her in an elegant brown suit and said, "Charlotte, I think you need to sit down."

"Why, what's wrong? Where's Tom?"

Just then, Tom's mother burst into the room shrieking hysterically.

"There was a private plane that crashed at Tri-State Airport and exploded on impact," Blaze said solemnly. "The two people on board were killed instantly. Charlotte...it was Tom's plane."

"No, no, no... this isn't happening!" Charlotte felt like she was going to vomit. She passed out into Blaze's arms. Suddenly she had a terrible, sick feeling in her stomach. She knew she was going to have an accident right there on Blaze. Her mind switched out of the dream and she realized she had to pass more prep, so she got out of bed and ran to the bathroom. The clock said seven a.m., and Blaze had already left for his campaign trip.

Charlotte got back in bed and lay there for a few minutes. Her procedure wasn't until one o'clock and she couldn't eat or drink, so there was no reason to hurry. She thought about Blaze. Weeks after Tom's funeral, he'd flown back to West Virginia to visit her. They were sitting on her parents' porch overlooking Ritter Park when he told her that he'd always loved her and wanted to marry her. He wanted her to live with him in Texas where he ran his father's oil business. She was surprised and confused and asked for time to think it over, but six months and numerous phone calls and visits later they were married in her parents' back yard. The wedding was the biggest and the best Huntington had ever seen, with even Senator Robert Byrd flying in from Washington to attend. Yet to Charlotte, amidst the happiness and promise attached to two people coming together to spend their lives as a couple, there was a feeling of loss she could never totally get over.

Charlotte stayed in bed awake but daydreaming. Over the years, the sadness had diminished as she and Blaze fell even more deeply in love and experienced life together.

Near her parents' sprawling mansion was the Huntington Galleries, an art and handicrafts museum. It was one of the jewels of Huntington, situated on a mountaintop overlooking the city. It had room after room of paintings and sculptures and offered arts and crafts instruction for children. Outside the museum was a real Indian teepee. Charlotte and Tom had often played in that teepee as children. Tom was the brave chief of their Cherokee tribe and Charlotte was his loving squaw who watched over their children and cooked the wild animals Tom brought home from his hunting trips.

Tom's family had added a wing to the back of the Huntington Galleries in his memory, and it housed visiting collections. Whenever Charlotte went home to Huntington, she visited the Galleries and wept when she entered the Tom Patterson wing. Her heart ached when she passed the teepee, which hadn't changed from her childhood, and she always laid a red rose on the pedestal of the life-size statue of Tom in his flying attire at the Patterson Wing's entrance.

BOOK TWO

MORNING

"One person can make a difference,
and everyone should try."
—John F. Kennedy

CHAPTER SIX

Gabriel finished seeing his last patient of the morning, a fifty-year-old woman sent for a colonoscopy for colon cancer screening. She was significantly aged by chronic illness. She had Type One Diabetes for thirty years as well as having hypertension and moderate kidney dysfunction. She was what Gabriel called a "semi-compliant patient," taking her medications sporadically when she felt they were needed. Her older-appearing husband accompanied her. He sat silently in the corner of the room wearing a red baseball cap which said, "Don't Ask Me About My Fucking Hat." Gabriel reminded her of the importance of following her internist's advice and taking the medications as prescribed. But she laughed and said, "Lot of good that'll do me now. World's coming to an end soon so what difference does it make? Ain't that right, Clarence?"

Her husband looked up from the floor, nodded, and then returned to studying the floor. He was obviously a man of few words, and even fewer words when his wife was around.

The patient was at least fifty pounds overweight and only chuckled when Gabriel suggested Weight Watchers and a regular exercise program. She'd tried Weight Watchers several times, but it didn't work for her. As for exercising, she had bad knees that hurt every time she walked and her back ached just from sitting in a chair. Her husband was lean as a rail, reeked of cigarettes, and had the lines of a life-long smoker on his face.

Gabriel got up from his chair and led the woman over to his assistant's desk to schedule her procedure. As he walked back to his office, Gabriel remembered that on her review of systems the patient had checked yes to prior abortion. Gabriel never understood why prior abortion needed to be listed under the review of systems for a gastroenterologist, but he knew it was very uncommon for women to check this as positive. He never asked the women anything about their abortion. He felt it was none of his business and had nothing to do with what he was taking care of them for.

Gabriel sat down at his desk and began thinking about the one abortion he'd been involved in. Six years before, when his son Ray was eighteen, the boy had knocked on the door of Gabriel's study, come in and asked Gabriel to take him for a drive. It was unusual for Ray to do this during the week as he spent most nights up in his room, studying or texting friends. Later when Gabriel was in bed and Ray had finished his homework, he would often come into the bedroom and lie down next to Gabriel and watch television until Gabriel fell asleep.

But at eight o'clock that Wednesday night, Ray had walked into the study appearing distraught and saying that the two of them needed to go for a drive. Without saying a word to Gabriel's wife, who was in her studio on the other side of the house working on her latest painting, the two of them went into the garage and got into Gabriel's Mercedes.

As they pulled out of the driveway he asked, "Where are we going?"

His son looked over at him and said, "Dad, I have a story to tell you. I made a terrible mistake and now I have to pay for it."

"Go ahead," said Gabriel, "but first tell me where we're headed."

Ray reached into his pocket and pulled out a scrap of paper with an address written on it in a girl's handwriting. The address was in the most expensive area of Highland Park, the exclusive, ultra-wealthy city located in the middle of Dallas. Gabriel's home was also in Highland Park, but in a more modest neighborhood. Gabriel entered the information into his GPS.

"I got a girl pregnant," he blurted out and then he began to cry. "Harvard, football, it's all over for me. My life is ruined."

"Calm down," said Gabriel. "What happened? You and I have had several talks about always wearing condoms."

"I did," said Ray, choking out the words. "But this one broke. It was our first-time having sex and there were circumstances that were beyond my control."

An image of Ray's girlfriend from the last couple of years flashed through his mind. "It wasn't Caroline?"

"No, said Ray, "her name is Mary. I met her at a party after a football game. The first thing I told her was that I had a girlfriend. Mary goes to the Catholic all-girls school, Ursuline. Caroline was away that weekend visiting colleges with her parents. Mary and I hit it off; she's drop-dead gorgeous, and I said I would drive her home. On the way home, she suggested we go walk around a park across the street from her house. After walking and talking we sat down on a park bench and started making out. We started going further, and she suggested we go back to my car. She took off her blouse as soon as we got into the back seat. We kept going and she never said stop. We were both naked, so I put on a condom and we had sex in the back seat. Something went wrong with the condom. It may have been all the positions we tried and her constantly playing with my dick. Whatever, the condom must have broken just as I came or right after because when I pulled out of her and pulled it off there was a hole in the condom and it had no cum in it. I drove her back to her house and kissed her good-night. I told her about the condom and she said don't worry because she was due for her period. Since then we've texted a few times back and forth but haven't hooked up again."

"Yesterday she called me and told me she was eight weeks pregnant with our baby. Her father wants to meet with you and me and Mary tonight to decide what to do. She told her father, who she says is an atheist, but not her mother who is a devout Catholic. Mary, by the way, has been raised Catholic."

Gabriel was stunned and said nothing. He'd met and liked Ray's girlfriend of two years, Caroline, and he enjoyed talking to her parents when they were together. Ray had confided in him that he and Caroline had sex on a regular basis, and that she was on the pill, but he still used condoms.

It took ten minutes to reach Mary's family estate, which was surrounded by a twelve-foot fence and had a wrought iron gate with a phone outside of it. Gabriel put his window down, picked up the phone, and after a few seconds heard a man's voice saying, "The gate will open away from your car."

The massive gates opened, and Gabriel drove around the long curving driveway up to the house. He parked under the covered entrance, and the two of them got out of the car and walked to the door. Ray was six feet three inches, but he was hunched over in shame. Gabriel rang the doorbell and it was immediately opened by a tall, red-headed man who appeared Gabriel's age. He was dressed in a pin-striped gray Armani suit with a grey and navy blue Brioni tie.

"I'm Andrew Wellington, Mary's father," he announced. He neglected to shake Gabriel's or Ray's hands. "Come with me to my office. We've got things to discuss." His tone was serious bordering on dangerous; he was presenting himself as a man who had been wronged and wasn't to be trifled with.

The home was magnificent, with an enormous foyer opening on the right to a dining room which could easily seat forty people, and on the left to a sitting room with two long golden couches on each end and a series of love seats, chairs, and small tables situated throughout the room. Gabriel would have taken in the opulence, but his mind was consumed with the idea of Ray having a child growing in some girl's uterus.

They came to a wood paneled study which lacked any books or warmth. Mister Wellington sat behind his desk and motioned for the two of them to sit down. They sat in two of the three armchairs arranged in front of the desk.

"My wife is out of town visiting her sister on Martha's Vineyard. I waited for her to leave before arranging this meeting."

Just then, a beautiful young woman, Ray's age, walked into the office and sat in the chair next to Gabriel. She had the most gorgeous shoulder-length red hair pulled straight back from her face. It curled into waves just as it reached her shoulders that gently caressed her back. Her eyes were sky blue and sparkled every time they moved. She had no make-up on and didn't need any. She wore a green and yellow flowered peasant dress with a full open blouse and a short hemline exposing shapely legs to the mid-thigh and beyond when she sat down. She weakly smiled at Ray and said, "Hi."

Wellington began to talk. "Mary is eight weeks pregnant. She came to me only when she found out and we've discussed this in detail. She'll be starting as a freshman at Yale next year where four generations of Wellingtons have gone. She isn't ready or willing at this stage in her life to take care of a baby and raise it. We have two other children who are older and have graduated from college, and I don't feel that we can raise a baby either. We have other plans for our lives. Mary's mother knows nothing about this. She would want Mary to keep the baby and probably raise it or at least put it up for adoption. Mary and I have discussed all options, and we feel it would be best for her to have an abortion."

Gabriel was stunned. He turned to Ray. "Did you know anything about this?"

Ray shook his head sadly and said, "No. Mary just called me last night to arrange this meeting and tell me she was pregnant."

"Do we have any choice in this matter?" asked Gabriel. "Would you consider allowing my wife and I to adopt and raise the child? You and your wife and Mary could visit the child anytime and play as big a part in its life as you wanted. We always wanted more children."

Mary spoke quietly yet coldly, "Ray, you're going to Harvard to play football and become a doctor. I'm going to Yale to major in Fine Arts so that when I graduate I'll own and manage one of my family's art galleries in New York, Paris, or London. This isn't the time for me to have a baby. I don't want my body to go through the changes of a pregnancy at age eighteen. My body will be different for the rest of my life. I don't want to give the baby up for adoption knowing that there was a child out there that was mine and who I had nothing to do with. I just couldn't take it. I was brought up Catholic and I believe abortion is a sin, but at this point for me and my family I feel it's the only option."

Gabriel looked at Ray who now had his head in his hands on his lap. Then he looked back at Mary. Her beauty was so overwhelming that he couldn't look at her for long. Despite that beauty, what she'd just said lit a flame of disgust deep in Gabriel's being. He worked so hard to save lives as a doctor and now a life related to him was to be snuffed out. Gabriel looked down at the floor. Words came out of his mouth without him thinking. "Ray, what do you want, what do you want?"

Ray buried his face in his hands to hide his tears. "I don't know, Dad, I just don't. I think Mary has to have the final say since the child will be inside of her."

Gabriel looked up from the floor and directly at Wellington. "Is there an option if Ray wanted to raise the child?"

Wellington pulled out a pipe and matches from the desk drawer, lit a match and put it next to the pipe's tobacco. He loudly puffed on the pipe as the smoke started to rise from it. When the pipe was properly lit he took a few slower puffs. "No," he said in between puffs, "Mary and I have decided she needs to have an abortion done as discreetly and as quickly as possible. I have a close friend who is an obstetrician in New York City who will do the abortion without anyone ever knowing about it. He has a Park Avenue practice and is considered one of the finest doctors on the East Coast. We'll fly up there this weekend and have it taken care of while Mary's mother is out of town."

Ray said, "I'd like to go with you. I'd like to be with Mary when this happens. I'm a part of this and I'd like to see it through."

"That's gentlemanly but unnecessary," said Wellington blowing smoke at Ray. "Mary and I will go alone. You stay and play in your high school football game and try to put the fact that Mary is undergoing an abortion out of your mind. My friend does charge a steep price for his skill and discretion. I need you to give me a check made out to cash for fifty thousand dollars."

"Fifty thousand dollars," Gabriel repeated incredulously, "that's a lot of money for an abortion."

"That is only half his fee. I'll pay the other fifty thousand. There will be no records, no one will know this ever happened. My friend is taking significant risk to help me out and should be compensated accordingly."

"There is no way to allow the baby to live? Do Ray and I have any say in the matter other than being extorted into handing over fifty thousand dollars?" Gabriel asked.

Wellington looked directly at Gabriel for the first time. "This is something that happened when a girl has sex for the first time in her life with a man she thinks she can trust who is supposedly wearing a condom."

"Then you're saying it's Ray's fault?" Gabriel interrupted.

"I'm not saying it's anyone's fault. I'm telling you that as Ray's father you should understand our feelings about this tragic incident and be a man and step up to the plate and help pay for the procedure. This is a matter that my daughter and I have already resolved. There doesn't need to be any more discussion or hand wringing."

Gabriel knew he could afford to pay the fifty thousand, but it was a lot of money. He was deeply opposed to the abortion of Ray's child but wanted to do what was best for Ray.

"Anything else you want to say, Ray?" Gabriel asked.

Ray started crying and tears poured down his cheeks like a faucet had been turned on. "Dad, it's all my fault. It's my fault the condom broke. It's my fault Mary got pregnant. Please dad, please. I'll pay you back someday but pay Mister Wellington the fifty thousand dollars so Mary can get the abortion and get on with her life and I can go on with my life. I'm so sorry for being so irresponsible and causing such harm and shame."

Gabriel looked at Ray and handed him a tissue from a box on the desk. "Okay," he said slowly, "we'll pay our part."

Gabriel reached into his wallet and pulled out his checkbook. He made out a check to cash in the amount of fifty thousand dollars. He got up and reached across the desk and handed the check to Wellington.

Then he turned to the girl. "Mary," Gabriel said, "I'm sorry to have to meet you under these circumstances. I certainly want what is best for you above all else. Since you and your father have decided that this is best, I think it's proper for us to help pay for the abortion, although I think it's the wrong thing to do. When things like this happen, it tests all of us. We must overcome it. Life is too short and too valuable to let one mistake –I don't know if I'd call it a mistake—to let one unfortunate circumstance ruin it."

Mary was crying also. She looked at Ray and then at Gabriel.

"You're right, sir," she said, choking out the words. "We'll get this taken care of. I appreciate your under-standing." She turned to Ray, regained her composure and stopped crying. "I'm sorry that you and I ever had sex. I knew you had a girlfriend. I don't know what got into me that night. I truly am a good, Catholic girl." She began aimlessly twisting the small golden cross she wore on her necklace. "I really do lead a clean life. I've never had sex before and I won't until I get married."

Mary turned to face her father. "Dad, I know I've disappointed you and I can't begin to express how sorry I am. I'll make it up to you someday."

Wellington puffed on his pipe. "Humph," he said. He pushed a button under his desk and within seconds a man appeared at the door who was obviously their butler.

"Romero, would you show Doctor Gold and his son the way out?"

Gabriel and Ray got up from their chairs. Gabriel wanted to only say good-bye and good luck, but instead he said, "Mary, I hope that you live a long wonderful life and have many children that you love. Good-bye and good luck with everything." He turned to leave the room, knowing that Wellington did not want to shake his hand.

Ray added, "Mary, I'm so sorry this happened. Please, don't let it stop you from becoming the person you want to be."

Mister Wellington said nothing. Gabriel and Ray walked down the long hallway and left the house. They got into the Mercedes and drove off. There was silence the whole ride back home. Gabriel thought about Ray; Ray as a father and what a child of Ray's and Mary's would have looked like. He even gave thought to himself and Sarah as grandparents.

They were greeted at the door by Sarah. "Where have you guys been? Go for a guy's night out?"

"Oh, we just took a ride around, talking about college and things like that," replied Gabriel. "We talked about Ray playing quarterback at Harvard and still making enough time for his classes and homework. College football is a big business now, but I think Ray is ready for the challenge."

"Great," Sarah said, "Ray, have you been crying?"

"No, just sneezing and coughing. Probably allergies. I'm going upstairs to do my homework." Ray walked up the stairs and they heard the door to his room shut.

Abortion, Gabriel now thought as he sat at his desk in his office. So damaging. Can change many lives. And yet, a woman had to have the right to make the decision herself, since she was the one most affected. But had Mary ever had the chance to make the decision or was it all her father's doing? Gabriel would never know. Time for some lunch now. He looked at his watch: twelve-fifteen. Forty-five minutes until the colonoscopy.

Since Ray died, Gabriel's wife made him lunch every day, so he didn't have to eat with the other doctors in the doctors' dining room. He'd just sit and eat his sandwich and potato chips at his desk, going through phone calls or signing dictations as he distractedly wolfed the food down. It had been a year since he'd eaten in the doctors' dining room; he didn't want to answer their questions or receive their sympathy.

Today, however, he remembered that his wife was in New York with her family for the Jewish holidays, so no sandwich had been made and no chips or pretzels were packed. He had no choice but to eat with the other doctors. He took the elevator down to the first floor of the office building and then walked across the corridor leading to the hospital and to the doctors' dining room. It was hidden in a hallway directly across from the morgue. He put his badge against the ID reader outside the door and the light changed from red to green. He walked into the dining room.

The dining room was just as he remembered it: full and loud. Most of the tables were square with four chairs, but the largest table, right next to the buffet line, was round, had twelve chairs, and always dominated the room with its noisy conversations. At this largest table, as usual, Guy McCord held court. Many years before Gabriel had nicknamed this joker "Guy McFuck." McFuck was a loud-mouthed, obnoxious, untalented vascular surgeon who had practiced at the hospital for fifteen years. How he'd gotten on staff and maintained privileges Gabriel never figured out, because his complication and death rate far exceeded the norm. He didn't operate on his own patients much anymore. Instead he assisted other surgeons on their cases. McFuck was talking about how the government was ruining medicine and how no one wanted to be a doctor anymore and how medicine would never recover from the government. *Just like your patients will never recover from your surgeries,* Gabriel thought. An infectious disease specialist from Iran sitting at the table asked McFuck about a patient he'd operated on for an abscess in the chest who died post-operatively. Guy launched into another tirade directed at the floor nurse who hadn't taken his orders off the computer quickly enough and done what he'd wanted. Gabriel could only think, *another death for you, McFuck.*

He'd had several common patients with McFuck, and many had not done well. He once called McFuck at midnight when McFuck was on call for the emergency room to see a ninety-two-year-old patient who appeared to have ischemic or infarcted bowel. At that time Gabriel was in the emergency room of another hospital getting ready to do an endoscopy on an eighteen-year-old boy who was bleeding massively in his upper intestinal tract. He gave McFuck the essentials of the case as they had been relayed to him by the emergency room doctor: ninety-two years old, writhing in pain, CAT scan read as showing infarcted bowel, high lactic acid level.

McFuck told Gabriel, "I'm not coming in to see that patient until you see him first. It's midnight and a ninety-two year-old gomer we're talking about. How long do you think he'll live anyway? You need to see the patient first and determine if the patient has dead bowel."

GOMER was an acronym for Get Out of My Emergency Room and had been immortalized in a book satirizing an intern's life as a new doctor, *House of God*. Gabriel told McFuck that he was at another hospital scoping a bleeder and would be tied up for another hour at least, and that the patient couldn't wait. But McFuck was adamant so Gabriel called a general surgeon who came in and immediately did a colectomy on the patient and saved his life initially, but the patient succumbed to complications two days later.

The food on the buffet was prepared by a chef the hospital had recruited to cook for the doctors. The food was delicious, but very rich and fattening. Today the entrees included steak with truffle sauce, sole with meuniere sauce, and roasted chicken breast with Pinot Noir sauce. Desserts included pecan pie, seven-layer chocolate cake and bread pudding. Gabriel felt like he couldn't tolerate any of these rich entrees, so he went to the two large refrigerated cabinets behind the buffet line and pulled out a Cobb salad with low-fat dressing and a bottle of water. He nodded at the occupants of the twelve-man table, including McFuck, and made his way to an empty table at the back of the dining room.

He ate by himself for the first few minutes, but then he saw Bruce Lam approach the table with his lunch. Bruce was Gabriel's go-to general surgeon and had been for his entire practice. Bruce was born in South Korea but had done all his training in the United States. Patients sometimes had a hard time understanding him due to his thick accent, but rarely were any disappointed with their surgical outcome. Bruce prepared extensively for every case and was technically brilliant. He'd done his surgical residency at Massachusetts General Hospital, and then somehow ended up in practice in Plano, Texas. His four children had all graduated first in their class from Plano Senior High, and two were now physicians in practice while the other two were successful owners of a medical software company that they'd started. Bruce's wife was on the board of the University of Texas at Dallas and was one of the leaders of the Korean Christian church they attended. He sat across from Gabriel at the table. His lunch also consisted of a salad and water with an apple and a banana for dessert.

"Gabriel, it's so good to see you eating in our cafeteria. I haven't seen you here in a long time. Probably not since your son's tragic death."

"I haven't been here since," said Gabriel choking nervously, "but today I didn't have any lunch to eat so I came down."

"How have you been?" asked Bruce. "As I told you before, I pray for you every day."

"Thanks. I'm still hanging in there," Gabriel replied. "I've got a colonoscopy at one that I'm worried about. It's a politician's wife."

"Oh, "said Bruce, "I'm sure she is an important person. I learned long ago, though, that once the case or operation starts you quickly forget who the face is at the other end of the table and you do the job just like you've done it thousands of times before. God made us all equal; we're all the same: same blood vessels, organs, colon. As a surgeon I see that every day. Once you start you'll be fine."

"It's more than that," Gabriel quietly replied looking Bruce directly in the eyes. "One year ago, I did a colonoscopy on her and cleared her colon of polyps. She wasn't supposed to return for five years at least. A week ago, I got a call from her internist. She presented to him with iron deficiency anemia and right-sided abdominal pain and the CT scan showed what looked like a right colon mass and multiple lesions in the liver. It probably means I missed the lesion a year ago and now it's had time to metastasize. It's just sitting there waiting to get me today. I'm scared, worried that due to my mistake she could die of the same disease that killed Ray. I keep telling myself it could be something else. The radiologist said the lesions in the liver could be atypical hemangiomas."

Bruce shook his head slowly from side to side. "You still can't tolerate mistakes, can you?"

Gabriel nodded. "Procedural complications or missing a cancer on colonoscopy would kill me," he said. "I've never learned how to emotionally or psychologically handle them. They can make me not want to get out of bed, not want to be in the company of another human being."

Bruce folded his hands on the table. "Doctors either perform procedures or make diagnoses. You and I perform procedures. I perform surgery every day. I do an average of fifteen to twenty operations a week. Not every surgery goes the way I want it to. I've had patients die on the operating table, in the recovery room, in the intensive care unit, or on the ward. All you can do is your best, which we both know you always do. Then you have to be willing to accept the consequences and move on."

"I do my best always," said Gabriel, "but I can't accept the consequences when they're bad. All I can think of is what I may have done wrong, and I play the scenario over and over in my mind. I went to a therapist once who taught me a technique of taking bad thoughts and putting them into a box and then storing them in a part of the body away from the brain where they can't be retrieved. Sounded good, but it never worked for me. Don't complications and patient deaths bother you?"

"Obviously they do," answered Bruce. "There are days when I go home and sit alone in my dark bedroom and think and think and think. I meditate to try and clear my mind. I try to concentrate on thinking about the people I've helped. But just like you, there are times I can't get it out of my mind completely and I suffer for days. However, I know that there are other patients depending on me to be capable and focused on their problems, so I erase it from my mind while I'm operating on them. I know this lady you're doing is famous since her husband is a politician, so if she does have cancer you'll get negative publicity. Remember, though, you did your best, you worked your hardest, and that's all you can do. That is all that God expects of any of us."

"Maybe I should have become just a diagnostician," said Gabriel, "although gastroenterology involves a lot of diagnosing."

"If you were a diagnostician you would go home nightly worried about the diagnoses you'd made and if you'd missed some small detail in a patient's history or physical exam." Bruce smiled. "You are who you are, and I am who I am and at our ages, we're not going to change. My advice is always move on and forgive yourself. Maybe she doesn't have cancer. Maybe she has colitis or something else. You know how notorious the radiology department is for overreading CT scans. Any spasm or contraction of the colon is a possible malignancy. Any spot in the liver must have a sonogram, CAT scan, and MRI scan done to look at it and then be repeated six months later to make sure it hasn't grown or changed. You know, CYA: cover your ass—and no one does it better than the radiologists."

"You're right, Bruce," said Gabriel, "that's the only thing that is keeping me going. I've gone into so many cases previously thinking that I missed a cancer because of radiology: cannot rule out cancer, cannot rule out cancer. The radiology department must cause more heartache and distress than any other department in the field of medicine."

Bruce nodded. "You're right. Not to change the subject, but have you heard about what is going on in the news today?"

"Briefly," answered Gabriel. "I didn't listen to much except that the terrorists are threatening to destroy the entire world unless the United States surrenders to their rule and all of Israel converts to Islam."

"That's right," said Bruce, "the world as we know it will cease to exist. It's just a matter of time. How much time no one knows. Days, maybe years. Maybe not for another generation. They're accumulating the nuclear and chemical weapons and they will unleash them when they have enough because they feel we are their mortal enemies. They feel that once they're dead they'll be in a far better place than they are now. You're Jewish, Gabriel. I think you need to save yourself before you die."

"What do you mean?" asked Gabriel.

Gabriel knew that Bruce was an evangelical Christian who believed in the Bible as being written by God and therefore should be followed to the letter. Bruce had preached to Gabriel many times that Jesus Christ had saved his life and turned him on to a spiritual, loving life once he'd arrived in the United States.

"I'm asking you to become a Christian now," said Bruce. "I know you're Jewish, but I want you to join me in being saved. You've become like a brother to me over the past twenty-plus years. You and I have laughed together, cried together, yelled at each other and then made up and become even stronger friends. I know that you need to accept Jesus Christ as your personal savior to join me and my family in Heaven. Jesus Christ has given my life meaning and hope. My personal relationship with him has brought me more contentment than anything else in my life. Being able to share his glory with my wife and children has been my greatest achievement, no matter how many lives I save. Jesus is love. Until you know Jesus and what he personally went through for you, you don't truly know what love is. You need to experience that love and that comfort and that sense of being whole that can only be achieved by turning your life over to Christ."

Gabriel was quiet for a moment. "Thank you, Bruce, I truly appreciate your love and concern. I understand what you're saying. I'm not a Christian. Like Jesus, though, I was born a Jew, lived life as a Jew, and will die a Jew. The things you speak about that Jesus brought to your life, Judaism has brought to me and my family."

"Today is Rosh Hashanah, your new year. If your faith is strong, why are you here at work?" asked Bruce. "Why aren't you at your synagogue praying to God and thanking him for this New Year?"

"I couldn't get myself to go to the synagogue," admitted Gabriel. "It's been a year since Ray passed away and maybe I'm still angry at God for taking him away. I thought the best way to deal with my anger was to avoid it, not confront it at the synagogue, and come to work."

"Don't you understand," said Bruce, "only those who believe in Jesus will be saved and live on in the kingdom of Heaven at his side. Your anger will disappear as you reflect his light. In Heaven, you and I can talk, spend time, be around the angels and Jesus, God himself. He has set up a kingdom for the righteous, the true believers, that makes anything on earth a mere pittance in comparison."

"I don't want to hurt your feelings, but I don't believe in that," said Gabriel. "I don't believe that you have to believe in Jesus to go to Heaven. I'm not even sure there is a Heaven," Gabriel continued. "This may be all there is. I do believe, though, in the idea of being part of the family of Judaism. I was born a Jew, that was a family I was born into, just like I was born a Gold. We're more of a family than a religion. We started off as a people and then we found a religion and we found a code of ethics to bind us closer together. We have one belief that we all share: the belief in one God. I follow that belief because it makes sense to me. The idea of treating others as you want to be treated, which Judaism originated, I believe in. Helping one's fellow man and doing what's right on this earth while we have the time and means to do it is what I believe in. I'm not willing to give up all the things that I've believed in over the years for a magical hope of being whisked away from eternal damnation. My idea of Heaven is a place where I can be reunited with Ray who died and was buried as a Jew and be with my wife, Sarah. Getting to see and talk to Ray and Sarah and holding them again would be all that I would ask for from any life after death."

Bruce shrugged. "Very well. I tried. I'll miss you, my brother, in the afterlife. I wish you peace and harmony always."

Gabriel finished the last bite of his salad and rose from the table. "I've got to get back to the endo center for my procedure. If the world does end today, maybe I'll see you in Heaven. So often clinically your judgement has been spot on. This one time, predicting the end of the world, I hope you're dead wrong. If you're right, I hope that all of us who have lived just, moral, righteous lives are allowed into the kingdom of Heaven. I believe those are the only criteria for admittance to Heaven if there is one."

Gabriel walked out of the doctors' dining room. As he closed the door, he heard the loud crash of a plate breaking at the table of twelve.

CHAPTER SEVEN

"Ten minutes, Adonis," came the booming voice of Jeb Fesela.

"Okay," replied Adonis, "I'll start cutting down on anesthesia, so he'll wake up soon."

Adonis was in the operating room working with Jeb, a podiatrist. They'd already completed seven cases. This was the eighth and final case of the day. It involved amputating the great toe from the right foot of a thirty-two-year-old Type One diabetic. The toe was gangrenous and well beyond salvageable, mainly due to complete lack of interest from the patient. The patient was a homosexual, drug abusing African American male with full-blown AIDS. Up until this hospitalization the man hadn't taken any drugs for his diabetes or AIDS. His CD4 count was dangerously low and he was under no doctor's care even though his AIDS had been diagnosed four years before. His brother had found him living under a bridge and brought him to the emergency room. Now he was getting a toe amputated, but Adonis knew this man's health issues would soon cut much deeper.

When the surgery was over Adonis held the patient's head as the operating room aide rolled the man from the operating table to the stretcher. Adonis was amazed at how little the man weighed, like they were moving a skeleton. His body had shriveled from the ravages attacking him and instead of the curves of fat and muscle, only the angles of bones jutting out defined him.

Jeb Fesala's booming voice brought Adonis back to the present. "I'll bring orders over to the recovery room in just a minute. If you don't mind telling the recovery room staff that this patient has multiple other health issues besides his toe and needs to be watched carefully. And they need to watch out for themselves." He winked at Adonis conveying that he was more concerned with this patient somehow transmitting AIDS to the staff than he was for the patient's health.

Adonis pushed the stretcher out of the operating room and into the long, cold hallway leading to the recovery room. Many doctors hated taking care of AIDS patients, he thought, not only because if transmitted the disease could be deadly, but also because most of the patients were male homosexuals whom many doctors despised.

In the recovery room, one of the nurses, Lisa, was waiting for them in a curtained-off area. She motioned for Adonis to bring the patient to her. She was the newest, youngest, and by far, the hottest nurse in the recovery room. She'd just celebrated her twenty-fifth birthday and her three-month anniversary working at the hospital in Adonis's bed after a wild night out dancing, drinking, and snorting cocaine.

She greeted Adonis in a sexy voice, "Well, Doctor Gonzalez, it looks like this is your last case of the day. How's your little body—I mean patient doing?"

"Well hello, Lisa. This is Mr. Charlie Brown who has just undergone a right great toe amputation by Dr. Fesela. It was done under general endotracheal and blood loss was minimal. He's slowly waking up. I've given him antibiotics during the procedure, ampicillin and gentamycin, and I know Dr. Fesela is going to want to continue him on antibiotics. He may want you to give him something if he's going to be here for long."

Lisa hooked Charlie Brown up to the monitors in the recovery room.

"His vital signs have been stable," Adonis continued, "and he's done remarkably well. He does have AIDS and a low CD4 count as well as having essentially untreated Type One diabetes for who knows how many years. The last fingerstick I got five minutes before the case ended showed a blood sugar of one fifty-seven."

Lisa looked at Adonis in amazement. "He's not really good at taking care of himself, you're saying."

"No, he's not," Adonis replied.

"And how about you, Donnie? I haven't seen you in a couple of weeks. Have you been taking good care of yourself or has someone been taking good care of you?"

"Well, yes I have. I've been around. Had to travel a little bit. Some family issues, but now I'm back. 'Course it's always good seeing you and hearing your sexy voice."

Lisa blushed as she touched Adonis on the arm. "Maybe we can hook up again sometime. That twenty-fifth birthday was my favorite birthday ever! First time I ever combined cocaine and sex; awesome combination and you were incredible."

"I had a great time, too," Adonis lied. He'd enjoyed the cocaine, but the sex was a show that was getting harder to perform.

Lisa had dark brown eyes and a surgically perfect nose which were the centerpieces of an exquisite face. She had wavy blond hair which touched below her shoulders Even scrubs couldn't hide the fact that she had a swimsuit model's figure: thirty-six D implants, no waist, and long voluptuous legs. Her pink scrub top was cut low enough that when she leaned over most of her breasts, encased in a lacy black bra, were revealed up to the nipples. The matching scrub pants that she wore were tight enough to see that two perfectly shaped cantaloupes comprised her ass. Adonis catalogued her beauty the same way he viewed the *Mona Lisa*; it was interesting to see and appreciate, but not at all tantalizing or sexy. She walked over to the other side of the stretcher and scribbled a note, then walked back to Adonis. She handed him the note. "Just in case you forgot, these are my home and cell numbers. I'm really looking forward to spending time with you again."

By now the patient was starting to wake up and sputtered and coughed a little. Adonis raised the head of the stretcher and asked for an oxygen face mask which he strapped over the patient's face as he removed the nasal cannula.

"He doesn't have pneumonia now, but apparently he's had pneumocystis pneumonia in the past," he told Lisa. "Infectious disease is following him, and they've got him on a cocktail of AIDS medications. Dr. Fesela will write orders that all of those need to be restarted when he goes back to his room. I'm going to grab a quick bite in the doctors' cafeteria. His vital signs look stable. Do you think you've got things under control?"

"Of course, Dr. Gonzalez," replied Lisa. "I'll take good care of your patient and you take really good care of yourself. Remember –" She put her right hand into the shape of a telephone and held her thumb up to her ear and her pinky up to her mouth.

Lisa briefly tugged on Adonis' surgical cap as he walked away. The cap had been bought for him the week after the 9-11 terrorist attacks in 2001 by the operating room manager. She'd bought all the anesthesiologists and nurse anesthetists caps with the American flag on them. No one wore theirs any longer except Adonis, who made it a point to wear it whenever he worked in the hospital. He took off his cap and put it in his pocket, then left the recovery room heading to the doctors' cafeteria for lunch. He realized that he smelled something on his arm, so he brought his arm to his face and smelled the fragrance of Lisa's perfume. He walked by a water fountain in the hallway and splashed water on his arm, erasing the smell.

It was twelve-thirty and he had one more case with Gabriel Gold in his endoscopy suite before he finished for the day. Adonis felt ashamed as he walked down the hospital hallway. *I'm leading that girl on*, he thought, *just like I've done with so many girls. Just to protect myself. She's going to be disappointed. Is it fair to her? I'm homosexual, not bisexual. I can still, miraculously, get it up for women, even though I'm not interested in them. Isn't it time? Why make enemies and continue to live like this? I'm living a lie.* Then another thought came into Adonis's mind. He'd heard on the news about the world ending, with terrorists blowing it up. He didn't want to die without setting the record straight. *People all over the country have come*

out as being gay, lesbian, transgender. Hell, the Supreme Court has come out with a law saying gays could marry. He'd hidden it for all these years. It was enough, he decided. *No more hurting women. No more trying to fool myself. I'll come clean sometime soon and find a place to marry Jean-Baptiste.*

He entered the doctors' cafeteria, took a plate, and studied the vast array of choices on the buffet. He glanced across the room. It was amazing how many doctors came from throughout Plano to eat here because of the chef's superb cuisine and because it was free. Adonis didn't know most of the doctors. Internists, family doctors, and pediatricians who practiced in the Plano area and only stepped foot in the hospital to get a free lunch since they had hospitalists in the hospital to take care of their patients. They mainly sat in the back, while the front table of twelve was filled by the doctors who worked in the hospital. Adonis rarely sat at the table of twelve because the doctors who sat there were loud, obnoxious assholes. He preferred to sit at a quieter table in the back of the room with one or two other anesthesiologists who also were gay and were non-confrontational.

Adonis got in line and got chicken breast with Pinot Noir sauce, buttery garlic green beans, and dauphinoise potatoes. He looked around the dining room for an empty seat, but every seat was taken. He saw Gabriel Gold at a back table in deep conversation with Bruce

Lam. He decided not to bother Gabriel since he knew they'd be working together shortly.

Suddenly at the table of twelve, Houston Steele, one of the orthopedic surgeons, stood and picked his plate up from the table. "Here, Adonis, you can take my seat. I'm done, and I've got to go to the emergency room and evaluate a hip fracture."

Houston walked away from the table and Adonis grudgingly took his place. As they passed each other, Houston patted Adonis on the shoulder and said, "Now you can join the conversation on the world ending today. That's all anyone wants to talk about, even though the threat has been there for years. I'd rather talk about anything else, even McCord's sex life."

"I'd much rather discuss the Dallas Cowboys," laughed Adonis as he sat down.

One of the other doctors at the table was Albert Putz, a family practitioner who snuck into the hospital for lunch but hadn't worked in the hospital for thirty years. He was brave enough to sit at the table of twelve—or maybe it was stupidity; he was often the object of their ridicule.

"What do you think, Adonis?" Putz asked, "do you think the world is going to end? Or do you think they'll bring the television show *Dallas* back for another go-round? We've been debating the odds on which of those two things will happen first. Third *Dallas* series or the world ends?" He laughed.

Adonis started eating. "I don't know," he said in between bites. "For some reason, those terrorists sound pretty pissed off to me. It's as though they don't want us to go on living. It's as though us being alive is an insult to them. How can you inhabit the world with people who are enraged by your very existence?"

"The Israelis have been dealing with that issue with the Palestinians for years," replied Putz. "They've tried to lead normal lives and build their own country up and make it prosperous."

Guy McCord jumped in. Adonis also thought of him as "Guy McFuck" after working for years with Gabriel Gold and hearing his nickname. "We have got to do something to kill all those terrorists," said McCord. "There is not one good thing about dem Ay-rabs!"

Two Egyptian neurologists in the back of the room looked up from their plates.

"The only good terrorist is a dead terrorist," Guy continued.

"How did they get so strong and how did they convert so many followers from all over the world?" asked Jim Kline, another anesthesiologist in Adonis' group. "It seems that they're all young people that they've recruited."

McFuck weighed in. "They're recruiting young people who don't give a damn about their lives. They feel they've been cheated out of their futures by governments that don't care. Kind of like my son: went to high school, went to college, graduated, got a Masters, got a PhD in psychology and now lives back at home with my wife and me. I guarantee you if these terrorists offered my son seventy-two virgins in the afterlife to blow up his father and his father's house he'd be the first in line to accept."

"Your son's that interested in virgins?" came Albert Putz's quick retort. "Doesn't he want women with a little bit of experience?"

"Hell," said McFuck, "one thing I can say about my son for certain: he may not be a hard worker but he certainly ain't no faggot! He'd take the seventy-two women anytime. For him that would be paradise."

The cardiologist, David Prusta-Shlub, spoke up, "Seventy-two virgins, young women, it's hard to give up. Especially after all of us have been married for so many years. I don't know about the rest of you sitting here, but seventy-two virgins could have come in really handy at about year ten of my marriage."

Adonis saw David look over at him. "Except Adonis, that is. He's smart enough not to get married and still screw around with the young nurses."

Adonis half-smiled at this with his mouth full of food.

"It would serve these terrorists right," McFuck said, "if instead of seventy-two virgins waiting for them up in

Heaven, there were seventy-two faggots just waiting to corn-hole them."

Everyone laughed loudly except for Adonis.

"Don't think that's funny, Gonzalez?" asked McFuck in a bullying tone. "Yeah, I can see it now," he continued spurred on by Adonis' lack of response. "Seventy-two faggots waiting for you. But at least they'd have your apartment in Heaven neat and orderly and your color scheme would be adorable."

"Yeah, right," said Arnie Shanda, the infectious disease specialist. "Your clothes would be stylish, you'd have a cute little lap dog and all your towels and washcloths would be shocking pink."

"Well," Adonis said, "whether they were faggots or virgins I still think I'd rather be in this world living my life. Hopefully all the talk about the terrorists is going to be just that, talk. How 'bout them Cowboys?"

"I hope you're right," said McFuck. "The terrorists have us right where they want us. It's fucking inevitable. The world is going to end, but maybe a few of us will survive. Someday they'll hopefully re-populate the world, unless of course those few that survive are fucking faggots."

Adonis could feel the steam inside his head as his face turned red. When they were talking about faggots waiting for the terrorists in Heaven, he could hold back his anger. But now he felt it boiling over inside of him.

The table of twelve was a dangerous place to sit, full of vicious, uninformed, opinionated assholes. They had a reputation for ridiculing every group from gays to women to people from India and Pakistan. Now he couldn't take it any longer. He finished his food, wiped his face with his napkin, and looked directly at McFuck.

"If you found out your son was gay, if you found out that he was a faggot, what would you do?"

McFuck was famous for answering questions by asking another question. "Why in the fuck would you think my son was gay? Because he lives at home? I've seen him in his room with women. He's not fucking gay. If he was, I can tell you he wouldn't be living in my house. I wouldn't support a faggot under my roof. He could go live with his faggot boyfriend. Would you support a faggot son, Putz?"

Putz seemed surprised to have the attention focused back on him and turned red. "One of my nephews is gay and he lives in San Francisco with his husband. They have a child, a little girl they adopted from Russia. They seem to be getting along well, and they seem to be good for their daughter." It was obvious Albert was choosing his words carefully as he spoke very slowly. "She'd have no parents otherwise. I'm not against gays. Each person has the right to make their own decisions on sexuality, and the right to have their sexuality be their own business."

"You're not against gays!" said McFuck, "I'm not so sure you're not a faggot yourself. Don't you see how they've ruined our country's morals? In some ways it's the gays and our acceptance of them that's responsible for what's about to happen. It's Biblical! Our country doesn't have a president who is man enough to fight off these terrorists. We've gone against the Bible's teaching with the fags and now anything is acceptable. Gay marriage, gay sex, bestiality. Nothing's off the table. And the man up above sees that, and he's going to bring it all to a shrieking halt. The terrorists know that our country has been abandoned by God because we have acquiesced to the Gay Agenda, and now they're going to destroy us."

Adonis stood up, lifted his plate and slammed it down against the table, shattering it and sending shards of porcelain flying all over. He pushed his chair further back and shouted, "So you don't trust faggots, huh? So, you wouldn't want faggots taking care of your precious family? Well let me tell you, McFuck, I'm a faggot and I'm tired of pretending I'm not and listening to crap from assholes like you. Just because I fuck men in the ass doesn't mean I'm any less competent a doctor than anyone in this fucking room. I'm declaring it here today. Whether the world ends, or it doesn't, I want to be truthful to myself and say that I'm gay. And the last thing I want to say, McFuck," as he stared directly into McFuck's gray eyes, "is that God hasn't abandoned this country or its people. The hatred that you espouse divides this great country and weakens it."

Staring at the astonished faces of the people around him, he continued, "My God is Jesus who is a loving God who loves us all and understands and accepts us. I didn't choose to be gay. I was a macho Cuban boxer when I was a kid. Being gay is a part of me, just like my eyes are part of my face and my love for my fellow man made me become a physician. I don't hold it against you that you're a racist, bigoted asshole, so don't hold my sexual orientation against me."

Adonis started walking out of the dining room. He expected McFuck to try and stop him, but the lowlife didn't have the guts. There were four other gay doctors sitting at the doctors' dining room as he left and not one stood up for Adonis. *They all still feel safer in the closet,* he thought. *One day they'll discover how liberating the truth can be.* Adonis looked at his watch; it was twelve forty-five and his case with Gold began in fifteen minutes. Just enough time for a bathroom break and the walk over to the endoscopy center.

CHAPTER EIGHT

The morning cases were done, so RC walked over to Carol and said, "Want to go to the cafeteria for lunch before Doctor Gold's next case? We've got an hour, and I didn't get much breakfast."

"Sure," said Carol, "let me get my wallet."

RC watched as Carol waddled off to the changing room. Carol was the pre-op nurse who got all the patients ready for their procedures. RC saw her as a surrogate mother, who unlike her birth mother, always listened to RC and tried to help her. She was short, stocky, and had straight white hair. Her blue eyes sparkled with kindness and the patients all loved her. Even the most neurotic, nervous patients felt more comfortable as RC wheeled them into the procedure room after spending time with Carol. She wore granny glasses which RC often jokingly told her she was too young for.

As they walked out the door Carol studied RC's face closely. "You're wearing a lot of make-up today, but I still see a fresh black eye. That sonovabitch beat you again?"

RC didn't want to cry but couldn't stop the tears from flowing as they got on the elevator to go down to the first floor. "I got too drunk to remember, but it must have been Randy. He gets drunk and mad and drunk and madder and takes it out on me. I think he knocked me out with a punch last night."

The elevator stopped on the first floor and the two of them walked down the corridor to the main cafeteria. Carol handed RC a tissue and she wiped her eyes and face.

"That crying washed away the makeup that was covering your black eye. Now you can see it easily. I can see his knuckle prints on the right side."

RC had her purse with her so when they passed by the ladies' room she said, "Let's stop inside a minute."

Inside, RC pulled out her make-up and powdered her entire face, putting a double coat around her eyes. "Is that better?" she asked Carol.

"Much better," replied Carol. "Can't even tell there was a bruise there."

"My father beat my mother," RC started saying as they left the rest room. "Every night he'd get drunk and then find some excuse to hit her. He hit her with his hand, a belt, once even a frying pan. When I was five I asked him why he hurt Mommy and made her cry and look ugly and he said it was none of my business and if I asked again he'd beat me, too."

They got into the lunch line and each ordered a hamburger, fries, and Diet Cokes. When they got to their table and sat down, RC continued, "Two months later on my sixth birthday I woke up and went looking for my mother, but she was gone. I couldn't find her anywhere. Dad was in a drunken stupor passed out on the living room floor, and on his naked back was taped a note addressed to me from my mother. All it said was that she loved me but couldn't live with my father anymore, so she'd gone and wasn't coming back. She'd taken all her personal stuff and whatever money my parents had with her. I never saw her again. I always wondered why she didn't take me with her."

"Did you try to find her?" Carol asked.

"Yes and no. Sometimes in high school when we were playing in other towns and I was cheerleading I'd pick up a phone book and see if she was listed under her married or maiden name. Never found her. I was too busy growing up and trying to survive my drunken, abusive father. I just wanted to grow up and get away like she did."

"She never contacted you?"

"Never. That's one thing different about her and me. I could have left little Joshua with his paraplegic father to be brought up mainly by his grandparents, but I would never leave him. Even when I found out he was autistic I could have run away and left him with Chip's parents. But I wanted him to have a mother, a good, caring mother who loved him. I was naïve enough to think that I could break the cycle of beating and abandonment. I can never tell if Joshua appreciates all I try to do for him, but I think he does. I even stay with that bastard, Randy, because he takes him to daycare and picks him up and keeps a roof over our heads. I hate it though, that Joshua sees his mother all bruised and torn up."

"Do you think that women who were abused as children or see their mothers abused gravitate towards that same type of man?" asked Carol. "My husband knows if he ever touched me I'd shoot him, and my mother would have shot my dad if he tried to hit her."

"I don't know if I'd say I gravitated to a Randy, but it doesn't seem that unusual for him to beat me or hurt me. I have less fear of his behavior than I probably should because it's all I've ever known. It almost seems natural, like I deserve it. My dad beat my mom, then he beat me, and now Randy beats me."

"You need to get away or he'll kill you one day. You and Joshua deserve a normal life. You make a good living as a nurse. Get your own apartment while you can."

RC munched on a French fry and pondered Carol's statement. "I guess I've been waiting all my life for Prince Charming to come and rescue me. I can support myself, and I can stand on my own two feet. I did it before I met Randy. You're right. I need to quit waiting for Prince Charming and move my life in the right direction myself."

"You and Joshua can come live with me until you get on your feet. All I've got in my big house is me, my sick husband, and my pooch, Goldie. It would be good for Joshua to be in a home with a backyard and around a dog. Dogs are a little boy's best friend, especially boys who are autistic or developmentally disabled. Thinking of it reminds me of growing up in East Texas and a boy I knew named Chris and his dog, Syrup." Carol stopped and wiped her eyes.

"Are you crying?" asked RC.

"A little bit. I was just thinking about Chris and Syrup."

"Tell me about them. I love to hear your stories about growing up in a normal home."

Carol started, "It will take a few minutes to tell the whole story, but if you want to hear it, here goes." She wiped her eyes and continued, "It was late spring in Tyler, Texas and school was within a few weeks of ending. It was a glorious day of sunshine with promises of athletic glory. My cousin Steven and I were in the second grade, my brother Russell and my other cousin, Kim, in the fourth. In gym class the last two weeks we played a new game, kickball, and I begged my mother to buy one of those big red rubber balls, so we could play in the front yard of my cousins' house. I had visions of kicking the ball over the hedges between my cousins' house and their neighbors, which of course I'd never accomplished with a baseball and bat. I remember walking over to my cousins' house with that big red rubber ball and bouncing it on the sidewalk.

"We picked teams for kickball; the girls, Kim and me against the boys, Steven and Russell. My other cousin Thad, a year younger, saw us playing and came outside wanting to play, too. Uneven numbers always meant one person was a permanent fielder and so we parked Thad next to the garden light that represented third base.

"We played for a while and were having a great time. After about thirty minutes, Chris Colley appeared at our ball field walking his dog Syrup. Syrup was a medium-sized tan mutt with a round face and perky ears that stood up as she walked. Even though he was somewhat slow, Chris was in my class in elementary school since they didn't have special education then. Everyone just went to school together except the coloreds who had their own school on the colored side of town.

"Chris didn't look retarded. He had jet black hair straight as a ruler, cut close to his head, but not quite a crew-cut. He had dark blue eyes, so dark they sometimes seemed black. His face was a small triangle with a pug nose and a large dimple on each cheek. He was slight of build and short. I was a head and a half taller than Chris and even though I was a slim tom-boy then, next to Chris I looked husky. He had tiny hands which were always in motion for reasons none of us could understand and which never looked coordinated. He still wore the kind of tiny red Keds sneakers that I wore in kindergarten.

"Chris rarely left his yard to join us for sports; however, that day he'd been in his backyard which was across the creek from my cousins' house and heard us yelling and screaming. He decided to cross the creek and climb the hill to see what was going on. He'd been playing with Syrup in his backyard and brought Syrup with him."

"I'd love for Joshua to be able to play with a dog," RC interrupted. "I think it would help him to develop emotionally. Maybe he could relate to a being that gives unconditional love all the time instead of a human being who gives love that comes with boundaries. Wish I'd had a dog growing up to love and to love me back. Maybe my life wouldn't have been so fucked."

Carol nodded. "Chris came over and stammered, 'I want play. I play in school. I can kick.'

"We added him to our team while Thad joined the other team and now he'd be allowed to kick, too. The game continued, and the day started getting hotter. I noticed Syrup ambling over to sit under a tree on the other side of the driveway. As she walked, I noticed that her legs were too long for her body. She seemed to wobble with each step like a newborn horse. It was as if she was scared to put her paws on the ground and had to make sure each paw was securely placed before the next one could be lifted. She lay under that big oak tree and seemed to go to sleep.

"When it was our turn to bat Chris would go over to the tree and hug and pet Syrup. Then he announced that he could only play one more inning; he had to go home for a peanut butter and jelly sandwich and to give Syrup a bath to make her fur look new. On the next play, I singled and was on first base and I yelled to Chris that he was up. Chris rubbed Syrup a few more times for luck and stepped up to the plate.

"Just then we heard the gunning engine of a car out on the street. The engine reached a crescendo and the car made a squealing turn and began racing down the street. I looked up the small hill to the road and saw a shiny black Chevy race by me with a teenage driver and another kid in the passenger seat. Then I heard barking and across the driveway saw Syrup galloping as fast as she could up the hill after the car. When she was running, those long legs could really pump.

"Chris started running after her. 'No!' Chris cried, turning and running after Syrup. 'No, stop Syrup!'

"The car's brakes screeched loudly as the barking intensified and then there was a sickening thud as the car ran over Syrup and crushed her. There was one loud yelp, and then silence. The driver had seen the dog too late out of the corner of his eye, and his swerve to the right only left more of the tire to crush Syrup.

"The car backed up and the teenagers got out. Chris was crying hysterically. He lay down on the street next to the dog, and stroked Syrup's head with his hands and kept saying, 'You be all right, girl, you be all right. Gonna give you a bath and clean you.' I walked up the driveway to where Chris and the dog were lying, and it was a gruesome site. Blood covered the street around Syrup and blood trickled down the driveway. The dog was motionless with no breathing, so even though her eyes were open, I knew she was dead.

"Kim ran down to Chris' house and brought his mother back. Kim had told her what happened, and she came with Syrup's favorite blue blanket that she'd knitted for her. The blanket had the name SYRUP knitted in white letters and Syrup slept with it. Chris' mother was also tiny and had dark hair with a kerchief tied around it. She always wore long dresses and white long-sleeved blouses, no matter the weather. She was always doing the laundry or cleaning their house or raking the leaves. She never came over to my cousins' house, so none of us really knew her.

"The driver was crying. 'I'm so sorry, so sorry,' the driver said as he cried.

"'We know you didn't mean it,' Chris' mother replied. 'It was an accident, we know. Jesus gave us Syrup for seven years; it was time for her to go back to God in

Heaven.' She draped her arms over Chris as he refused to let go of Syrup in the middle of the street. Chris' striped blue and white tee shirt and his white shorts were now brown from the dog's blood.

"'I've got to take her home, momma and give her a bath,' Chris sputtered, and his mom nodded her head. I looked at her to see why she hadn't said anything, and her face was ashen and covered with tears. 'She be okay when I get her home, momma, won't she? Her fur look new after a bath?'

"Chris' mom stroked his hair. She loved her Chris just like you love your Joshua. The driver of the Chevy was pounding his hand on the hood of the car and crying in rhythm to the pounding. All of us were crying.

"Chris took the blanket from his mother and wrapped Syrup up. He held Syrup in his arms even though she was about as big as he was. He walked slowly down the driveway, blood spots dripping onto the driveway with each step. His mother had her arm around Chris, and he hugged Syrup closer and closer to his chest. They went down the hill at the back of my cousins' house and crossed the creek. I could still hear them crying. They disappeared behind the big pine tree in their yard. I lived in Tyler for six more years and never again remember Chris joining us to play sports. I still saw him at school, and he eventually got another dog, but he never left his own yard."

"Does your story mean you're saying it was good for Chris to have a dog?" asked RC. "Emotionally that had to be a heartbreaking experience for a boy with limited intelligence and few friends."

"That dog Syrup was his best friend. So was the dog they got after her, Mustard. Boys with special needs can bond with animals. They share a love that is expressed in gestures and deeds, not in words. Chris may never have forgotten the pain of losing Syrup, but the dog helped him develop and learn to love someone other than himself."

"Syrup's death was tragic, but it taught all us kids that life can be over in the blink of an eye. Don't think that didn't leave a lasting impression on me and how I live my life. I refuse to put off the things and people that matter in my life because I don't know what the next moment will bring. You'll come live with me, and Joshua will have a dog to bond with and you'll be safe. You have no reason to feel guilty. You're not to blame for your mother leaving and not coming back, for the fact that your ex-husband is a paraplegic, or that Joshua is autistic. You don't need to feel guilty. You don't deserve to be beaten. It's time for you to live and love again. What is that famous saying? 'Today is the first day of the rest of your life.'

They got up from the table, deposited their cartons in the garbage can, and started walking back to the endoscopy center. Neither spoke at first, as each was deep in thought. RC thought about what would be best for Joshua and for her in the future. Randy had been a protection blanket for RC and Joshua, dangerous but always there. Did she want Joshua to grow up in that environment? Couldn't she meet a nice man who wouldn't beat her?

"You're right," said RC, "I finally see the light. I don't deserve this and neither does Joshua. Randy could end one or both of our lives today. Joshua needs to be around a dog and with people who love him. Now he knows love from me and disdain from Randy. At least with Chip and his parents, he's with people who love him and care about him. After Gold's colonoscopy I'm going home to pack, and I'll be at your house tonight before Randy knows I'm gone."

The women smiled at each other; it was the special kind of smile reserved for people who would be starting life together away from hatred and destruction, and with the common goal of enjoying every moment.

CHAPTER NINE

ester walked out of the endoscopy center and started his journey to the hospital cafeteria. At the end of the long hallway was a six-foot six-inch, two-hundred and ninety-pound African American young man with a shaved head. *Can't miss Abraham,* Lester thought. *He looks like he could still be the defensive end for Plano's high school football team.* He wore dark blue scrubs with Plano OR and his name, Abraham, embroidered on the shirt pocket.

"Been waiting for you," Abraham said.

"Last case ran a little late and I had to clean up the room for a one o'clock case," replied Lester, "but I've got an hour off now for lunch and to visit my mother in the hospital."

"She's back in the hospital?" asked Abraham. "Didn't she just get out two days ago?"

"She was readmitted last night with a blood sugar of nine hundred and seventy and severe abdominal pain," replied Lester. "Let's walk outside to the hospital instead of cutting through indoors. It's such a beautiful day and we're inside working all day."

"Sounds great," said Abraham.

Lester thought about the man walking beside him. Abraham had been brought up Christian, going to church every Sunday and even singing in the choir. He had a beautiful baritone voice and it was a pleasure to hear him speak. But four years before, after studying with a former high school coach who was Muslim, Abraham had converted to Islam and changed his name from Marshawn Patrick to Abraham Ali. The coach and other members of the mosque had taken in Abraham like he was family, he told Lester, so the conversion was easy and very enjoyable for him. He now prayed five times a day, facing Mecca, and he daily advocated to Lester to convert to the Muslim religion.

They opened the building door and the radiant sunlight made them look down as they walked on the sidewalk. *What a gorgeous, glorious day* thought Lester. They started down Coit Road and then would make a left on West Fifteenth Street, and then another left into the entrance of the hospital.

Halfway down Coit Road, a Ford F-250 truck pulled up beside them. A young white man with a beard and scraggly blonde hair leaned out the passenger side and shouted, "Hey, can you two niggers give me directions to Harlem?" He then shot them the bird with both hands.

The truck immediately went into high gear, racing away. The truck had a Confederate flag painted on the back window. Its license plate was a custom Texas plate that said DIXIE.

Abraham shook his large head slowly. "Still such prejudice… still such hatred. My religion doesn't allow this. Allah preaches love for every man. Hatred takes one straight to hell. Love guides man on the path to Heaven."

Lester slowly shook his head back and forth as he looked up at Abraham. He had an incredible physical presence that would stand out no matter where he was. The sunlight beamed off his bald, glistening head.

"It's amazing," said Lester, "one hundred and fifty years after the end of slavery there's still such hatred, such bigotry against African-Americans in this country. So many white people have never gotten over the Civil War. How can people still hate? So many African-Americans have died defending this sacred country of ours. Why do people still hate? Here we are working in a hospital and endoscopy center to make people of all colors, races, and religions better. Yet all they look at is the color of our skin and they direct hatred towards us. They'll never get over the fact that for eight years this country had a black man in the White House. They will never forgive themselves for letting their guard down and letting that happen."

Abraham laughed. "The prophet Mohammed's life needs to be followed by all of us. We must all live in faith following the words of Allah as they are recorded in the Quran. Allah says we must love each other. We must also follow all of the laws and edicts that he proclaimed."

"Yes," said Lester, "I understand your belief. You've talked about your religion for years. We both went to work instead of going to college, and you chose to convert to Islam. At least you had the opportunity to play football at a junior college."

"I didn't want to be in school anymore," replied Abraham. "I needed to get out and start making money. I have five brothers and five sisters younger than me and I wanted to help my parents support them. Three of my brothers have converted to Islam, and I'm working on the rest. You should convert, too. African Americans aren't slaves in Islam. We're not looked down upon like the White Christians look down upon us in America. African Americans in Islam are equal. We have equal rights and no one person in my religion looks down on another."

"I often wonder," said Lester as they walked into the hospital and made their way towards the cafeteria, "why man hates man. How is it that the difference in skin color causes one to despise another? Where does hatred come from? I recently read an article that said that the DNA making up whites and blacks only differs by 0.1 percent. Yet rather than celebrating our similarity, we focus on the miniscule difference and use it as a reason to divide."

Abraham looked down at Lester and smiled. "My kind friend, you always have such deep philosophical questions and thoughts. You would make the perfect Muslim. Plus, after the destruction of the world you would go to Heaven. In our Heaven, the body accompanies the soul. You would be around others who love and don't hate, and you would be with Allah, our God."

"Think about it," continued Lester, "remember that tape of fraternity boys on a bus at the University of Oklahoma singing about lynching niggers? They sang about putting ropes around our necks and letting us hang from a tree until we died. That's happening now. What about those poor black high school students from Dallas who went to Texas A and M looking to better themselves and they were crushed by racist slurs uttered by the college students? Not only did the white students make them feel unwelcome, they also insulted them and stripped away their human dignity."

"I think that there has to be hatred in this world," said Abraham, "so that love can be practiced and appreciated. Hatred is passed on. A baby doesn't come out of his mother's womb with hatred—he must be taught. Love must be passed on from generation to generation, and that can only be done by believing in Allah. The easiest thing in this world is to learn to hate; you and I see that every day. Think about the racist slurs you and I just had to endure. The hardest thing is to love. Black, white, red, yellow, purple, it doesn't matter. People look for someone that they can hate, look down upon. Putting that person down with an insult or slight makes them feel superior. Islam teaches that only through love and following the life that Mohammed lived can we achieve happiness and fulfillment. Not through hatred or divisiveness, but only through love."

The Christian and the Muslim sat down and ate lunch together.

"Can you imagine your life without Islam?" asked Lester.

"No, man," replied Abraham. "My life now is orderly and stable. No longer do I let alcohol touch my lips or go out looking for easy women. A marriage will be arranged for me when it's time for me to have a family. I'll marry someone with strong beliefs like mine and we'll raise children and instill in them our beliefs. The month of Ramadan is a special month for me. I fast from morning until dark and pray. Someday I will make a pilgrimage to Mecca with my wife and children. There I will see first-hand the greatness of Mohammed and feel the love of Allah. There is a peace and contentment that I feel now as a Muslim that I never felt as a Christian. Just like Islam grew out of Christianity and Judaism, so, too, have I grown out of Christianity into the Muslim faith."

"I was born a Christian, and I'll probably die a Christian," said Lester. "But I don't go to church now. My mom always says how important Jesus Christ is and how Jesus has done this for her and Jesus has done that for her, but I can't see that he's done anything for her. I'm the only one who cares about her and she'd be long dead if it wasn't for me. Sometimes I think that Jesus was just a seed that was planted in her brain when she was a child, but she never nurtured it or allowed it to grow to mean something. I believe in the teachings of Jesus Christ that I learned from attending Saint Mark's and being around relatives, but I know I need to learn more. It's interesting; I've always considered myself an African American first and a Christian second. I think that's because I've had to fight because I'm black, but never because I was a Christian."

"Yes," said Abraham, "Jesus was a great prophet. So were Abraham, Noah, and Moses. Jesus was a prophet but not the last or ultimate prophet. The ultimate prophet is Mohammed. Sure, Jesus was a great prophet, but the religion of Christianity—where has it gotten you? What has it done for you? You seem unsettled. You don't have the peace of mind that I've attained. Only by changing your beliefs will you go to Heaven." He paused, looked up at the cafeteria ceiling, and then looked back at

Lester. "I'm going to tell you something now and you're the only person I'm going to tell. From conversations I overheard in the mosque, today is the last day that you can change your belief. By reciting one verse with me you'll become a Muslim and you'll be entitled to the same things in Heaven that I'm entitled to. We'll enter the realm of Allah as equal brothers."

"Let me think about it," said Lester. "Let me think about it. Somehow, it's starting to make sense to me to become a Muslim. I've got to go up and visit my mother now in room 406. Can I talk to you later?"

Abraham looked intensely at Lester with his charcoal eyes and smiled. "I'll wait for you outside your mother's room when I'm finished praying. We'll talk then. Before you go, I need to ask you a question that I've never asked you before. What made you decide to go into medicine and want to become a doctor?"

Lester laughed. "It's a long story. Do you really have the time to hear it?"

"Sure," came Abraham's eager reply, "you tell me the story and then we'll both go our separate ways."

"It started when I was a sophomore in high school and had just transferred over to Saint Mark's. I was living with my grandfather at that time; he was the only one who had room for me and I was supposed to take care of him in exchange for room and board. Everyone called him Pappy. It all happened one morning; I went from not knowing what I wanted in life to knowing that if I couldn't be a professional football player, I wanted to be a doctor.

"I was awakened by the sound of my grandfather gasping for air. I pulled the electric alarm clock close to my eyes and read the time—it was five twenty-five in the morning. Almost time to get ready and then take the city bus to Saint Mark's School. I got out of bed, went over to the window, and pulled the curtain to one side. The window was streaked with rain and felt cool. Outside the street was barren. Even the barbeque stand across the street was dark, and its parking lot was empty. I walked over to my grandfather's bed and knelt beside him.

"How can he sleep when he makes so much noise? I thought. His head was tossing and turning. I lay my hand on his arm. I had raised the head of his bed with blocks just like his doctor, Dr. Porter, had suggested, but it didn't help at all. My eyes were now adjusted to the darkness and I could make out my grandfather's curly yellow-white hair and dark black face as he tossed his head from side to side, spitting, choking, snorting and coughing. *Poor Pappy!* Small wisps of white hair now appeared on Pappy's face, the result of me not having shaved him in several days.

"Pappy," I yelled.

"He grunted something unintelligible.

"The covers were thrown off the bed and the sheets were in disarray. I could see his ankles now; they looked like giant grapefruits at the end of long, slender sticks.

"I knew he'd been getting worse and worse. I knew I needed to call Dr. Porter, his cardiologist. My alarm clock started beeping and I shut it off.

"'Hmm, bug guhya,' was my grandfather's response.

"Pappy, you don't sound good," I said.

"He took a deep breath and there was a moment of silence and then, 'What?'

"Pappy, you need to see Dr. Porter. Your breathing is awful."

"He said, 'Boy, what you talk 'bout. Don't know your damn ass from, (cough, cough). Don't you be feeding me none of your lip, you ole frizzle-haired (cough). Ya ain't got no sense but talk down 'bout Pappy.'

"Here, Pappy, let me help you sit up."

"'Don' need your help.' But I helped him sit up anyway. 'I'll send you back to live with your uncle, much help you been givin' me,' he said.

"Pappy, you sounded really bad last night. Doctor Porter said to come back to the hospital when you sound like that again. And your ankles are swollen up again."

"'Boy, you nappy-headed goat. If I war ten years younger, I'd rap you op side your head. No doctor gonna tell me what best for ole Willie Sims. Give me my pills and I take 'em.'

"I walked over to the lone dresser in the room and opened the top drawer on my grandfather's side. Inside were two bottles of pills. I removed one pill from each bottle and returned the half-filled bottles to the drawer. Then I stepped around my grandfather's bed and walked into the kitchenette. I turned on the light and saw three large roaches in the sink. I opened the cabinet and took out a glass with a large roach scrambling around inside of it. I turned the glass upside down and the roach fell on the floor and I crushed it with my foot. I filled the glass with water and brought it back to the bed along with the pills.

"Here, Pappy."

"'Wuthless boy. When I was your age I be a man already. You ... ' He gulped down the pills with the water. He fought to catch his breath, but all that came out were high-pitched shrieks.

"Pappy!" I yelled as I patted him on the back. "Pappy, you need help now."

"Pappy stopped wheezing after a minute. 'Turn on the light, boy.' I reached over and turned on the lamp which sat on the table between our beds. Pappy looked terrible. His chest was heaving in and out and he alternated between making gurgling sounds and wheezing. His eyes were bloodshot.

"He said, 'Boy, why don' you make me my meals and jes' be head'n on to that fancy private school. Don' wancha round me all day, stirring up trouble. Jes like your momma before she 'came an addict. Always lookin' for trouble.' Pappy started coughing again and bent over at the waist while holding his chest. His face turned red and then a scary blue color.

"Uncle sent me to live with you to take care of you. I'm going to call Doctor Porter and see what he wants me to do." I put on my clothes and my shoes and headed for the door to go make a phone call. We didn't have a phone in our tiny apartment.

"'Boy, (cough) (cough), come back here.'

"I closed the door to the apartment and was engulfed by darkness. There was only one light in the entire hallway, and since its shade had been broken years before, all that was left was a burned-out light bulb. I felt my way along the wall to the stairway and opened the door leading to the stairs. The stairway was dark and smelled like vomit. I carefully climbed down five flights to the sixth floor, and made my way to apartment six -twelve, and knocked on the door. After a minute the door opened and there stood Jarmille Dixon wearing torn jeans and no shirt. Jarmille and I had gone to middle school together, and he'd played wide receiver on our football team. 'Mother-fuckin Lester. What chew doin' heah? Thought you was at that fancy private school now.'

"Jarmille, I need to use your phone and call Pappy's doctor. He looks really sick this morning."

"'Come in then. The phone's right there,' Jarmille said, pointing to a table just inside the door.

"'Who theah, Jarmille?' a woman's voice called out from the darkness at the end of the small hallway.

"'Lester heah to use ar phone.'

"A small boy walked out of the darkness into the hallway holding his crotch with his right hand. 'I gunna use bathroom, Jarmille.'

"'Lissen, Beetle. You jes hurry up cause I'm getting ready for school.'

"The small boy walked by me without looking up and went into the bathroom and closed the door.

"I forgot the doctor's number. I'm gonna go back and get it," I said as I started towards the door.

"'Wait a mother-fuckin' minute. Here.' Jarmille pulled out a large phone book from under the table and handed to me. 'Look in here for the number.'

"I took the phone book and started flipping through the pages until I came to Dr. Porter's office number.

"Jarmille said, 'Beetle, get your mother-fuckin' behind outta that bathroom and back in bed 'fore I come in there.' The commode flushed, the bathroom door slowly opened, and Beetle walked back into the hallway. Jarmille sniffed the air.

"'Beetle, you made a stink, you little mother. It smells like something done crawled up your ass and died. Now I gotta wait for the smell to go down. You can go ahead and dial the number.'

"Thanks" I said. I dialed the number as Jarmille went into the bathroom and turned on the faucet. Someone answered right away. "Doctors' answering service for Dallas Cardiology. Can I help you?"

"I'd like to speak to Dr. Porter. My grandfather is doing very poorly," I said.

"'I'm sorry. Dr. Porter's office isn't open yet. It will open in about three hours. Unless this is an emergency, you'll have to wait until then.'

"This is an emergency. My grandfather suffers from congestive heart failure and I think he's in failure again. I lay out his medications for him every day, but I'm never sure if he takes them. Dr. Porter said when Pappy looks like this, he needs to go back to the hospital."

"'Would you call this an emergency?' the operator asked.

"Yes. It's an emergency!" I gasped.

"'What's your name, please sir, and your grandfather's name?,

"Lester Jones is my name and my grandfather is Willie Sims."

"'And this is regarding your grandfather, Mr. Willie Sims. At what number can Dr. Porter reach you?'"

"Hey, Jarmille, what's your telephone number?" I shouted.

"'Sssshhhh. You're gonna wake up everyone. Jamille walked into the hallway and whispered to me, '972-684-3276.'

"I repeated the number into the phone. The lady on the phone said, 'I'll have the doctor get back to you as soon as possible. Good-bye.'

"I hung up the phone just as Jarmille's twenty-year-old sister, Ruby, stepped out of the darkness and into the hallway. She was about five feet six inches tall and beautiful. She had straightened her hair and wore it pulled back. She had a gorgeous face and perfect white teeth. She worked downtown as a secretary in a law firm. She wore a giant purple bath robe which had a large hole over her left hip. As she passed by me I looked down into the hole and saw her chocolate-colored skin.

"'Jarmille, it's my turn in the bathroom,' she said, without noticing me. Jarmille was buttoning up his shirt and looking at himself in the mirror. 'Come on, Jar, I'm gonna be late for work.'

"Hold on. Mother-fuckin' Beetle got in heah and stunk place up and Lester been bother'n me, so hold on."

"Ruby looked at me for the first time. 'What chew want, Lester? You the one be makin' all that racket out heah? Mr. Private School, Lester.'

"Just then the telephone rang. 'This is Dr. Fred Porter. I understand you called my answering service about your grandfather. What's going on?'

"He's not doing well, Doctor Porter. He's struggling to breathe. He's been coughing and wheezing the last few days and today he can't catch his breath. I think his congestive heart failure has worsened. I just gave him his morning medicines, but so far, they don't seem to be helping."

"'Has he been taking them every day?'

"No, sir. He only takes them when he feels he needs them. He still has a half-bottle left of each of them. His ankles are more swollen than I've ever seen."

"'He needs to be admitted to the hospital again, Lester. Get him over to Presbyterian's emergency room and I'll meet you there later this morning.'

"He's not going to want to go," I said. He just got out of the hospital a month ago."

"'I know, Lester. But your grandfather is a very sick man, and he needs help right now. I'll see you in the emergency room.'

"Okay, Dr. Porter. Thank you. Good-bye," I said. I hung up the telephone.

I looked around the corner of the hallway into the kitchenette where Jarmille was leaning against the stove and eating a piece of buttered white bread. 'You finished?' he asked.

"Yes. I'm going to take Pappy to the hospital now. Thank you for letting me use your phone."

"'No sweat, Lester. I sure wish we still had you on our football team. With you running the ball and me catching the passes, we'd be unbeatable.'

"I walked out of Jarmille's apartment and hurriedly felt my way back to our apartment. When I got there, I tried opening the door, but it was locked. I loudly knocked on the door. "Let me in, Pappy," I yelled.

"'Go away,' was the only part of Pappy's response I could make out. I knocked even louder.

"You've gotta go to the hospital, Pappy."

"'You ain't getting in that door.' Pappy was now on the other side of the door. I heard him struggling for air again.

"Dr. Porter says you need to come to the hospital now. I'm going to take you and miss school. Now, let me in!"

"'You nappy-headed (cough) (cough). I can't breathe cause (grunt), (cough). I need to lay down.'

"Now Pappy. I'm going to get the manager to let me in." I stopped and remembered that I had left my keys in my pants pocket the night before, so I took the key out and opened the door. I walked back into the room. Pappy was back in his bed, his head propped up on the pillow and his body quivering with each cough.

"'Nah, gah, ya nappy ole,' he stammered.

"Pappy get dressed. We're going to the bus stop and I'm taking you to the hospital."

"'Ain't going nowhere. You big, lazy good for nothing. You jes get on to your school. What (cough)…what you want (snort, several quick breaths) wif me?' Pappy opened his mouth revealing a total of twelve yellow rotting teeth evenly distributed between the top and bottom and placed so that there were at least two empty spaces between each one. 'I'll bite your fool head off!'

"I went to the dresser and opened the top drawer on Pappy's side. I pulled out a pair of dark gray pants and a red flannel shirt. I brought them over to my grandfather's bed. "Put them on," I demanded.

"(Cough) (Deep breath). 'Ya gonna kill me.'

I took off Pappy's nightshirt and replaced it with the red flannel shirt. I reached down to pull off Pappy's pants, but Pappy knocked my hands away. 'I do myself, ya wuthless (coughing fit).' He doubled over at the waist, coughing. I unbuttoned his pajamas and pulled them off.

"Dr. Porter said you need to go to the hospital, and I'm going to take you. They're going to get you better." I pulled Pappy's pants over his legs and snapped the buckle on his belt closed. "Where are your shoes?"

"'Boy, if I had one them right now I'd kick your behind. You ol' stubborn lazy mule.'

"I reached further under Pappy's bed and pulled out a pair of shoes with a sock in each one of them. The shoes were black and covered with dust with holes in both and with part of the heel missing from the left shoe. The left shoe had a brown lace extending through two of its four holes, while the black lace in the right shoe was tied into a bow at the three-quarter point. I put the socks on Pappy's feet and then slid the shoes on.

"Pappy looked down at his feet. 'I ain't gonna wear no Sunday, church shoes to no hospital, boy. Wha you be doin'? These ma church shoes and…I gonna kick'em off.' He made a weak effort to kick his feet and then lay back in his bed.

"I got Pappy's small brown suitcase out of the closet and filled it with his clothes. I snapped the suitcase shut. "Let's go, Pappy."

"'Boy, you a bigger fool than I thought. I gonna walk down 'leven flight of stairs? Jesus, Mary and Joseph! Now ya jes leave me in peace and git yur wuthles hide that fancy white boy school.' I handed Pappy the suitcase.

"You hold this. I'm going to carry you." I bent down and picked my grandfather up. In those days I was strong from all the weight-lifting I did for football.

'Wait, I need my hat.' I carried Pappy back into the bedroom and held him over the dresser while he picked up his Dallas Cowboys' baseball cap. He looked at himself in the mirror and adjusted the bill of the cap. Then I carried him out of the room and into the hallway. I had to rest a couple of times and set Pappy down, but I carried him down eleven flights of stairs.

"It was still dark and raining when we got outside the building. Cars sped by, splashing the sidewalk with water. I carried Pappy down the block to the bus stop, and by the time we got there, both of us were soaking wet. The bus stopped in front of us. We got in and I set Pappy down and I sat down next to him. We were the only souls on the entire bus, and after a moment the bus driver looked back at us and said, 'Fare, gentlemen.'

"I got out my wallet and realized I didn't have any money. "I forgot my money," I said.

"The bus driver was a serious black man who looked upset. "Shit. How you expect to ride the bus with no money? Where you and the old man going?"

"'Who he callin' old man?' Pappy yelled indignantly.

"We're going to Presbyterian Hospital emergency room."

"'Shit. This here bus don't go nowhere near that hospital. You need number thirteen. Git off now and wait for thirteen. Should be along soon.'

"I helped Pappy stand up and the two of us started walking off the bus.

"'Hey, kid.' I turned around to look at the driver who was reaching into his pocket. 'Here's a buck for you and a buck for the old man for the bus ride. He doesn't look too good. Get him to that hospital pronto.'

"Yes sir, thank you sir," I said as I took the two dollars. We stood in the rain waiting for number thirteen.

"'Gonna git ammonia cause you, boy.'

"What did you say, Pappy?"

"'Gonna git ammonia and die cause yaw nappy-headed ways. Can't trust my own flesh and blood. Jes like yaw mammy, you'se be the same 'cept you not an addict, yet.'

"Pappy, you just rest now."

"'Dontcha be tellin me what do. Eighty year-ole need be takin' orders from no frizzle-frazzle. Heah 'nother bus.'

"That's number twenty-two. We need number thirteen."

"Pappy sneezed. "I'se good as dead wif my 'monia and congestive failure. Boy, when I feelin' better I whip you.'

"Here's thirteen. Get on, Pappy." I handed the bus driver the two dollars as we got on. "We're going to Presbyterian Hospital, sir."

"'Sit down son,' he said. 'When we get there, I'll let you know.' There were two black ladies dressed in nurses' uniforms sitting towards the back of the bus talking to each other. Each woman was enormous, easily over three hundred pounds, with big round faces and giant breasts. They looked at us for a moment, and then they resumed their conversation.

"When I looked over at Pappy, his eyes were shut, and he was softly snoring. As the bus travelled down the street, Pappy's body leaned more towards me until his head rested on my shoulder. I fell asleep also. I dreamed I was at school and I'd forgotten my homework and had forgotten to study for the final exam that day. I started to sweat even though it was cold and rainy. Suddenly I felt something brush against my shoulder and I looked up quickly. The two nurses with enormous butts were waddling off the bus.

"Is this the stop for the hospital?" I shouted out.

"One of the ladies turned to look at me. 'This is the stop for Presbyterian Hospital, sugar.'

"I carried Pappy off the bus and we followed the nurses to the hospital. I saw a large sign that said, 'Emergency Room' and we went in that door. We walked down the hallway to the emergency room.

"A young Hispanic nurse sat at a desk just outside the large area marked emergency room. 'May I help you?' she asked.

"Dr. Porter told us to come to the emergency room and said he would meet us here later this morning. My grandfather has congestive heart failure and is doing poorly."

"'What is your grandfather's full name, please?'

"'William Virgil Sims,' Pappy answered.

"'Oh, yes, Mr. Sims. Dr. Porter called and told us to expect you."

"A tall young man wearing a white lab coat walked up to the nurse. 'Need any help, Sharon?'

"'Nope, just a patient of Dr. Porter with congestive heart failure. Do you have your Medicare card, sir?'

"Pappy reached into his wallet and pulled out his card and handed it to the nurse. She filled out some paper work and then gave it back to Pappy. Pappy started gasping for air. 'I can't breathe,' he whispered.

"The nurse quickly responded by addressing the young man in the lab coat. 'Ron, how 'bout taking him into the treatment room and helping him lie down in a stretcher. Dr. Porter said to give him some oxygen if he needed it and I think he does.'

"Ron led us into the treatment room. It was a large room with three stretchers and was equipped to handle all types of emergencies. Ron led Pappy to the middle stretcher and helped him lie down. Then he placed an oxygen mask over Pappy's nose and mouth. 'Just a little oxygen to help you breathe better. Just relax and breathe slowly.'

"Ron took out his stethoscope and listened to Pappy's lungs. 'Sharon did Dr. Porter say anything about starting some Lasix IV?' he shouted.

"'You know he doesn't like anyone to do anything to his patients but him,' Sharon shouted back. 'He did call in orders for labs and a chest x-ray.'

"'Now just relax,' said Ron. 'I'm sure Dr. Porter will be with you soon. Son, if he has any problems, just get the nurse outside. I'll go ahead and hook him up to all the monitors.'

"Pappy and I waited in silence for Dr. Porter. After a while I noticed a magazine on the floor behind Pappy's stretcher, and I went over and picked it up. It was a medical journal with the cover stating in large print that this issue was dedicated to medical students' thoughts and views. I rifled through the pages until a drawing caught my eye. It was the picture of a middle-aged black woman with a disfigured face lying in bed with a band-aid covering her right eye. Seated next to her in a chair was a black medical student with a white coat and a stethoscope around his neck. On the page across from the drawing was printed: Mrs. R---a poem by Derrick Harris, medical student at the University of Miami Medical School. The poem made such an impression on me that I ripped those pages out and folded them into my wallet. Here's the poem."

Lester pulled out and unfolded several papers from his wallet.

How could her daughter sit there so calmly knowing?

Only twenty, the daughter shouldn't be exposed to this.

And yet, her manner. Her way of studying my face as I asked each question.

Studying my face, as if from me would come
the answer.

Why? Why should her mother be so torn by
this cancer?

So disfigured; her face no longer smooth
and finely structured like the daughter's.

Instead, full of masses of that deadly disease.

I'm sitting in a chair in the hospital room
with the mother and daughter,

Knowing that when my questions are
answered and my probing complete

I can leave this tragic scene. "How long has
she been sick?"

I ask no one in particular, trying desperately
not to mention tumor, cancer, mass.

The patient looks at me with her eye. The
other eye is hidden by a wide band-aid.

"I was well till two thousand and nine."

"And what were your first symptoms?"

"Mama ain't felt too good for quite some time."

The patient's eye travels back to the television set.

She is the mother of thirteen children, ten girls and three boys.

Her barely-touched lunch try sits before her. "Not hungry, huh?"

She studies me a moment. Her daughter's head is bowed.

"Mama ain't had much appetite since she been sick this past month."

"You feel you've gotten worse lately?" Both heads bow down.

Not wanting to ask more questions, I start to examine her.

"Turn your head towards your daughter." She turns her head towards me.

"No, the other way, please.

"You gonna find out what wrong with me?"

"I'm sorry, I couldn't hear you."

She turns to look at me with her left eye.
She starts to speak, but the phone rings.

Her daughter picks it up and whispers into it.

I shine a light into her eye and she blinks.

"Now you just tell me if anything I do makes
you uncomfortable," I say,

Trying to avoid saying the word pain to a
woman who is going to die soon.

"Ruby Ann want talk you," the daughter
whispers.

The mother gazes at me with her eye. "Tell
her I'm with my doctor."

Suddenly I feel renewed. I'm her doctor.
Maybe I can help her.

I don't have the knowledge, yes, but my
caring, my decency, maybe…

"I need to look in your other eye. May I
remove your bandage?"

"Okay…doctor.

IN THE END

I remove the bandage and find myself gazing into the head of a fifty-two-year old black female.

No eye is there to stop my view, no nerves, no vessels, nothing.

I'm looking inside the head of a living human being.

A cold chill starts at my shoulders and sweeps down my body.

I grasp the bed for support.

I take my penlight and shine it into the inner regions of this lady's head,

Through the hole created by the removal of her malignant eye.

For a moment I'm looking through the carved-out eye of a jack-o-lantern.

Nothing could prepare me for this. The smell of something rotting

hits me, but still I look.

I shine the light around the inside of the woman's head one more time, slowly.

Several of the structures are familiar to me
from seeing them in anatomy class.

I want to remember this view, not for the
anatomy,

But because it will serve to remind me how
thankful one must be to be healthy,

And to be spared from suffering the terror
I now behold.

I put back in place the band-aid which
covers this portal,

Step back from her for a second and breathe
deeply. She says nothing.

Her daughter still whispers on the phone

Sitting in the chair by her mother's bed in her
plain white dress with her legs uncrossed.

"My sister want know how mama is."

"I can't tell you. I'm only a student."

Lester folded up the papers and put them back into
his wallet.

"It was that experience helping my Pappy and coming across that poem that convinced me I wanted to become a doctor. The poem made me realize that it takes a tremendous amount of education to really help someone. The student appreciates his position, but leaves you feeling that he craves to know more so that one day he can help that woman. I, too, wanted to improve others' lives like only a doctor can, and I wanted to achieve that level of education. Pappy lived two more years and had to be hospitalized many more times. But through it all, I saw what difference a kind, caring, decent health care professional could make."

"What an incredible story, "said Abraham. "I wish you well in all your pursuits. This world needs noble doctors like you. I only wish you would have the time. But in Heaven, there will be unlimited possibilities."

The two of them finished their lunches and went their separate ways, Abraham to get his mat and pray, and Lester to visit his mother.

When Lester got to his mother's room, she was lying in bed, drugged and asleep. An unopened tray of food sat on the table in front of her. In the last month she'd been in the hospital every day except for two. In between her last discharge and being readmitted there had been twelve hours. His mother refused to follow the diet and medication guidelines that she'd been given for her diabetes, so after a short time she returned to the emergency room with blood sugars ranging between five hundred and one thousand. She had to be dialyzed three days a week. Although a van picked her up and took her by stretcher to dialysis when she was home in their tiny apartment, she always felt better in the hospital.

Lester knew that his mother loved being in the hospital. She was in her forties, but she loved the idea of being an infant again and having all her needs taken care of. And of course, there was the Dilaudid, the powerful intravenous pain medicine which his mother had long ago become addicted to. She had the emergency room doctors trained to give her this the moment an IV was secured in her body.

"Mother, mother!" he shouted as he shook her shoulders. "Wake up, it's Lester and I'm here to see you."

"Jesus, what a racket," his mother said as her eyes fluttered open. "So, it's you, Lester. How are you? It's good to see you, son."

"Mother, are they taking good care of you? Are they getting you better?"

"Jesus be praised, I'm feeling much better. My sugars are under four hundred and my dialysis is going good." She yawned and stretched her arms straight up in the air. "If only they could control my pain. Every two hours I hafta call my nurse to give me my Dilaudid shot. With my lupus, I jes hurt everywhere."

"Where's your pain now?" asked Lester.

"It's mainly in my back but creeps around, and it's also in my front. Physical Therapy is coming by this afternoon after I get my Dilaudid to get me up and try and walk me using my walker. They think getting me up and offa my back will help the pain. Sometimes now I even get hip pains shooting down my legs like a bolt of lightning. Bottom of my feet feel all tingly and 'electric, too. Doctor says if I control my sugar that will get better."

Lester looked at his mother. Her hair was black and gray, with wisps growing out in all directions. She usually wore a shiny silk scarf over her head to cover her hair, but now it was missing, probably dropped off on the ambulance ride to the hospital. She had no teeth but had a full set of dentures. She wore two light blue hospital gowns, one put on forwards and the other backwards. Her skinny legs were hidden beneath the blankets. In her left arm was the IV—a PICC line going into a central vein since she no longer had any peripheral veins left in her arms.

"Why don't you eat some lunch?" asked Lester. "Maybe a little food in your stomach will help you feel better. I know you get nauseated from the Dilaudid, but I'm sure they've been bringing you Zofran for nausea every four hours. They always write for the Zofran when you're admitted."

"Gimme my teeth," replied his mother, "and I'll try a few bites if I don't get to feeling sick."

"Where are the teeth?"

"Look in the top drawer of that cabinet," his mother replied, pointing to the small bedside cabinet.

Lester opened the drawer and pulled out the blue plastic container that the hospital had given his mother months ago to hold her dentures. The top of the container had a worn piece of surgical tape with faded letters spelling out her name. He gave her the container and she opened it and put in her dentures.

Lester took the cover off her lunch plate. Her lunch consisted of a turkey sandwich with low-salt potato chips, a salad, and sugar-free Jell-O. She began to eat a little of the salad.

"Mom, how can we ever get you out of the hospital and keep you out? I want you at home with me. You and I can spend time together and get to know each other better. I can help you manage your diabetes if only you'll follow my instructions. There are so many things in this world to see and do; I want you to have the opportunity to do them."

His mother looked at him and smiled. Her wide-open mouth showed lettuce stuck between each upper tooth. "Lester, son, I love you. I'm the one who brought you into this world and took care of you as a baby. But I really need to be in the hospital. It's where I'm taken the best care of. You can come by and visit me as often as you like and tell me about what's happening in the world and in your life."

"Mom, you're addicted to the Dilaudid. We've got to get you off it. You don't think properly on it. Your life is at a standstill. You went from being addicted to street drugs to becoming addicted to Dilaudid."

"I know, I know," said his mother. "But I like it here. In the hospital I'm taken care of. The doctors and nurses see me and do what's best for me. I just push this button (she pointed to the nurses' call button right next to her right arm) and someone comes in and gives me my pain medicine. You're working. You're not home during the day. I need someone around all the time to keep me out of pain. Believe me, Jesus, if I wasn't so sick I'd be at home with you and doing the stuff you're talking about. Don't you forget, though. I've experienced a lot. Anyone that's lived out on the streets for years has seen it all and probably done it all. Maybe even done it all twice. And I think the doctors have run out of tests to put me through, so I don't have to go here and there in the hospital and be prodded and probed. I can just stay here and be as comfortable as possible with all my issues."

"Mom, I'll help you when I'm at home and when I'm not, you can get up and take care of yourself. I'll lay out all your pills. I talked with Dr. Gold about setting up home health to have nurses see you every day. I'll buy us food, I'll buy us a brand-new television, I'll buy us…"

"Yes, child," his mother interrupted, "but you can't buy me my Dilaudid. And without my Dilaudid, what good is anything else?"

"What about the other pain pills? What about all the Vicodin you have at home? We could open up our own pharmacy with all the Vicodin pills you have."

"I like Vicodin. It's a good drug. I've taken Vicodin for over twenty-five years now. First it was Morphine and then Demerol and now Dilaudid. It's the only drug that really controls my pain."

"Why do the doctors give you such a powerful narcotic? I remember at one point Dr. Gold said to get you well they had to get you off the Dilaudid. It makes your GI tract not work properly; it causes nausea and vomiting and constipation. It keeps everything in your body from working right."

"It may do that," replied his mother as she closed her eyes and shook her head slowly. She opened her eyes again. "But the one thing it keeps working properly is my brain. I sleep, but I think great thoughts on the Dilaudid. It lifts me up like riding aboard a flying carpet. I love it. Everything can go on around me and it doesn't matter to me. And they can give me other medicines to control the effects of the Dilaudid. The Zofran takes care of the nausea and Miralax keeps my bowels moving regular. They just have me take the Miralax three times a day here in the hospital and my bowels work like clockwork."

"You're an addict!" cried Lester. "An addict who refuses to be helped."

"An addict is right. It's the doctors who did this to me. They got me addicted to Dilaudid sure as that pimp Drayton got me addicted to heroin thirty years ago. If the doctors had tried harder to help me and not just give me drugs to shut me up, I wouldn't be an addict. And when one emergency room wouldn't give it to me, I'd just go to the next one and they would give it to me. I'd go from hospital to hospital until they admitted me and gave me Dilaudid. I could get my blood sugar high enough within hours that they *had* to admit me. I work the system and get what I want. See, your mother ain't dumb. I know what I want. I like my life. Now, instead of having to go from hospital to hospital, I jes' come here to Medical City of Plano where they know me and put me right in the hospital and start my Dilaudid immediately. I jes' tell the ambulance driver, 'Take me to Medical City of Plano,' and here I am."

She pulled a tiny gold cross on a necklace out of her hospital gown and began twirling it between her fingers. "I know I'm gonna die young and be with Jesus soon. My mother died young of kidney failure and sugar, and my sister died young of cirrhosis. I'm gonna die young, so let me live my life the way I want while I'm still alive."

Lester thought for a moment and then spoke. "Mom, at one point you and I were going to try and live in a real house together."

His mother laughed. "Lester at one point, when you were in high school, and I came back into your life from the streets and crack houses, I thought you were gonna be a professional football player and make tons of money. Or at least go to that college, Harvard, and become a rich, rich, man. Then you tore up your knee and all that went down the drain. I went to church and got forgiveness from Jesus, and then I went back to my life on the street. I'm not addicted to street drugs. You're not finding me dead in a crack house. You rescued me from the street life. I'm here in a fine hospital where it's legal and right for the doctors and nurses to give me the drugs that I need."

Lester shook his head angrily. "Someday Mom, someday, we're going to get you off the Dilaudid. You and I are going to build a life together, make up for my childhood that you missed. I never got to have a mother and father like the boys at Saint Mark's. I forgive you. I just want us to be together and live regular lives, in a real house with a refrigerator full of food. You'll have your own bedroom and bathroom. There will be a front porch, and I'm going to buy the most comfortable rocking chair for you to sit on and watch what goes on in the neighborhood. I'll even give you grandchildren, you'll see."

His mother straightened up in bed. "Sounds good, but it will never happen. The life you describe was never meant for me. Please don't be mad at me for being the way I am. Oh, and I just remembered, Lester. If you reach into my purse in the top drawer, there's some papers. I found them crumpled up in the back of your drawer when I was putting your underwear away last time I was home. I thought you might want them."

Lester reached into the purse and pulled out the crumpled pages. He opened them up and immediately recognized them. It was the speech he'd given when he was a junior at Saint Marks School for Boys and was running for president of the senior class. He hadn't seen the speech in over seven years, and as he read it he started to chuckle. He'd gotten the poem from Ray Gold who said he'd found it in an old comic book. The rest of it Lester had come up with himself. Even though he'd lost the election, he was still proud of this speech. Ray had told him that if he was going to run for president, his speech needed to be witty and interesting enough to keep everyone's attention, and this speech certainly did. Lester read:

I come before you
To stand behind you

To tell you about something
I know nothing about.
Next Thursday
Which is Good Friday
There will be a men's meeting
For women only.
Admission is free
Pay at the door.
Grab a seat,
Sit on the floor.

What does this have to do with running for senior class president? Each line has important relevance as to why you should elect me.

I come before you with my record fully open. Not only have I spent almost seventeen years living on this planet Earth, but I have worked hard in student government and have accomplished a lot for you. I was the vice president of our junior class and I helped organize the activities for Homecoming and McDonald's week.

To stand behind you. You need to know that no matter what, I will stand behind you, my fellow Marksmen, and do everything in my power to make sure this is a better school. I've got your backs.

To tell you something. The something is a brief look at my plans for our future. I plan to make our senior year the best senior year any class has ever had. I plan to have mixers with our sister schools, Hockaday and Ursuline. I plan to work with the administration to help make the college admissions process less daunting and more enjoyable. I talked to seniors last year and many of them said that the college application and admission process was the one thing they wanted more guidance with here at Saint Mark's.

I know nothing about. I know I don't have all the answers. No one does. I work best when I work with others and I'll continue to do so as your senior class president.

Next Thursday which is Good Friday. Your vote for me makes whatever day you vote a good day.

There will be a men's meeting for women only. Saint Marks is a school for men and I'm proud of that. But I'm also proud of the first Ursuline tenth grade mixer which I planned and put together and of other opportunities I had as class representative to interact with the fairer sex at our sister schools.

Admission is free. No charge to cast your ballot in this great country of ours or in this great school of ours.

Pay at the door. We all pay for the privilege to attend the best school in Texas and one of the best in the country. I intend to keep our school the best in Texas.

Grab a seat, sit on the floor. Grab a seat and hold on for the time of your lives, because with me as your leader, the sky's the limit and we will share many exciting adventures together.

Thank you for your support.

Lester smiled as he finished reading the speech. He'd done a good job—it was funny and caught your attention. He made it to a run-off with the most popular boy in the class, a lacrosse player who had a reputation as a partier, and Lester had lost. The lacrosse player's father was on the board for Saint Mark's School and had been chairman of fund-raising for the last ten years. His winning opponent's family was the type of family that every private school needed, one who gave the real money for the big projects. They already had one building on the campus named after them and rumors were they were planning on building a new Fine Arts building with their name on it. Since he was popular, and his family was so involved in Saint Mark's, it was no surprise that his opponent had received more votes. Everyone said that Lester's speech was the best and he was proud of his political campaign. He folded the pages and put them into the front pocket of his scrub pants.

"Mom, I've got to go back to work. I've got one more case this afternoon with Dr. Gold scheduled for ninety minutes, and I've got to do some cleaning around the endoscopy center and order supplies. I'll try and get back to see you later, but if I don't, I'll see you tomorrow."

His mother had fallen back asleep on the pillow and nodded her head at the sound of Lester's voice. Lester

kissed his mother on the forehead and said, "Bye mom."
He left the room and saw Abraham in the hall.

"How's your mom?"

"The same," answered Lester. "She's addicted to
the Dilaudid. It's such a common problem in this hospital. I've heard Doctor Gold talk about it so many
times. Patients like my mother come in for one reason
or another and are given narcotics. That shuts them
up and keeps them happy. But it also turns them into
addicts and zombies. Doctor Gold says that doctors
are the main cause of drug addiction in this country; both prescription and non-prescription. When he
trained, he says, narcotics were given for terminal cancer patients with pain or post-operative patients for a
specified time after surgery. Otherwise, they weren't
prescribed. Now they're given on a regular basis to
anyone who shows up in the emergency room and
complains about any kind of pain. It's ridiculous. It's
turned my mom into a zombie who has no hope for a
future outside this hospital. She talks as if she wants
to spend her future life drugged here in Medical City
of Plano Hospital."

"Let's talk about *your* future," said Abraham. "The
world is going to end today. I know that from the best
sources. Several men at the mosque warned me that
Yawm al-Din, the day of Judgement, will happen today
when the annihilation of all the living will be followed

by their resurrection and judgement by the only true God, Allah."

Lester looked up at him. "You're really convinced of that? You think these friends of yours know more than the President of the United States and the Prime Minister of Israel?"

"The jihadists are going to end the world today. All will die. I heard it at the mosque repeatedly. They've got the technology and are willing to destroy everything. Today is the day. They wanted to celebrate one more Ramadan. This is the day they've been waiting for; they will carry out their plan symbolically on the Jewish New Year Holiday. I only came to work today to have one last chance to get you to see the light, to become a Muslim."

Slowly they walked back to the endoscopy center. When they got there Abraham said, "I want you to be with me in Heaven. I want you to enjoy the afterlife. The last four years, you and I have become friends and have eaten together and enjoyed talking with each other. You are my only non-Muslim friend, and I want you to have everything that I shall have. Please convert now. Christianity is a precursor to Islam. You haven't yet attained the highest religion, the most that Allah can give you. Now is your last chance."

Lester looked in Abraham's eyes which were staring back at him, into his soul. "For some reason, I think you're right. I think the world is going to end today and I think I would have a better chance at Heaven as a Muslim. Christianity hasn't gotten me much. My relatives took me to church, but it seems like it was more for singing and socializing and having a good time than it was for praying and getting to really know Jesus. I never really identified with Jesus as my personal savior. My mother always cries, Jesus this and Jesus that, like Christianity was just an excuse to say Jesus' name. I don't know anything about your religion; is that okay? "

"You will learn in Heaven. You will be with Mohammed and all the great caliphs. You will have up to four wives."

"One would probably be more than enough for me," said Lester. "I haven't done much dating since I graduated from high school. No time, money, or women. I guess you could say I'm a loner, but I don't want to be one."

"Everything will be better once the world is destroyed. You'll see. Once we're with Allah and Mohammed in our final designated places, things will be perfect."

"Okay," said Lester, "how do I convert?"

"It's very easy. Repeat after me. This is the Shahadah: I testify that there is no God but God, Muhammad is the messenger of God."

Lester repeated the Shahadah word for word.

"Now," said Abraham, "you are a Muslim. When the world ends, you and I will be together to share the beauty and holiness and physical pleasures of paradise. As-Salamu Alaykum, peace be unto you."

"As-Salamu Alaykum," Lester assuredly replied as he walked into the endoscopy center. He felt a peace and inner calmness that he had never felt before. Whether all that Abraham had said was true was not as important as the feeling that the pieces of his life were falling into place.

CHAPTER TEN

"Pearl," said Charlotte Traylor as she walked into her enormous kitchen in her Highland Park mansion, "it's almost time for me to go for my colonoscopy and find out whether I've got cancer like the doctors think I do."

Pearl stopped buffing the marble counter top and shook her head. "You don't have cancer, Ms. Traylor. I know you don't. You gonna live a long, long time. Rich people don't die young. Just us poor, don't know better folks who die young. People rich like you get the best possible medical care, see the best doctors and live long, healthy and happy lives. Poor folk like me just go to bed and wake up dead."

Pearl had been one of the Traylors' maids for thirty-five years. There were three maids who cleaned the mansion and Pearl was their chief. She was a short, obese black woman who dyed her hair black to hide the gray. She had huge arms on which the fat jiggled every time she moved.

Mrs. Traylor walked up to a broad set of windows in the kitchen which overlooked her favorite garden. A darkly tanned young man with stringy blonde hair covered by a Cowboys baseball cap was trimming the hedges in the garden. He wore an olive tank top shirt that was soaked with sweat, and red shorts. Each of his arms was adorned with a full sleeve tattoo, made up of objects and people painted in neon shades of orange, yellow, green, red, blue, and purple.

"I never could understand the appeal of those tattoos," said Mrs. Traylor. "When I was growing up, tattoos were one color and the people who had them were either men in the military or who had been in prison. Then, I think it spread to gangs. For some reason, now it's the thing to do. I know women who go and get tattooed for their sixtieth birthday. I think it's cheap. The art in the tattoos isn't something I'd hang on the walls of my home, much less put all over my body. And I just read it can be dangerous having your whole arm tattooed like that gardener. It keeps your arms from being able to sweat which you need to be able to do."

Pearl walked over to stand next to Mrs. Traylor and looked out over the gardens. "You're right," Pearl said. "People just wanna stand out, show they've got a dangerous side to 'em."

"Course I didn't mean you, Pearl," Mrs. Traylor said, noticing the tattoo on Pearl's arm.

On Pearl's fat right arm was a crude tattoo from the sixties with "Pearl" written in cursive dark blue and a round blue pearl below her name.

"I had my sister put this tattoo on me over forty years ago. It hurt like you wouldn't believe. I can still remember the pain. Back then I was young, thin, pretty, and stupid. I had nice solid arms and wanted to show them off. Forty years later and it just reminds me how low-class I am."

Mrs. Traylor didn't know what to say, so she said nothing. She looked at Pearl, who was wearing the house's standard maid's uniform. She had a lace white headband holding her hair back and a black dress which went below her knees with a white collar. She wore black pantyhose and black suede shoes.

Mrs. Traylor sat down at the kitchen table which was made from an enormous piece of Italian marble. "Those tattoos are one thing I'll never understand, Pearl. Course I'm not including you in this conversation, but I do associate them with a certain stratum of society."

"Well," said Pearl, "maybe it's low class. But they're a way for some people to express themselves who can't afford no better. Now you and Mister Traylor got plenty of money and you express yourselves with this beautiful big house that twenty families could live in. And all the cars and all the things you own. You don't need no other way to express yourselves. Mr. Traylor could sport a tattoo if he wanted to, though. He's got muscular arms that would fit a barbed-wire tattoo nicely."

"Hmm," answered Mrs. Traylor.

"Ms. Traylor, forgetting about tattoos, how else could I say how I feel? What I live in is squalor. I been livin' in the same house or shack for the past forty years. It's in South Oak Cliff and believe me when I tell you it's in the middle of the ghetto. I've got five rooms, a small kitchen, a room to eat in and watch television in, two bedrooms 'bout the size of this break-fast table and a bathroom so small when you sit down on the commode your knee bangs up against the sink. Now I've raised nine children in that house. Believe me, Ms. Traylor, it's tough being poor. I don't under-stand why, after all these years, God hasn't seen fit to give me more…to give me a better house. I raised nine children in that shack. My husband was a hard worker and a good husband and father, but you know he died young of a heart attack. He never saw a doctor. Just came home one night from workin' hard, ate his din-ner, went to bed and never woke up. Now it's just me and my oldest daughter, Diane, living there, and I'm sixty-eight and she's fifty-two. Course, all the time we have my other children coming in to stay with us who lose their homes or apartments. But why, with all the money you and people you associate with have, why should I have nothing?"

"It's the American dream like Blaze says in his campaign speeches," said Mrs. Traylor. "People like me motivate people like you to work harder to try and get wealthy and get a bigger slice of the pie."

"But I've worked hard all my life. I still work hard cleaning your house and it hasn't gotten me anywhere."

"I'm sorry for you, Pearl," said Mrs. Traylor. "I truly am sorry. You did raise nine fine children, though. That's nine more than Mr. Traylor and me. Look at it this way: I've got all the money, but you've got the children. You know that saying, the rich get richer and the poor have children. I guess that applies to the two of us. I remember my father once talking about the coal miners who worked for him in all the mines he owned in West Virginia. He didn't know any of them personally, and he said he didn't want to know them. They were risking their lives every day to feed their families, and he said they were all still poor as dirt. He had company stores where he sold them the food and other goods they needed, and he even made a huge profit from them at his stores. He paid them in currency that could only be used at his stores.

"I remember there was a disaster when one of the mines caved in and thirty-seven men were killed instantly. My mother said my father should at least go visit their families and offer his condolences, but he didn't go. He said they knew what they were getting into by working in the mines. He felt it was enough to send each of them a full Kentucky turkey for Christmas. Poor stay poor, he said, and unfortunately, I think that makes sense."

"I guess it does," said Pearl sadly. "Some of my children did turn out fine, with good jobs and children of their own. I've got thirty-one grandchildren and two great-grandchildren. Two of my kids are dead now. One, Cletus, was in the wrong place at the wrong time and got shot by a gang with a machine gun. Twenty-eight bullet holes in Cletus, the police counted. And Sheila, she died young of female cancer. Doctor said weren't no hope for her from first day she went to the hospital. She never saw doctor before goin' to that hospital neither. Never had insurance or any way to afford a doctor."

"I'm sorry for your losses," said Mrs. Traylor.

"Thank you, ma'am. If I can ask you without offending you, how come you never had any children?"

"We tried but it didn't work out for us. I was pregnant when I was twenty-five. I went through labor and delivered a stillborn baby boy, Micah. After I delivered the dead baby they couldn't stop the bleeding from my uterus, so I had to have an emergency hysterectomy right then to save my life. They had to pry lifeless little Micah out of my arms to take me to surgery. I'll never forget what it felt like to hold him. I wanted to adopt, but Blaze always said no, so we never did. It's just been the two of us becoming wealthier and more successful. Blaze accumulating more and more oil and property and banks and political offices, and me by his side accumulating more and more weight. You know, when we married, I was a size two. I was five feet seven inches and weighed one hundred and twenty-five pounds. I've gained one hundred pounds since we got married. I'm two hundred and twenty-five pounds now, fat as can be."

"Humph," said Pearl, "preacher down at church said in ancient times being fat was a sign of being wealthy. I guess here in this room we got two opposites, in you, weight signifies wealth, in me it signifies eating crap and being poor."

Just then Fenton, the driver, walked into the kitchen from outside. "Mrs. Traylor, which car you want to take to your appointment today?"

"Has the new Rolls Royce come in yet?" asked Mrs. Traylor. "I know that Blaze ordered it a few weeks ago. Most expensive Rolls ever made and most luxurious, Blaze told me."

"We just got it yesterday and it's a dandy!" Fenton was a tall black man measuring six feet eight inches. He walked with a slight stoop betraying the fact that he was now in his seventies. He was a superb driver who always wore a chauffeur's cap and white driving gloves.

"Gee, that car is great!" he continued. "It's got a big engine that purrs like a pussy cat and the inside is sparkling pearl white. The steering wheel and dashboard are dazzling red."

"Let's take the new Rolls," decided Mrs. Traylor, "and ride in style."

"I'll go to the garage and bring it around." Fenton walked outside to the seven-car garage. They had three Bentleys, two Rolls Royces, a custom-made Mercedes limousine, and a Tesla.

"You don't think I'll die today, huh?" asked Mrs. Traylor of Pearl. "You don't think they're going to tell me I have cancer?"

"Dying is for poor people," replied Pearl. "I don't think you got cancer and I don't think you're gonna die."

"What do you think about the terrorists? You think they're going to end the world today?"

Pearl shook her head. "I jes don't know. Crazy people can be rich or poor. Doesn't seem to be any separation of brains by money. But if the world ends, I know I'm going to Heaven to be with Jesus. I go to church every Sunday, I sing in the choir, and I brought up my children to be good Christians, too. When all else failed, we had very little to eat, no games in the house, no nothing, but we always had the church. I could always count on my friends at church to slip me a dollar or two and help with the children. Especially after Ronnie, my husband, died so young. My belief in Jesus has kept me going through more tragedy than I can tell you about. I always remember the Passion of Christ and what he went through to give me eternal life. Knowing his sacrifices always kept my faith strong and my needs small."

"Why didn't you ever remarry?"

"Who'd want a poor fat black woman like me with all those mouths to feed? C'mon. What am I good for? I'm good for cleaning your house. You got three of us maids with me in charge and I do a good job. But no one ever thought to marry me. I envy you, Ms. Traylor, I envy the wealth that you have. I envy the fact that you can do whatever you want with whoever you want. You travel all over the world, and you always go first class. You eat in the fanciest restaurants, even though you have Pierre as your personal chef. And, no one minds that you're fat since you're so rich."

"A lot of what you're saying is true. But did you know that I've had two men in my life that I've loved? One boyfriend who became my fiancée and one husband. Both men came from families that had billions of dollars. My family had billions of dollars. I was raised going to the finest places in the world, travelling in the most luxurious planes and cars. That's the way my life has always been. I wouldn't know any other way to live. I graduated as one of the first women from the University of Virginia and I was the homecoming queen.

"But you know something I don't tell many people? I had a four-point-zero grade point average—that's straight A's and no B's or C's. I graduated Phi Beta Kappa, which is the honor society for the smartest students and that's why I have this little key on my bracelet. I could have gone to medical school, law school, or run the family business. Every opportunity was available for me, but I decided that I wanted to be a wife and have a family and support my husband in whatever he did. And you want to know something else? Life hasn't always been perfect, but my life has certainly been an adventure."

"Mine sure hasn't," said Pearl. "I travel by bus to get to your house here in Highland Park and I still hafta walk almost a mile to get from the bus stop here. Sometimes Fenton will give me a ride to the bus stop at night, or sometimes I jes walk. I've never been on vacation. Only place I ever been is Fort Worth and I only went there for a cousin's funeral. It's pure hell being poor. I don't know what the rest of the world is like. All I've got is me, my children, my grandchildren, my great-grandchildren, and Jesus."

"Would you trade all that for being rich?" asked Mrs. Traylor.

"I don't know that I'd trade for being rich. I'd never trade my family or my belief in Jesus for anything. But I think it's only fair that people like me who've worked all our lives should get to share some of the American dream."

Fenton came to the door. "It's time," he said.

Mrs. Traylor was dressed in her Prada sweats and carried her Hermes Birkin Python handbag in which she had her cellphone and another pair of Prada sweat pants, just in case she needed them. It also contained her wallet with her insurance information and the paperwork she'd filled out online for the colonoscopy.

"Good-bye, Pearl."

"Good-bye, Ms. Traylor and good luck. I'll make sure to leave an extra comfy pillow on your side of the bed, so you can rest easy when you come home."

"Good luck to you, Pearl. I know we'll see each other tomorrow, but for some reason I feel I must thank you today for all that you've meant to me in my life. You have always been here to work and to help wherever you were needed. I know we were never friends, but I do consider you someone that I've always felt closer to than any other employee."

Mrs. Traylor reached into her wallet and pulled out a twenty-dollar bill and handed it to Pearl. "Go see a movie or do something fun with your daughter tonight. Live it up on me."

"Thank you," said Pearl quietly as the door closed behind Mrs. Traylor.

As they took the tollway from Highland Park up to Plano, Mrs. Traylor started to talk to Fenton. Besides his chauffeur's hat and white gloves, Fenton wore a starched white dress shirt and a black bow tie and black perfectly creased pants. His shoes were buffed shiny black and his black socks were pulled tight.

"Fenton, tell me, what do you think of this Rolls Royce?"

"I love it. I just love it. I think they get better and better. Their cars are the best and they drive so sweet. Only thing can compare to them are the Bentleys. This car is worth every penny that Mr. Traylor paid for it."

"You're so right. It's so comfortable here in the back seat. And I've got a phone, television, bar, everything I could want back here. Too bad Dr. Gold can't do my colonoscopy right here. It would be a lot more comfortable than that cold stretcher."

"Yes, ma'am, yes."

"Fenton, how long have you been working for us?"

"Ma'am, I've been working for you almost thirty years. I've been your chauffeur for that long."

"Thirty years. And Pearl's been with us for thirty-five. It's amazing how time has passed. It seems like yesterday we hired Pearl. Petite black woman looking for a job to feed her family. She was a maid for the Fords who moved from Highland Park to Beverly Hills. When I was younger, time passed much more slowly. I remember summers in Huntington, West Virginia, running around Ritter Park day after day. We played in Four Pole Creek until the creek got polluted and dirty, so we couldn't go down there anymore. We climbed in the hills in the park like they were mountains. We'd go out to our country club, the only one in Huntington, and swim and eat barbecue and play tennis. It seemed summer was endless.

"Then I became a teenager and time speeded up. I'd go away to our place on Martha's Vineyard and spend most of the summer there. I'd go to the beach and swim in the ocean. Daddy would take me out sailing and sometimes fishing. There'd be a giant fireworks extravaganza over the ocean on July Fourth. We'd visit with the Kennedys and the Bushes and all our family friends in that part of the country. By the time I'd get back, it was time to get ready for school. Still I'd run around with friends and date Tom. I guess I never told you about Tom, did I?"

"No, ma'am, I don't know nothing about Tom."

"The time we spent together then seems like a blur, it went by so quickly. Like it was here and gone and he died so young. I can still see him when I think about him. He'll always be twenty-two to me. He never got older like I did. He never got fat or lost his hair; he just stayed Tom."

"Yes, mam," said Fenton, "people who die young, they stay the same age forever. They're always that way in our minds, even as we get older and we know they would have gotten older. I had a son, Jessie, who was shot standing by our apartment house by gang bangers when he was nineteen years old. Still got his picture at nineteen in my wallet. Still got his picture in a frame at home. When someone dies like that they're frozen forever in time."

"You're right," said Mrs. Traylor. "Once I married Blaze and moved to Texas it seems as though time again slowed down. We were going to have a baby, and all my time was spent planning, going to baby showers, setting up the baby's room. Then the time came to have the baby, and we drove to the hospital, and the baby was stillborn. Little baby Micah, so tiny yet looked just like Blaze. There we were, just the two of us left to build a life alone. The next twenty years, from twenty-five to forty-five, went by fast, what with Junior League and me chairing the Crystal Ball Charity and the Cattle Barons' Ball. We travelled all over the world and Blaze got more and more successful and rich and politically active. I just turned forty when my father passed away. We got the call that he died suddenly while tending to the rose garden behind his house. He had every color of rose you could imagine, and Daddy kept them in beautiful condition. It was a lifelong hobby of his. I went back to Huntington. Hadn't been there in five years, and you know something, Fenton?'

"What's that?"

"Time didn't change Huntington. Oh yeah, Marshall University got bigger and took over more of the city, but everything else was the same. It's as though in some places time stands still and only the people age. The houses in Huntington were the same, downtown was mostly the same. We buried my daddy..." She paused and wiped a tear from her eye.

"Yes, it's always hard to bury someone that you love," said Fenton, "hard to say that final good-bye."

"I remember going to the funeral and then looking at our family plots in the cemetery. The same cemetery that the Marshall University football team that was killed in the plane crash in nineteen seventy was buried in. The bodies they couldn't identify, burned beyond recognition, were buried there."

"Yes, ma'am, I remember that plane crash. I remember all the young men that were killed. What a tragedy."

"Our family plot is just up the hill and on the other side from that Marshall burial site. If we want, there's two places reserved for Blaze and me. Blaze wants us to be buried in his family plot here in Texas, and I'm not going to argue with him. Doesn't matter much to me where I'm buried. When you're gone, you're gone. We don't have any children to come visit our grave sites and leave flowers."

She paused to look out the window before continuing. "The last eleven years life has gone by so, so quickly. Time sped up. People told me when you had children and grandchildren time sped up; I had neither.

Still, it'd be Christmas and then suddenly the Fourth of July, then Thanksgiving and Christmas again. Year after year, marked by the holidays and the charity balls and of course, by Blaze's political career. Becoming mayor, trying to bring about change to make Dallas a better place..."

"He *has* made Dallas a better place," said Fenton. "Dallas has more parks now, places for people to go safely. Mr. Traylor has done a very good job. The roads are better, I hear the schools are better. He's quite a man, your husband."

"You know," Fenton continued, "time has passed differently for me at different times of my life, too. When I was a boy growing up I was a star basketball player. I had a college scholarship waiting for me, but my daddy said, you gotta go to work. So, I did. I worked in Galveston in a shipyard—back-breaking work. Boy, did time pass slowly then. Each day getting up at five in the morning, stomach growling from not eating enough. Going to work and keeping at it till six at night and then getting off and going home exhausted. Got married when I was twenty, had four kids, raised those kids and kept working in the shipyard till I was forty. Got that little bend in my back from working in that shipyard," he chuckled.

"Then moving to Dallas after my wife left me with the children, and she moved by herself to Kansas. I asked her if we could move as a family and she said she didn't want to be around me or the kids anymore. Never could understand that woman or why she left. But I wanted to stay in Texas anyway. I'm a Texan, through and through. I couldn't work in Galveston anymore, so I moved here to Dallas. Worked as a waiter for a few years. Time started speeding up a little bit then. Again, like you said, the holidays, birthdays, having the kids visit me after they grew up, all marked the part of time I can remember. Otherwise, most of it is still a blur."

He paused. "I got older; fifties and sixties seemed to pass so quickly, ma'am. Came to work for you folks when I was forty-five, and the last thirty years, time has speeded up each year." Fenton took off his cap with his right hand and scratched his gray, thinning hair with the same hand.

"Still got my hair, though," he laughed. "Still got my little apartment above your garage and still get to drive the two of you."

"Are you happy with your life, Fenton?"

"Am I happy? What is happiness?"

Mrs. Traylor paused and then said, "Happiness is if you can look back and say you enjoyed things."

"I'm enjoying things now," said Fenton, "but to me happiness is peace of mind. Happiness is knowing that I'm going to have something to eat, that I've got a job and a place to live. Happiness is getting to see my kids when they want to see me and seeing my grandkids when they want to see me, too. Happiness is knowing that my family is healthy and safe. Time passed quickly in my life. I never thought I'd spend the last thirty years of it as a chauffeur. I knew I'd work, work hard in Galveston, raise a family. I always thought if I worked hard, I'd get a better job and a better job and a better job. But it never worked out that way for me. Never had much money or many possessions. Shoot, you could easily put all I own in this car. But I think I've always had a good frame of mind. I've always been happy, like you would say. I've always enjoyed the moments, even though some of them passed so quickly."

"Here we are, ma'am, "said Fenton, as the Rolls Royce pulled up in front of the doctors' office building in which the endoscopy center was located. "I'm not going to let the valet touch this Rolls."

"Here's a tip to give him," said Mrs. Traylor, handing Fenton a fifty-dollar bill.

Fenton put down his window. "Here's fifty dollars if you just let me park this car myself in your valet area."

"Okay," the valet said, "there's the valet area over there." He pointed to a parking lot on the other side of the office building.

"Do you want me to wait in the car, or should I help you in?" asked Fenton.

"Stay in the car," answered Mrs. Traylor. "You know one more thing that's interesting? How you and I have spent so many important times together. Times when Blaze was out of town or out of the country, out on business or politics. It was you and me driving here and there. Going to parties, to balls, to fundraisers, even to doctors' appointments. You know, you may be the oldest member of the family we put together. When I say family, I mean our servants, drivers, lawn people, chef, Blaze and me. If the world ends today, you'll be the last one in the family that I'll have a chance to say good-bye to. So, good-bye, Fenton, and thank you. I hope we treated you with respect and kindness."

"Yes ma'am," said Fenton, "you and your husband always treated me well. I'll see you in a few hours. Good luck."

Mrs. Traylor got out of the car with her Hermes bag slung over her shoulder and walked into the office building. The sliding glass doors opened, and she went straight through them and walked to the elevators at the back of the first floor. She pushed the up button and an elevator door opened. She got in alone and pushed the number four.

Meanwhile, Fenton pulled the Rolls Royce over to the valet area and parked the car in two spaces, so no one would scratch it by carelessly opening a door. He took out the morning paper from under his seat and started to read. He read the sports section and then got out of the car. With a thick, soft towel, he began wiping off the dirt the car had picked up from the drive. He had to stoop down, and sometimes get down on his knees as he went around the car, but finally he was satisfied that it was clean. He took off his chauffeur's cap for a moment, scratched his gray thinning hair with the same hand, wiped his brow, and then got back in the car and slammed the door shut.

BOOK THREE

AFTERNOON

The Moving Finger writes; and, having writ,
Moves on: nor all thy Piety nor Wit
Shall lure it back to cancel half a Line,
Nor all thy Tears wash out a Word of it.

And fear not lest Existence
Closing your Account
Should lose or know the
Type no more. The Eternal
Saki from that Bowl has
poured Millions of Bubbles
like us and will pour.

—Omar Khayyam

CHAPTER ELEVEN

Lying on a stretcher in the endoscopy center, Charlotte Traylor felt more vulnerable than she ever had in her life. She was the only patient in the pre-op area, but they still had curtains surrounding her, protecting her privacy. She lay there wearing only a hospital gown which barely covered her buttocks and the tops of her legs, and she felt a chill. Her nurse, Carol, had been wonderful. She was about the same age as Charlotte, but she assumed the role of a kind, caring grandmother who fussed about and took care of Charlotte's every need to make her experience as pleasant as possible. Carol listened to Charlotte's history, helped her take off her clothes and put on the hospital gown, and then magnificently slipped in her IV with only a tiny stick which Charlotte didn't have time to react to. Throughout all the preparation, Carol reassured Charlotte that Dr. Gold was a wonderful doctor who would take excellent care of her.

Carol even remembered Charlotte from her colonoscopy the previous year. She discussed Charlotte's West

Virginia upbringing and inquired about the friends and family she still had there. When Charlotte spoke of West Virginia, her face took on a radiance and her voice became joyful. The upper part of the stretcher was at a right angle with the rest of the stretcher, so Charlotte was sitting up when the curtains opened and in walked a young, heavily muscled black man who introduced himself as Lester. He said he'd be Dr. Gold's assistant during the procedure. A minute later a beautiful young woman with dazzling long red hair and sparkling green eyes and what looked like heavy theatrical make-up came through the curtains and said that she'd be the nurse in the room during the colonoscopy. RC checked Charlotte's armband to make sure it matched the name and birthdate on her chart.

"Do you have anyone you want to kiss or say goodbye to?" RC asked sweetly as Lester kicked up the brake pedal so that they could move the stretcher.

Charlotte laughed. "My husband is off campaigning for governor in Austin, and my chauffeur, Fenton, is downstairs waiting to drive me home when the procedure is done. I doubt that Fenton would want to give me a kiss."

"How about I give you a kiss," Carol joked as she leaned over the stretcher and gave Charlotte a peck on the cheek.

"You really do everything to make a patient feel at home," Charlotte laughed.

With Lester behind the stretcher and RC in front, they wheeled Charlotte out of the pre-op area and into the hallway separating pre-op and post-op from the endoscopy room. Charlotte gazed up at the ceiling made up of acoustical tiles. As a child one of her favorite things to do was to look up at the ceiling or down at the floor wherever she was, trying to find patterns that evolved into people's faces or other objects such as houses, boats, or even airplanes. She looked up at the acoustical tiles and quickly picked out two eyes staring down at her.

"Stop for a second," she heard herself say.

Lester stopped pushing and RC turned around to look at her. "Is there something wrong?" RC asked as she moved from the front of the stretcher to Mrs. Traylor's side.

Charlotte continued to look at the eyes she'd found in the tile, and slowly realized that it was an entire face with eyes, a nose, and mouth. She ignored RC and Lester who were now on either side of the stretcher.

"It's Tom," she gasped. "Tom, I haven't seen you in forty years." She looked back at RC who was looking at her with surprise and uncertainty.

"You okay?" RC asked. "Can we go into the procedure room?"

"I'm so sorry," said Charlotte. "Just a little game from childhood. I saw a face in the tiles I hadn't seen in forty years. My first love, Tom. Please, let's move on."

As they took their places again, she blew a kiss at the face in the ceiling in the hallway. She felt a surge of joy. *Maybe this is an omen and maybe I will be reunited with Tom soon.*

They started to push her again. To Charlotte's left was a large white ceramic medical sink with foot pedals on the bottom, one red and the other blue, and a large faucet rising out over the sink. Water was dripping from the faucet and hitting the bottom. Drip... Drip... Drip.

Charlotte again saw Tom's face. She thought of the drip, drip, drip of water as it slowly eased across the pebbles and stones in Four Pole Creek in Ritter Park. When she and Tom were children, less than ten years-old, one bend in the creek had been their favorite. Here were stones and bigger rocks that formed a diagonal pathway across the water that could take you from side to side without getting wet if you were nimble enough to negotiate it. She and Tom would skip back and forth across the stones, sometimes by themselves and sometimes together, holding hands so tightly that their two hands became one. At that age Charlotte took ballet and dancing and was so coordinated that she never fell into the water. Once or twice she remembered Tom falling in, and she would walk him back to his house on the other side of Ritter Park with his shoes and socks soaked. They still laughed about it as they made their way home, and it gave Charlotte an excuse to hug Tom close to her to keep him warm. Even with all her love and shared experiences with Blaze, she knew she'd never forget Tom and how much he meant to her. He'd been her first love and was the man she was supposed to marry and spend her life with.

The stretcher turned left into the endoscopy room and Charlotte noticed an X-Ray screen on the wall to her right. There were two signs posted on the screen. One said, "Five Moments for Hand Hygiene" and gave instructions for keeping hands clean. The other sign showed techniques for abdominal pressure during colonoscopy to help advance the scope around the colon. Charlotte was sure they'd have to use all these techniques on her, and maybe more since Dr. Gold had told her repeatedly what a difficult colonoscopy she was. She looked over the sign and saw hands pressing in all parts of the abdomen, either one hand alone or both in combination. There was a definite science to getting the colonoscope to go around the colon, she realized. The amount of pressure placed in the areas of interest seemed a lot to her since the abdomen pictured was forcefully pushed in. She bet that having big muscles like Lester would help in this process.

Below the X-Ray screen was the crash cart. Charlotte recognized it from seeing similar ones on television medical shows. The defibrillator was a menacing presence on top with a thick paddle on each side tucked into a special groove, and the middle of the defibrillator contained an assortment of buttons and knobs and red lights that were now all in the off position. Sitting right next to the crash cart was a large white binder on which "Crash Cart Instructions" was printed in bold red letters. Above the x-ray screen was the fire alarm light which consisted of two spotlights bound together in a steel, baffled frame.

The young black man broke the silence. "You're a tough colonoscopy," he said. "I remember you from last year. Dr. Gold booked you for ninety minutes today. He usually only books colonoscopies for forty-five minutes. But RC and I both just had an hour off for lunch, so we're more than ready for this challenge."

"Well," Charlotte smiled, "I guess if you have to be tough at something this isn't the worst possible thing. Hopefully, since you were here last year with me you probably remember all the right places to push."

They wheeled Charlotte's stretcher into the middle of the room and Lester pushed down on the brake, locking the stretcher in place. Charlotte looked to her left and saw a white sheet listing all of today's procedures in that room. Even without her glasses she could pick out the one procedure that had not been crossed off the bottom of the schedule. By squinting she could barely make out her name and beside it the word colonoscopy. Next to the printed schedule was a telephone and below that were the light controls for the room.

Charlotte had always had a talent for remembering details and for some reason she felt the need to remember each detail in the room. She wanted to be able to tell Blaze all about her experience and hopefully top off her story with a happy ending.

In the middle of the back wall was a large black clock which read exactly one o'clock. On the wall to Charlotte's right was the procedure cart. Prominently hanging on the front was the colonoscope. This was the instrument that would be soon be coursing through her colon. She felt a chill go down her spine and suddenly felt cold all over. It was larger and longer than she'd imagined, and all the knobs and buttons frightened her. *This will be the instrument that determines my life or death,* she thought. *I choose life.*

Charlotte looked up at the ceiling and saw there was an operating room light perched over her. Charlotte remembered asking the previous year if she was in the wrong place and they intended to do surgery on her, but the nurse replied no, all endoscopy centers had to have these surgical lights by government standards, even though they were never used.

Charlotte shivered. "It's cold in here. Can I possibly get a warm blanket?"

"Sure," replied Lester, and he quickly left the room. He came back with a warm blanket and covered Charlotte's body. "Better?" he asked.

"Much, much better," Charlotte replied. "I don't see how you can work in here since it's so cold."

"We wear gowns and gloves which are warm," RC replied, "plus we're working so hard we heat up quickly."

Charlotte nodded her understanding.

Lester said, "Okay, it's time to get you ready now."

Lester took the green oxygen nasal cannula out of the drawer, removed it from its plastic covering, and hooked one end to the oxygen outlet on the wall. Charlotte felt the cannula in her nostrils. She felt Lester pull the strap over her ears and then securely behind her head. To Charlotte, the oxygen smelled like a beach ball. In the meantime, RC took the EKG monitoring pads and put them on Charlotte's chest, abdomen, and arm. She attached wires to each of the pads and then hooked the wires to the EKG machine next to the stretcher. Charlotte's heart beeped regularly, matching the line of QRS complexes marching along the monitor.

Charlotte felt better with her body completely covered with the blanket. She didn't like people to see her naked body with its drooping fat, so being covered made her feel more at ease. She was confident Dr. Gold would find what was going on with her and get it taken care of so she could rejoin Blaze on the campaign trail. She loved being with Blaze and hearing him speak. Everyone said that he'd win the race for governor handily, and she knew he'd be a superb governor. After that, the sky was the limit. She might very well be the first lady of the United States someday. Now warm and covered, she turned away from the frightening colonoscope and focused on other objects in the room. She just wanted this ordeal to end.

Lester listened as RC talked to Charlotte and again explained to her what was going to happen. Lester had always had a crush on RC but had never said anything about it. He remembered Ray, Dr. Gold's son, talking about RC and how he'd nailed her a few times. Ray never displayed any emotion or love in his voice when he talked about sex with RC. This lack of sensitivity lowered Lester's opinion of Ray, since Lester had such strong feelings for her. She was a beautiful woman, which made it even harder for him to see her come to work battered and bruised. He once left a Women's Shelter Hot Line card in her locker in the hope that she'd use it. As far as he knew, she'd never followed up on it and still lived with that beast, Randy. Lester had met Randy once and immediately realized what a jerk he was. He was big and strong, though, and looked like he'd been in his share of brawls. Randy had implied that Lester's job was more suited for a woman, trying to elicit a response from Lester. But Lester had learned long ago never to get into a pissing contest with a drunk bully, so he let the comments go unanswered. Still, Lester felt that if

RC ever asked for him to help protect her against Randy physically, he wouldn't hesitate to do so.

Lester remembered Mrs. Traylor very well. She was one of the hardest colonoscopies Dr. Gold had to do. Instead of the usual colonoscope Dr. Gold had ordered a pediatric colonoscope because the twists and turns in her colon were far too difficult to negotiate with the adult colonoscope, which was larger in diameter and less flexible. Hopefully, starting with the smaller and more flexible scope would take some time off the procedure. They'd spent thirty minutes trying to maneuver the adult colonoscope last year without getting out of the sigmoid colon. Dr. Gold had finally made the change to the pediatric scope. Lester remembered the work-out he'd gotten from turning and moving Mrs. Traylor and from applying pressure to her abdomen. He was glad the morning cases hadn't been too difficult, so he had plenty of energy now. He was also glad he'd had plenty of time to eat a good lunch. But the powerful talk with Abraham and his fateful decision weighed on him.

Lester started planning his afternoon after the case was finished. First, he'd clean the scope and perform his other duties like ordering the supplies for the endoscopy center. He would then go over to visit his mother again and tell her that he was now a Muslim. In her pharmaceutical haze she'd look back at him with her best, "I can't believe what you're saying" look, and then smile and slap him gently on the face as if it were all a joke. But it wasn't a joke. Lester was determined to learn as much as he could about Islam. He was distracted by Mrs. Traylor as he saw her toes wiggling outside the blanket. Her toes were perfectly manicured and painted bright red. He looked up at her fingernails which were also bright red. Lester knew that she was a wealthy woman whose husband was a very powerful and influential man. But to him, all the patients were the same and he had to do his best to take care of them. He had to supply the pressure on the outside of the abdomen to allow Dr. Gold to advance the scope around the colon. Lester also assisted the doctor by using biopsy forceps to remove small polyps from the colon; this was rather easy as Lester just had to open and close the forceps on command. Far more challenging was using the electrocautery snare which he had to open and close precisely to capture larger polyps. Then he had to close and burn through those polyps at the right rate so that there was a clean white burn and no bleeding or perforation.

Lester felt very confident in his abilities with all the instruments and enjoyed the more challenging cases which proved his expertise as a GI tech. Yet he knew that there was much more that he wanted to accomplish in life. He wanted to become a nurse and then a doctor. He wanted to have his own patients. He'd decided he wanted to be an orthopedic surgeon, specializing in sports medicine so he could help young athletes who had suffered horrific injuries like he had. He felt he had received excellent care from his doctors, but the personalities of the orthopedic surgeons were lacking. They all tried to portray themselves as a mixture of a rough cowboy and a tough professional football player. They weren't warm and personable like Dr. Gold and Dr. Porter. He wanted to be an outstanding surgeon but still retain those humanistic qualities he saw in Drs. Gold and Porter. He also wanted to be able to take good care of his mother and give her a real house for the first time in her life. He wouldn't be able to reach his dreams by playing professional football, but he felt nothing could stop him from fulfilling his new ambitions.

He'd gotten the application to nursing school online, and he'd finish filling it out tonight. Dr. Gold had already said he'd write Lester a letter of recommendation. His plan was to attend nursing school at night while he continued to work days at the endoscopy center. Then he'd go to medical school on scholarships and probably loans and from the money he saved from working part-time as a nurse. Then orthopedic surgery residency. He knew it would be a long road and a tremendous commitment, but after his experience taking care of Pappy and his mother, he felt it was well worth it. Dr. Gold and his partners all loved being doctors and helping sick people, and their only complaints seemed to involve the insurance companies and the government.

Lester's thoughts were interrupted by Mrs. Traylor's voice. "Excuse me, sir, do you know where my doctor is. I see it's five after one and he's not here yet."

"Dr. Gold will be here any minute. He's usually early," Lester replied. "He must be caught up in something. He may be over at the hospital making rounds, treating his sick patients or answering emergency phone calls in his office."

Just then into the room walked Dr. Adonis Gonzalez, the anesthesiologist. Lester had always admired Dr. Gonzalez, not only for his skill as a doctor, but also for his good looks which caused all the women to love him, and his easy-going, joking personality which made the time go by faster. He was always super-nice to Lester and asked Lester's opinion on everything from sports to what was going on in the world. Having him in the room meant it would be an enjoyable case with engaging conversation. Some of the other anesthesiologists would put the patient to sleep and then just sit back and read the newspaper or get on the internet on their phones. One of Dr. Gonzalez's partners was notorious for falling asleep on a regular basis during cases. Dr. Gonzalez was different, and it was reassuring. He put the patient under and then hovered over them during the entire procedure, making sure that the patient did well.

Dr. Gonzalez walked to the side of Mrs. Traylor's stretcher and looked down at her with a big smile. "Mrs.

Traylor, I'm Dr. Gonzalez and I'll be doing your anesthesia for this procedure when Dr. Gold gets here. He usually beats me to the room, but I'm sure he'll be here shortly. Don't worry, I'll be with you the whole time and you'll wake up just as beautiful and charming as you are now. We'll let you go home and have something good to eat. Now I need to ask you a few questions after I read through your chart."

Dr. Gonzalez put the chart down after a minute. "It seems like you're very healthy and you've been through this procedure before. Have you or any family members ever had any problems with anesthesia?"

"No," replied Mrs. Traylor.

"Last time you had anything to eat or drink?"

"Last night for supper, I had clear liquids. I haven't had any solid food in almost two days."

"Any drug allergies?"

"None."

"All right, then. Open your mouth as wide as possible. Very good, you can close it now. When Dr. Gold gets here we'll get started. Any questions for me?"

"No, I just want this to be over. I know the worst part is the prep, and I have all the confidence in the world in Dr. Gold. If he chose you to be my anesthesiologist, then I also have total confidence in you."

RC looked around the room, double-checking that everything was in place for the colonoscopy. She'd had a crush on Dr. Gonzalez since she'd first met him, and when he walked into the room her heart skipped a beat. He was the kind of man she'd love to marry and spend her life with. Not like her abusive, alcoholic boyfriend, Randy. She listened to Dr. Gonzalez talk and she loved the sound of his voice. He spoke English perfectly, but still had a hint of a Cuban accent. He always talked with a smile on his face, showing his whiter than white teeth. He had an air of extreme confidence in his abilities. Anyone who was lucky enough to have anesthesia by him had to be enthralled by his looks and manner. She had suggested a couple of times that the two of them meet for drinks after work, but Dr. Gonzalez had always been busy with other cases and politely turned her down.

She had everything set up for Dr. Gold because she knew how particular he was. This was the last case of the day but it was scheduled for ninety minutes, so she knew it was going to be tough. She hadn't been in the room last year when Mrs. Traylor was scoped, but she'd heard from those who had been there that it had been horrible. Dr. Gold had had to turn this obese woman multiple times and had to bring in other nurses and techs to give pressure on her abdomen when Lester tired. She knew they were in for a battle, but when the case ended she'd go home and pack all her and Joshua's things for the move to Carol's house. If Randy was at their apartment she'd confront him about what he had done to her the previous night. She thought she better have a couple of glasses of wine before she did that to get the courage to stand up to him.

Randy wants me to live with him, she thought, but only on his terms. It was fortunate that Joshua was in Houston and not at home when her breakup with Randy occurred. She missed Joshua a lot. He loved to see his mother when she came home from work and sometimes would allow her to hold him close. Other times he'd be in one of his moods and wouldn't want to be bothered. She loved him so much that she couldn't imagine a mother loving her son more than she loved Joshua. She wished he was normal and could do the things boys his age could do, but she knew that would never be the case. But anything he did do, from pointing a finger at a bird flying in the sky to smiling when she fed him his favorite chocolate ice cream, made her feel wonderful. It made her feel that he was enjoying the limited life he had and somewhere deep within his brain the center that created pleasure was being activated.

She saw Dr. Gonzalez staring at her. *Does he see the extra make-up covering my black eye*, she thought?

Dr. Gonzalez smiled and said, "Okay, RC. You're looking good today and so are you, Lester. Lester, every time I see you it looks like you've been working out more and you look more buff. Now all we need to get this party started is the honorable Dr. Gold."

As if on cue, Dr. Gold walked in through the door. "Sorry I'm late," he said.

"No problem," answered RC, "let's do a quick time out. This is patient Charlotte Traylor and she is a sixty-one-year-old white female who is undergoing colonoscopy by Dr. Gold. She has no known drug allergies. Is everyone in agreement?"

Drs. Gold and Gonzalez said yes together. RC put Mrs. Traylor's chart on the back table where Dr. Gold had his computer opened to his procedure note from Mrs. Traylor's colonoscopy a year ago.

Dr. Gonzalez spoke to Mrs. Traylor. "Okay, Mrs. Traylor, it's time for you to go to sleep. Do you have any questions for me or for Dr. Gold?" He asked this while filling up the large syringe he held with Propofol, the anesthetic.

"No, no," said Mrs. Traylor. "I've done this before. I know what to expect. Just make sure I wake up."

"That's what you're paying me for," replied Dr. Gonzalez. "Anyone can put you to sleep, but the waking up part is a why I get paid the big bucks." He laughed. "Don't you worry, though. You'll wake up and you'll be fine and ready to go to Schmaltzies and get a nice juicy cheeseburger."

Dr. Gonzalez guided Mrs. Traylor as she turned onto her left side, assuming the left lateral decubitus position. As she turned he was struck by her nudity; most women wore their bras for these procedures and often a shirt. She wore no shirt or bra, just a naked chest with large pendulous breasts and tired pink nipples that drooped. He observed her nakedness as an entomologist might observe an insect he was studying. It gave him no titillation. He realized that he'd just come out of the closet, and soon word would spread to everyone about it. He didn't know if he'd mention it during the colonoscopy; he would see how things went. Somehow, though, he felt a tremendous load had been lifted off his shoulders. He no longer needed to go around pretending, flirting with women and taking them out on dates. Now he could be who he really was. Gays had the right to marry and he'd marry Jean-Baptiste and have him move to Dallas and set up a salon here. The two of them would live in Adonis' condo together and become an active part of Dallas' social scene. He felt proud that someone as beautiful and talented as Jean-Baptiste had chosen him to spend the rest of his life with. He could hardly wait. The thought of it made him feel so good he broke into a broad smile.

"Okay, this medicine might sting a little bit as it goes in," he said, "but this is the numbing medicine." He looked down and saw the gown barely covering

Mrs. Traylor's enormous buttocks dimpled with cellulite. "Now comes the good stuff," said Adonis. He began injecting the Propofol into Mrs. Traylor's IV. He saw the clear fluid in the IV tubing quickly turn the color of milk. He watched carefully as the blood pressure cuff went up, squeezing Mrs. Traylor's arm and then deflated registering a blood pressure of one forty over ninety. Her pulse was steady at eighty-three and her oxygen saturation was ninety-nine percent.

"Sweet dreams," he said, "you'll wake up in the recovery room and be able to drink any kind of juice you want."

Dr. Gold sat at the back table going over Mrs. Traylor's procedure notes from the previous year. He looked at Adonis and wondered if he'd had anything to do with the loud crash he had heard when he left the doctors' dining room. He'd already put on his gown and gloves while Dr. Gonzalez was putting Mrs. Traylor to sleep. He wore a face shield with a mask at the bottom to protect his face. He looked at the pictures he'd taken a year ago of the right side of the colon. The colon had been poorly prepped; there was a large amount of dark brown liquid and even some dark brown stool covering the walls of the colon. But there was nothing big he could see that he could have missed. Of course, the pictures on the report were each only two inches in diameter, making it hard to appreciate much detail. He sighed. *Now I'll find out if I missed cancer last year. Probably the most important lady in the city and soon to be the most important lady in the state. Her fate is entirely in my hands.* He had tremendous respect for the sanctity of life and the idea that anyone's death could be attributed to him caused him great trepidation.

He got off the stool and walked over to stand next to Lester. "You okay, Lester?" he asked.

"Fine, just fine, Dr. Gold," Lester replied. "Life is beautiful."

"When do you think we're going to be able to get your mother out of the hospital and home for more than a day?" Dr. Gold asked.

"Don't know, don't know," replied Lester. "Saw her at lunch and she seemed so comfortable asleep, but complaining of pain, as usual, when awake. May take a bomb under her to get her home," Lester laughed.

"What about those Mavericks, Lester?" Dr. Gold asked to change the subject.

Lester laughed. "Doesn't look like it's going to be their year again, does it? They've already lost five games in a row three times."

"No, it doesn't look like they will even make the playoffs," Dr. Gold replied. "Is she asleep, Adonis?"

Dr. Gonzalez took his right index finger and gently brushed it across Mrs. Traylor's eyelashes. There was no movement "She's asleep and we're ready to rumble," he loudly announced, using his best Michael Buffer boxing ring announcer voice.

Lester put down the railing on the stretcher. Dr. Gold took a deep breath and wiped his brow with the sleeve of his gown. He looked over at RC and noticed that her left eye had a shiner underneath it which she'd partially covered with make-up.

"You okay, RC?" he asked.

"I'm fine, Dr. Gold. Let's get going."

CHAPTER TWELVE

Gabriel took a deep breath. He'd been taught from the first year in medical school that a doctor should be calm in all situations. Getting upset or stressed did nothing good for the patient or for the doctor. He remembered being the code blue doctor during his rotation at the Veterans Administration Hospital in Houston. The hospital's main floor was over one-mile long with wards and ICU's and various other departments radiating off the first floor like tentacles off an octopus. Due to its length, getting from one place to another in the hospital could take twenty minutes. When his code beeper went off in the middle of the night he'd put on his white coat and start running as fast as he could to the ward where the code was called. At the entrance to the ward, he'd stop for a moment and collect himself, take three deep breaths, calming himself down and reminding himself that he was in charge and knew exactly what to do. Now he knew that this colonoscopy was going to be challenging and he dreaded the possibility of finding cancer in her now after giving her a clean report a year ago. But no matter what, he'd stay calm and see the procedure through to its end.

He briefly remembered an article he'd read years before about the famous North Carolina basketball coach, Dean Smith, and how he had endured terrible failure initially as a coach. He'd even been hung in effigy on the North Carolina campus after a loss. Finally, after reading and praying, Coach Smith concluded that he would do all he could do to help the team be successful, and then he had to turn it over to God. There were things in life, Smith realized, that he had no control over, and he had to learn to accept that and leave it in God's hands. Once he accepted this way of living, Coach Smith became one of the all-time greatest college basketball coaches. Gabriel looked at the ceiling for a moment and said to himself, *I've done all that I can. I'm turning this one over to you, God.* Maybe Rosh Hashana was a good day to talk to God after all. He looked back down at the patient and began the procedure.

The room was chilly, but since Gabriel and Lester wore plastic gowns over their scrubs, they were comfortable. Gabriel advanced the scope to the recto-sigmoid junction, just over a foot in, and immediately encountered problems. There was no opening to push the scope towards now. This next part would have to be done blindly, relying on feel and experience. Carefully Gabriel observed the way the colon folds were aligned up to that point and concluded that the opening had to be to the right and slightly upward. He pushed to get the device moving in this direction, but the scope wouldn't go. It just buckled, with the leading edge of the scope falling lower. Gabriel pulled the scope back and tried again. Again, it buckled; he got a glancing look at where he needed to go but the path was elusive. This was a pediatric colonoscope which was the most flexible instrument, and even with this, he was failing to negotiate this turn.

"Lester," Gabriel said calmly, "give me some abdominal pressure really low and let me see if I can get the scope around this turn."

Lester reached around Mrs. Traylor's back and pushed down on her abdomen in the left pelvis. This kept the scope from buckling at the turn, and Gabriel pushed the scope through the opening. He breathed a sigh of relief.

"So, you been doing okay, Gabriel?" Adonis asked as he jotted down the latest vital signs on the anesthesia record.

"No complaints," answered Gabriel, as he looked intently at the view of Mrs. Traylor's colon now showing on the television screen. "You've been gone for a while, haven't you?" Gabriel asked, not wanting to mention the sounds he had heard in the doctors' dining room.

"Yes," replied Adonis, "just got back from Paris and had a great time there. Oh, and by the way, since you may have heard this and the rest of you will probably be hearing about this soon, I just announced to the entire doctors' lunch room that I've come out of the closet. It's the most liberating day of my life! I can now be honest with the people I work with and with the people that live in Dallas and proclaim I am gay!"

"Good for you," said Gabriel. "As long as you're happy, that's all that matters. Smashing a plate in McFuck's face was a great way to come out of the closet!"

RC took a deep breath and felt her heart race. She looked at Dr. Gonzalez. How could he not be straight? He'd always been a model for a macho, handsome, suave, perfect male specimen and available doctor. "Y-Y-Y-You're gay?" she stammered.

"Sorry RC, I am. But that doesn't mean I still don't think you're beautiful. When I was in Paris I was with my lover, Jean-Baptiste, and I think I'm going to ask him to marry me and move to Dallas. He's a hair dresser and he is very talented. I think he should open a salon here. Gabriel, I think he could do a lot to help your, how shall I diplomatically say it, your somewhat ungroomed hair."

Gabriel was concentrating so intently on Mrs. Traylor's colon that he barely heard the conversation going on around him. He was now in an area of the sigmoid colon that no matter how much he pushed in, the scope wouldn't go any further. It was very frustrating, because he was looking at the exact same wall, no matter what.

"Can you help Lester give pressure?" he asked RC.

RC moved from the computer she was sitting at to the opposite side of Mrs. Traylor's stretcher. She put the railing to the stretcher down on her side and began pushing on Mrs. Traylor's abdomen.

"You both ready?" asked Gabriel.

"Yes," they answered in a chorus.

He again tried to push the scope in. "No, not working," he said, "it's just staying in the same place. Try pushing in different places."

Both RC and Lester moved their hands lower and pushed again. Gabriel tried a couple of times, but after putting in twenty to thirty centimeters of scope each time, he knew that it was futile.

"We're going to have to roll her onto her back," Gabriel said.

. "Thank goodness we've got a sheet under her we can roll her with," said Lester. "Dr. Gonzalez, would you mind helping RC on her side?"

They turned Mrs. Traylor onto her back.

"Good," said Gabriel as he pulled the scope back a few centimeters, "let's get you guys to give good pressure again."

Lester and RC gave pressure but nothing happened.

RC said, "Let me get a stool and stand higher and see if I can get my hands further into her belly. She's got a lot of belly to push through." RC pulled a stool over and began giving pressure again, and after she did, Gabriel was able to advance the scope ten centimeters further into the colon before it stopped moving again.

"All right, that's good!" Gabriel said. "Relax for a minute."

While Lester and RC relaxed, Gabriel became aware of the sweat on his T-shirt and under his arms. They were just starting into the sigmoid colon, maybe a quarter of the way around the entire colon, and already he felt like he'd done ten colonoscopies.

Lester wiped his brow with the back of his arm. Dr. Gonzalez turned on the nineteen-nineties boom box radio which sat below the television screen on the same moveable stand. They always listened to the same station which had no talk, few commercials, and Dr. Gold's favorite rock music from the seventies and eighties. He turned up the volume and the room was filled with "House of the Rising Sun" by The Animals.

"There is a house in New Orleans… Oh mother tell your children…Not to do what I have done…"

"Let's try the pressure, again," Gabriel said. "Let's see if we can get any further."

RC and Lester pushed again. RC was pushing down so hard that her elbows trembled. The scope advanced a few centimeters and then stopped. Gabriel was now again in an area where he could not see in which direction the lumen of the colon went. He pulled back and tried to push in a couple of directions, but all he could see was the whiting-out of the scope against the wall of the colon which meant he was pushing into the wall and not advancing. He knew that if he continued to push in the direction of the white-out he would perforate her colon. He pulled back again. "The House of the Rising Sun" was over, and "Let it Ride" by Bachman-Turner Overdrive came on.

"Let it Ride" had been Gabriel's favorite song since it came out. It was released in nineteen seventy-four during his sophomore year of high school, and the thought of letting something ride, forgetting about it, and moving on to the next thing in life—whether it was a relationship, a class, or a job, had always been his motto. At least until Ray's death, that was. Even then, he'd partially worked through and seen the light as the lyrics sang, and here he was working today. He was listening intently to the song as he pushed into the area where he thought the opening had to be. It barely opened allowing Gabriel to quickly push the scope into the junction between the sigmoid colon and the descending colon.

"Let's take a break for a second," Gabriel said as they all relaxed and listened to the harmonies of "Let it Ride."

"And would you cry if I told you that I lied and would you say good-bye, or would you let it ride…"

"Congratulations Adonis," said Gabriel. "It had to be miserable living a lie all those years. You have a great work ethic and worked so hard to get to where you are now. You deserve the happiness that comes from being able to openly live with and love the person you truly care about."

Adonis smiled and said, "I'm amazingly happy. I feel like a burden has been lifted off my shoulders."

Lester chimed in, "You're still a great doctor, Dr. Gonzalez. Gay, straight, hetero, homo, bi, transgender, it doesn't matter. All that should matter to anyone is how you take care of your patients, and you've always done an outstanding job. If I ever needed to be put under, I'd want you to do it."

"Why thank you, Lester," said Dr. Gonzalez, "I appreciate that. You two don't know how good it makes me feel to hear your compliments. My father is dead so I won't have to tell him, but my mom is still alive in Miami Beach so I'll bring Jean-Baptiste there to meet her. She'll be shocked at first, but happy for me if she knows that I'm happy."

"Well, enough compliments for now. Let's get back to work," said Gabriel.

They had Mrs. Traylor on her back for another five minutes before Gabriel realized that the scope wasn't going any further no matter where they pressed or how much scope he pushed into her. "Let's turn her back on her left side," he said.

RC shook her head and then grabbed her side of the sheet. With Lester doing most of the pulling, they got Mrs. Traylor back on her side.

"Lester why don't you and RC switch positions?" asked Gabriel. "That way Lester can apply pressure directly to the abdomen without having to reach over Mrs. Traylor's body." RC and Lester changed positions.

Lester began pushing. He was in the exact right spot because the scope went through the area of the descending colon and made the turn into the transverse colon which Gabriel identified by its triangular-shaped folds.

The announcer came onto the radio and said, "Happy Rosh Hashanah, happy new year to all of our Jewish listeners!" Then the station went to commercials.

"Hey," said Dr. Gonzalez, "you're working today, Gabriel. Don't you usually take off for the Jewish holidays?"

"Yes," replied Gabriel, "I usually do. This year was somewhat different, though, and I just couldn't go. Lot of work. Lots of things I just wanted to get caught up on. My mind wasn't where it needed to be. All right, Lester, push right there."

Gabriel didn't want to admit that he was still so angry at God for Ray's death that he couldn't pray on this holy day. That was something between him and God, and not something he wanted to share.

Lester began to push and Gabriel was slowly able to advance the scope another ten centimeters. There were three settings of increasing tightness which made the scope more rigid and easier to push. In the sigmoid colon Gabriel didn't use these settings due to fear of perforation with an inflexible scope. But now that he was in the beginning of the transverse colon he turned the tightness up to the maximum setting of three.

Gabriel had Lester pushing Mrs. Traylor's abdomen from the front and RC pushing Mrs. Traylor from the back to make sure she didn't fall off the stretcher. They came to an area where the transverse colon was redundant and looped on itself. No opening could be seen.

Gabriel put in more and more carbon dioxide gas to insufflate the area until Lester said, "She's so distended with air now I can't push down on her abdomen. It's too tight."

"Give me a minute to take out some of the air," Gabriel said. Gabriel pushed on the suction control button with his index finger to get the air out and suctioned up dark-green fluid. "Is that better?" he asked Lester.

"Yeah, I think that's better," Lester replied.

"Try to give the pressure again."

Lester gave the pressure again and Gabriel reached the area where the colon folded on itself. Finally, Gabriel found a sliver of an opening at the eight o'clock position. He veered in that direction and the colon opened. Once he got through this area, the scope stopped moving again.

By now, both Lester and RC were sweating profusely. Adonis was at the head of the stretcher, intently watching Mrs. Traylor while singing along to Blue Oyster Cult's "Don't Fear the Reaper."

"I don't fear the Reaper," said Adonis. "I do fear that now that I've come out as gay people will shun me and I won't have my same straight friends."

"Your friends are your friends," said Gabriel, "your co-workers are your co-workers. We're not going to desert you. To be honest with you, I always thought you were gay, but it never mattered. Your work has always been outstanding, you've always been a pleasure to work with. That's all that matters to me. If I'd known for sure earlier, I would have encouraged you to come out a long time ago. Life is too short. I think we're going to need to put her back onto her back."

"Okay," Lester said as he blew out a long breath. They pulled Mrs. Traylor onto her back while Gabriel held the scope in place.

Just then the Emergency Warning Signal blasted from the radio.

RC said, "I didn't think there were any storms in the area. I wonder why the Emergency Warning is going off."

Suddenly the deep voice of the station's manager came on the radio. "We have just learned from credible sources that the terrorists have set off nuclear and chemical weapons throughout the world. It's estimated that the terrorists have at least ten strategically targeted nuclear weapons. We have seen video that Paris and London are in flames, and that New York City and Washington, D.C., are destroyed. Unfortunately, our president and the rest of our government have been completely wiped out. Therefore, I have no statement to read to you from Washington."

The radio went silent for a minute. The endoscopy room was silent and its occupants stunned. After a minute the announcer's voice returned. He was crying and it was difficult to completely understand him. "We have just learned that the terrorists were able to hack into the nuclear arsenals of the United States, Russia, and the United Kingdom. Over fourteen thousand nuclear weapons owned by these countries are on their way to destinations throughout the entire world. It's a nuclear holocaust! Word coming now from governmental nuclear physicists is that no human beings will survive the nuclear attack and its effects. They are also saying that chemical weapons were released in the atmosphere destroying life as we know it."

There was another pause, much longer this time, and broken by the sound of people screaming and crying at the radio station. The announcer's voice came back. "To all of you I say good-bye and good luck. I guess that was a fucking stupid thing to say, good luck. There is no more luck. It's the decision of the management of this station to continue to play music until either we are dead or our signal is gone. Good-bye to you listeners, good-bye to my family, Delilah my wife, Eve, Jonah, and Noah, my children. I won't be able to see you again on this earth, but I'll see you again someday in the future. Our spirits will be joined again in a more loving world in an alternate universe. To stay alive as long as possible, stay inside your house or place of work. Let me repeat, it's the decision of the management of this station to continue to play music until we are dead or our signal is gone.

"I understand from reports that there are still more nuclear weapons reaching their target sites as I speak. I want my family to know how much I love you and that I've always loved you. You gave me more happiness than one man could ever deserve. Keep your heads up, children, and your keep your faith in the teachings we have discussed over the years. Now here's the music we leave this earth with. Enjoy the last music you will hear and kiss and hug your loved ones if possible for the last time. I'm supposed to do a spot for Al's Auto Repair Shop now, but fuck 'em. They did a shitty job on my BMW when I brought it in, so whether you're still alive or not, don't take your car to Al's!"

CHAPTER THIRTEEN

"No Sugar Tonight" by the Guess Who came on and the radio went dead for a moment. Then there was loud static and finally no sound at all. The four awake people in the room looked around at each other. They all had looks of wide-eyed disbelief.

Just then Carol burst into the room. She'd been waiting in the recovery area to recover Mrs. Traylor when the procedure was done. "Did you hear what's happening? I looked outside the windows and the whole sky is smoky and gray and dark and the sun is gone. There's wrecks all over the streets with people getting out of their cars and dropping dead. We're all going to die! I've got to try to get home, though. I've got a husband with Alzheimer's who's all by himself. I need to take care of him. I need to hold him in my arms one last time. I love you all. Goodbye and trust in Jesus." She ran out of the room. There was silence.

"I guess there's no reason to go forward with this colonoscopy," said Adonis, breaking the silence.

He looked over and RC was now curled up in the corner of the room, crying hysterically. "My son, my Joshua, my son. I've got to see him but he's in Houston. How can I die without saying good-bye to the person I love the most and care the most about?"

Lester looked at Dr. Gold and said, "My mom's in the hospital next door, you know. I've got to see her before we all die. Good-bye. I've enjoyed working with you and you have all taught me a lot. I'll never forget you and all that you have done to help me."

"I'm so stunned that nothing I say will make sense," said Doctor Gold. "I've enjoyed working with you, Lester. I want you to know I always tried my best with your mother, but sometimes it seemed she didn't want to be helped. Good-bye, forever."

Adonis said, "I've got to try and call Jean-Baptiste and say good-bye to him. I'll come back, but I need to leave the room for a few minutes. Do you want me to just let the patient wake up on her own, or should I give her more drugs to knock her out until this is all over?"

"I guess let her wake up," replied Doctor Gold. "I'll keep the scope in until she complains."

RC and Lester ran out of the room. They almost tripped over each other running down the four flights of stairs. There was no electricity so the entire building was dark. The endoscopy center was the only place with power now, since it had its own generator. RC and

Lester looked outside and the scene was devastation. Everyone was lying on the sidewalk, grass, or driveway, dead. Carol was lying dead on her knees on the sidewalk just outside the door, her body leaning against a bush with her arms upstretched, so it looked as though she was pleading with her maker. She had draped a scrub top over her head to try and protect herself from the radiation and chemicals, but the scrub top now lay half on her and half draped on the bush beside her.

Lester ran over to the door which connected the office building to the hospital. Waves of intense heat pushed him back from the door. The hospital was a giant ball of fire and no structure resembling a building remained. There had been a direct hit of a nuclear warhead a few blocks down, and the fire had spread to the hospital but not yet to the adjacent office building containing the endoscopy center. Lester's heart sank as he realized there was no way he'd be able to say good-bye to his mother. He tried his cell phone to call his mother's cell, but his cell phone was dead. He tried not to, but thoughts of her last minutes on earth kept filling his mind. Hopefully, she slept through everything in a narcotic-induced haze. It troubled him to think she could have been awake when her room exploded or when a giant fireball engulfed her body. No, he decided, she was in her drug-induced euphoria when the ending came and she never knew what had happened.

Meanwhile, upstairs at the endoscopy center, Adonis left the procedure room and ran into the break room. He called Jean-Baptiste's cell phone in California and then his salon's number, but both lines were dead. Adonis put his head in his hands and started crying. He pictured Jean-Baptiste bravely trying to console his clients as the salon lost power and then was decimated. Jean-Baptiste had a comforting, reassuring way about him that certainly would have helped ease the misery of others. But what of Jean-Baptiste himself? Had his death been quick and painless or had he been forced to suffer? Adonis could only hope and pray for the former. He cried for Jean-Baptiste and for the life that the two of them never shared together.

Lester and RC looked numbly outside at the cataclysm. Dozens of people were screaming and running aimlessly around the lobby. RC put her arms around Lester's waist and he put his arms around her shoulders and they both cried. They continued to hold each other as RC chanted, "What should we do? What can we do? I've got to get ahold of Randy and see if he's heard anything about Joshua." She got out her cell phone, dialed her home number, and miraculously it rang.

Randy picked up the call. "RC," he said, "RC, good-bye. I love you. I know that the world is ending…"

RC interrupted, "Have you heard from Houston about Joshua?"

"Yes, they've got him inside Chip's house until the end. I told them to tell Joshua that you loved him more than anything."

"I wish I could come see you," said RC, "but if I go outside I'll immediately be dead."

"I know," said Randy.

"I've got to ask you. Randy. I've got a black eye today. Did you hit me last night?"

"No," answered Randy, "I didn't punch you last night. You got drunk and fell and smashed your face on the bedside dresser. Don't you remember? I had to pick you up off the floor and put you in bed."

Out of her shock from the world ending and out of the alcohol-induced stupor from the previous night, some neuron in RC's brain fired and she remembered being picked up by Randy's powerful arms and put into bed. A movie began playing in her mind of her stumbling out of their bathroom and tripping before she made it to bed and hitting her face on the dresser. It must have knocked her out, because the movie in her mind ended abruptly.

"Randy, I know we've had a roller coaster of a relationship, but I guess in the end you were the best for me and Joshua. I just wish you hadn't been so abusive to me."

"I'm sorry for all I've done," said Randy. "I'm sorry for the life I've lived. I grew up being abused, too. I should have tried to do better to stop the vicious cycle. I won't get that chance, now, so all I can do is apologize and tell you that I always loved you and everything about you. You turned me from a wild male beast into a human being and made me feel things I never felt before. Good-bye, RC, and please find it in your heart to forgive me."

"Good-bye," replied RC, "I do forgive you, just like Jesus taught me to forgive. The next time I see you it will be in Heaven with our Lord and Creator, Jesus Christ. I'm going to dial Chip's number to say good-bye to Joshua."

She began dialing but the line was dead, and although RC screamed, "Joshua, Joshua" into her phone, she knew there would be no reply. She looked at the screen saver on her cell phone. It was a picture of Chip in his wheelchair holding Joshua, with RC standing to his side. The picture had been taken at his parent's ranch when she and Chip were still together. Maybe I should have stayed with Chip, she thought. Maybe I should have gutted it out and been his caretaker and wife. No, no way I could have survived that life. I did what was best for me and hopefully for Joshua. It would have been nice to be able to say good-bye to Chip and apologize to him for leaving years ago. So many different thoughts rushed through her head that she had to sit down in the lobby amidst all the screaming and terrified people. She curled up into a ball and put her hands over her ears. Lester stood next to her, watching her, not knowing what else to do. Finally, he sat on the floor next to RC and wrapped his right arm around her waist and put his head next to hers.

CHAPTER FOURTEEN

Gabriel was alone in the room with Mrs. Traylor with the scope halfway around her colon and the business end of the device coming out of her buttocks. He sat on his stool. He looked at the black clock on the wall. It had been thirty minutes since the colonoscopy started. Should he continue to go on? Should he just pull the scope out and spend whatever short time he had left doing nothing? He sensed that Sarah was dead since she was in New York City and it had been obliterated.

"Sarah, I love you," he whispered to himself. "Wherever you are, I will always love you."

He pulled out his cell phone to call her, but it went immediately to her voice mail. He didn't know if she'd ever get this last message, but he felt he had to leave it.

"Sarah, I know I'll never see you again, but I need to tell you a few things from my heart. You have been and will always be the only love of my life. You brought love and beauty and comfort to me, and there's no way

I can tell you how much you have meant to me. It took me a long time to find you, or did you find me?"

He laughed. "Either way, like you once said, we were meant to love one another and share our lives. Thank you for Ray. He told me when he was a young boy that you were his favorite person in the world, and I always knew why. You were improbable, unexpected, joyous and caring. You gave the two men in your life more love than we could ever have hoped for as a wife and as a mother, and I thank you from both of us. We'll meet again someday, of that I'm sure. I know I'll recognize your soul: it will be the only one wearing camouflage gear. I love you. Shalom." He set the scope down on Mrs. Traylor's stretcher. The television screen went blank for a minute and the scope went silent as all the electricity went off, and then the screen flickered back to life and the scope made its usual sound as the emergency generator kicked back in.

Gabriel sat down. "I can't believe it. Last day of the world and I'm all alone." He closed his eyes and began to think of meeting Sarah and their early life together.

The Dallas Young Jewish Single's Group was having an outing at the Dallas Museum of Art, and Gabriel had decided to go. There was a Monet exhibit featured at the museum, and the flyer promised guided tours of the exhibit as well as coffee and dessert after. Gabriel was a gastroenterology fellow at Southwestern Medical School in Dallas and had been so busy in the last few months with work that his already anemic dating life had screeched to a complete halt. He hadn't gone to any of the Jewish singles events before, but figured it was worth a try. Even if he struck out socially, there was still Monet, whose paintings he loved.

When he got to the museum he went inside and followed the signs to where the group was meeting. There were about one hundred people milling about, and after five minutes of standing with his hands in his sport coat pockets, he was relieved to hear someone in charge make an announcement. "Welcome to our Monet Mixer Event at the Dallas Museum of Art. I'm Beth Epstein, and I'm the president of the Young Jewish Singles Organization. Today we have a special treat, a closed-to-the public viewing of the visiting Monet collection. We are honored to have five art professors from SMU to lead groups of you through the exhibit and give you an intimate look at the genius of Monet."

Five women stepped forward. Four were in their forties to fifties and wore frumpy age-appropriate dresses. The fifth appeared to be in her twenties and wore a camouflage blouse and skin-tight green army pants.

One of the older professors spoke. "We'll divide you into groups of twenty." She counted out the first group and said, "You'll go with Isabelle who is one of our professors of art history. She counted out a second twenty and pointed to the younger professor dressed in camouflage and said, "You next twenty up to the man in the sports jacket will go with Sarah, one of the Professors of Creative Art at SMU."

Gabriel was the man with the sports jacket, and he was somewhat disappointed not to be included in the young professor's group. He'd already sized her up and down and was very impressed by what he saw. She was tall, slender, had long red hair, and lively blue eyes. As he waited to hear who would lead him in the next group, he was surprised to hear Sarah speak.

"I think you counted wrong, Professor Clay. Number twenty for me is the gentleman in the light blue sports jacket with his hands in his pockets. Now you all come and follow me."

Gabriel was delighted to be with such a young, beautiful guide. She told the group her name was Sarah Brownstein, and she was Jewish and one of the artists in residence at SMU. She'd just moved to Dallas a few months before after being on the faculty of her alma mater, Yale, and was a huge fan of the Impressionist movement in general and of Monet in particular. She took them through the exhibit, treating each painting with joy and surprise as though it was a present being opened by a child on Christmas morning. Gabriel had taken art history as an elective in college eons ago, so he knew a little bit about Monet and his work but was learning much more.

The group stopped at one of Monet's most famous works, *Parisians Enjoying the Parc*. Sarah said, "If anyone can tell me where the setting for this painting is, I have a prize for them."

Without thinking, Gabriel shouted out, "At Monet's home in Giverny, France."

"Very good, that's correct," replied Sarah. "What's your name?"

"Gabriel."

"Well, Gabriel, see me after the tour for your prize."

When the tour ended everyone met in the large hallway outside the Monet exhibit for dessert. Gabriel went up to Sarah who was surrounded by five men and said, "Pardon me, I have to leave. But I'd like to know if I'm getting some sort of a prize."

Sarah walked away from the five men completely encircling her and came right next to Gabriel. She was so close to him that he reflexively crossed his arms in front of his chest.

"Your prize is you get to rescue me from talking to all these other single men and you get to buy me a decent cup of coffee."

"That's my prize?" asked Gabriel. "Shouldn't you be the one buying the coffee?"

"Your prize is for being so cute you get to meet me and learn the mysteries of my life. Buying the coffee is a small price to pay for that adventure."

"I get the feeling you like me," said Gabriel. "You made sure I was included in your group and now you're getting me to take you out. Only someone as gorgeous as you could get away with this."

"I don't necessarily like you," replied Sarah, "but I think you will fall in love with me and I'll learn to at least tolerate you."

Sarah smiled with her whole face. She had beautiful eyes and facial features that probably could have supported a career in modeling. Gabriel had never met someone so direct and sure of themselves. They walked from the museum to Gabriel's car holding hands the entire way.

Dating Sarah was like trying to capture the wind: each time you thought you had her in your grasp there was something new, exciting, and dazzling about her that made her seem too amazing to hold on to. She was from Greenwich, Connecticut where her parents lived. Her father was a wealthy property owner in Manhattan. She'd gone to Yale undergraduate and had been an artist in residence for three years before accepting the offer to join the faculty at SMU as an assistant professor. This was her first time living outside the Northeast, and she was having a ball. She loved doing everything, from going to the stockyards in Fort Worth to eating corn dogs at the Texas State Fair to going shopping at the Neiman Marcus store. She made every date fun and an adventure.

She told Gabriel that in college she thought she was bisexual, and had had some lesbian sex, but now felt she was into guys and was saving herself for the right man. Luckily, Gabriel became the right man on their third date. He'd taken her to dinner downtown, and then she invited him back to her apartment which was also located in downtown Dallas. The apartment was in an old warehouse building, which had been turned into individual units, with each apartment having a downstairs and then a loft for the bedroom.

They walked into Sarah's apartment and the entire first floor had been converted into a studio for her to paint. There were four easels set up in different parts of the room with paintings in various stages of completion.

"I'm very into painting abstract art," Sarah said. "I'm mainly working with old chalk boards as my canvas and creating diptychs and triptychs. Each of the easels contains one chalkboard which, when I'm finished with it, will be joined with one or two other chalkboards."

Gabriel went up close to one easel and could easily see that it was, indeed, a black chalkboard onto which had been etched various abstract figures and designs mainly in white, but also, sparingly, in other colors.

"If you want to see what one looks like finished, come over here." Sarah took Gabriel's hand and led him to a corner of the room where numerous diptychs and triptychs were assembled. There was no frame, just the square chalkboards with abstract drawings, some with many drawings and some with just a few. They took a while for him to get used to, but the more he looked over them, the more they appealed to him. In one he could almost see the ocean and a fish swimming with some circles inside a circle of a different color painted next to the fish.

"I like them," Gabriel said, "have you had any shows of your works?"

"I have," replied Sarah. "I just had a very successful show in Greenwich where I sold all the displayed paintings. Now I'm preparing for a show in Scottsdale. My work has been auctioned off at major auction houses and I've had 2 museum exhibits. Let me show you the upstairs of the apartment."

Gabriel gazed up at the ceiling and saw that it was the typical industrial ceiling of a warehouse, totally unfinished and with no aesthetic features at all. Sarah took Gabriel's hand and led him up the winding,

wrought-iron staircase to the second floor of her apartment. She'd designed the staircase and her father had
had it built and installed for her. The entire upstairs
was filled with fresh cut flowers in vases all over the
room. Petals of all colors and shapes covered the floor
and bed.

"Where on earth did you get all these gorgeous
flowers?" Gabriel asked, turning to Sarah with delight.

"There is an orthodox Jew named Moishe who
owns a floral shop right around the corner. Every
Friday afternoon before Shabbos he lets me come
into his shop and pick from the unsold flowers to
adorn my home with. He says they will fill my apartment and my life with the beauty of Shabbos. I bring
him finished paintings every so often to express my
gratitude. It's kind of like Monet's garden, don't you
think?"

"Absolutely. Only Monet never had anyone as beautiful as you to occupy his garden. It smells so wonderful
in here. This must be what Heaven smells like."

The large room contained a bed, the largest bed
Gabriel had ever seen, and beautiful glass lamps on the
bedside tables that had been made by Chihuly. On all
the walls were Sarah's original paintings in a variety of
genres and photographs of Sarah and her family.

"Did you paint all these?" Gabriel asked pointing
to the multitude of art works.

"They're all mine. Various stages in my life when various artistic styles consumed me. Enjoy looking at them while I go to the bathroom."

Sarah walked down a narrow hall and Gabriel walked around the bedroom. He could see how talented Sarah was. She could paint well in a variety of styles. By looking at the art and seeing her paintings downstairs he could see how she'd matured as an artist and was finding a style she was comfortable with now. Sarah emerged from the bathroom wearing only a white terry cloth robe that came down to nowhere near her knees. Her hair was completely undone and hung loose below her shoulders. For a second Gabriel thought about the boxer, Mike Tyson, and how he came out of his dressing room for fights dressed only in a terrycloth robe, but then he got the image of Mike Tyson out of his brain and realized how amazingly beautiful and sexy Sarah was.

"If you're wondering why I have a king-sized bed," she said, "it's because I enjoy sex so much and I enjoy being able to experiment. I want to fulfill my wildest fantasies and yours. When I first saw you, I was very, very physically attracted to you, especially that perfectly rounded tush. But, kidding aside, you're a handsome hunk and I love being with you. I want you to make love to me."

Gabriel began unbuttoning his shirt.

"Not so fast. I know you took art history in college and think you know something about art. Let's role play.

I'll take off the robe and pose as a famous painting. If you can tell me the name of the painting and the painter, I'm yours."

The terry cloth robe slowly came apart, revealing large firm breasts with perfect pink nipples and then a flat, muscular stomach and slender hips. The robe fell to the floor and Sarah leaned back and raised her arms above her head, opening the small triangular thatch of red hair where her legs met. Her legs were shapely and long, completing the best piece of art in the apartment. Gabriel reached out to touch her, but she pushed his hand away.

"Remember, the painting and the artist. Don't worry, if it takes too long I'll give you clues."

Sarah sat down on the gold armoire at the foot of the bed. She leaned back on her right arm and put her right leg out straight in front of her on the bed. She turned her head to the left and bent her left leg at the knee. On her left knee she extended her left arm and hand, with the index finger reaching out in space.

"Michelangelo's *Creation of Adam,*" Gabriel shouted enjoying the beauty on display in front of him.

Sarah crawled onto the bed. "I'll have to come up with something more challenging next time," she said, as she sat on her knees and undid the buttons to Gabriel's shirt.

They ended up making love in the giant bed twice that night. Gabriel could tell that Sarah loved the feeling of him inside her since she made sure that he lasted as long as possible before coming by pinching the tip of his penis with her fingers every time he pulled out of her vagina. When they had both come for the second time they fell asleep in each other's arms.

They dated for three more months before Gabriel proposed. Sex continued to play an important part in their relationship, occurring only at Sarah's warehouse apartment and only after she'd appeared totally nude except for the terrycloth robe. Sarah portrayed da Vinci's *Mona Lisa,* Grant Wood's *American Gothic,* Botticelli's *The Birth of Venus, Whistler's Mother* and others before they would make love. The only painting Gabriel didn't recognize in the three months was *Napoleon Crossing the Alps* by Jacques-Louis David. For this painting, Sarah straddled a hobby horse completely nude except for the Bicorne hat she'd picked up at a flea market. She'd given Gabriel clues and he recognized Napoleon but didn't know the name of the work or the artist.

"No intercourse tonight," Sarah told him after giving him the painting's name and artist. "That means oral sex only." She crawled up on top of Gabriel in the sixty-nine-position and he quickly pulled off his clothes.

"Maybe I should have known fewer of these paintings," Gabriel joked.

"Maybe you and I should get married," came Sarah's reply as she began licking his penis.

Gabriel sat up straight in bed and Sarah fell off him and onto the bed. He looked in her eyes. She wasn't joking. They kissed passionately and when he drew back his mouth he said, "Will you marry me, Sarah Brownstein?"

"Of course, of course, yes. When you have time in your busy schedule, just pick out a big diamond engagement ring to make it official. Not too big, though, because I want to wear it while I'm painting."

Three months later the two of them were married in the backyard of Greenwich estate belonging to Sarah's parent's, right on the water. They'd been inseparable ever since, until now when they would die apart.

Gabriel thought of their last time together. Sarah was in her art studio which they'd added onto the east side of the house. Gabriel had to get up early the next day for work, and Sarah was getting up even earlier to catch her flight to New York City. She was still working as an artist and had her works displayed in galleries and museums throughout the country. She was no longer on the faculty at SMU, having left the university ten years before to concentrate on her painting.

Gabriel looked at her canvas and realized that she'd just completed her latest painting. Its style was completely different from anything she'd done before, but it was outstanding in composition and design. It was titled *Orbits* and the background of the painting was sky blue. The middle of the portrait was filled with eight squares, each of which contained a complex abstract series of curves which represented the orbits of the eight planets in our solar system besides Earth. For this painting, Sarah still considered Pluto a bona fide planet.

Below these squares was a larger square in which the orbit of Earth was displayed in abstract. At the bottom of the painting was a short paragraph which looked like it could have come from a scientific textbook, but which Sarah herself had written and designed in textbook fashion. On the left side of the orbits were stacked three silhouettes of women's heads, all of whom seemed to have their heads cocked to the right side, as though listening to the middle of the painting. For balance, on the right side of the painting there were three male heads, one on top of the other with their heads bent to their left, in the listening position. Gabriel looked at the painting for a long time before speaking. Somehow, it made sense to him. The orbits represented the enormity and mystery of our solar system and the heads represented our desire to meet that vastness. Gabriel often wondered what other worlds were out there.

"It's amazing," Gabriel said. "How did you make it?"

"Several new processes I've been working on. The orbits are from pages of one of Ray's physics textbooks from college. It's a monotype; one of a kind. I used solar plates as well as linoleum block to display the images. It's printed on BFK Rives Printmaking paper from France. The paper itself was soaked and had to be damp for printing the orbital images on a press. I've already sold it to an art dealer who came to look at it yesterday. It will go into a private collection in Beverly Hills."

She paused a moment. "It's special because it connects me to Ray and gives me hope that with the vastness of the universe and the greatness of God, you and I will be with him again."

She put down her paint brush and hugged Gabriel. Of the two of them, time had treated Sarah far more kindly. She dyed her hair the same color red as when they had met, and still wore it free-flowing down to her shoulders. Her blue eyes still sparkled, although now Gabriel felt a tear drop from one of them onto his face. He hugged her tightly and then kissed her passionately. Their last act together was making love on the sofa in her studio with the cosmos looking down upon them.

Adonis sat alone in the break room, staring out the window. "I can't believe it, I can't believe it," he stammered as the tears welled up in his eyes and raced down his cheeks. He kept calling Jean-Baptiste, but the calls went immediately to voice mail. He was too choked up to leave a message, so he decided to compose himself first, and then call again.

Moments later he tried Jean-Baptiste's cell phone and again got his voice mail. Now he was prepared to leave a message.

"Jean-Baptiste, this is Adonis, of course. I know we won't see each other again in this world, but I promise to find you in paradise. I'll search through all of Heaven until I find you. I love you with all my heart and the thought of never seeing you again makes me sadder than words can express. You completed me; you made me whole. I wish we could have grown old together and faced all the changes that life brings as two human beings are forged by love into one. Our lives may end but our love will endure throughout eternity. Good-bye, my sweet prince."

Adonis pushed the red button on the cell phone ending the call. Why had he only found true love so late in life? Why couldn't he have met Jean-Baptiste years before so they could have spent a lifetime together and not just a couple of years? Adonis thought about these questions, but then pacified himself by remembering that some people never find a mate in this life and never experience the high that true love can bring. The high had been short for the two of them, but it had been real and it had been dazzling. His Catholic upbringing gave him hope that there was an afterlife, and he prayed that in Heaven Jesus would want all sexual orientations to be happy. He would introduce Jean-Baptiste to his parents, and he believed that in Heaven his father would have only respect and admiration for Jean-Baptiste. Adonis pictured Heaven as a place where his parents and Jean-Baptiste would unite with him as one family. He hated the fact that he hadn't practiced Catholicism as an adult, because he was sure he would have uncovered even more of the love and enchantment that Heaven had to offer.

Lester and RC held hands as they trudged up the dark stairs to the fourth floor where the endoscopy center was located. Both were crying. RC's make-up was completely gone and the fresh bruise under her eye was visible.

"The world's ending, the world's ending. My whole life is over," sobbed RC. "Why did this have to happen to me now? I had plans to turn my life around and get it moving in the right direction, and now the plans are worthless."

"Everyone's life is over," replied Lester. "What should we do? We might as well go back to the endoscopy center and spend our last few hours there. There's really no other place to go that will have power."

"How could this have happened?" asked RC. "How can people be so stupid? How could people not want to live? Not let others live. If they want to end their own lives, fine. I wouldn't stop them. But to destroy the entire world? That is beyond comprehension. It reminds me of when people kill their families including their children and then commit suicide. Why can't they kill themselves and let others live? What could drive people to do this unspeakable act?"

"Hatred, I figure," said Lester. "Such hatred. Uncle Russell always told me easiest thing to do in life is to hate. Hardest thing to do is to love. Love is the hardest emotion. When I told Uncle Russell I wanted to be a doctor I thought he'd laugh at me. But he didn't. He said that I had so much love and caring in my body that I'd make the perfect doctor. He said it was sad that so few people had the kind of love I had."

"Have you ever made love to a woman, Lester?" asked RC, wiping the tears away from her eyes.

"If you mean have I ever had sex, no," said Lester. "I guess I never found the right woman."

The two of them walked through the wide-open door into the endoscopy center's hallway.

RC looked at Lester. Here he was, a handsome young man who had never had sex. They walked together into the recovery room where there was one stretcher with a sheet covering it and a pillow at the head, waiting for tomorrow's first patient who would never come.

RC took Lester's other arm and turned him towards her. She closed her eyes and let her face drift up next to Lester's so that their lips touched. She put her tongue into Lester's mouth and began kissing him, and he kissed her back. He freed his hands from hers and put them under her chin, gently cradling her head and moving it slightly closer to him.

RC pulled off Lester's scrub top and began fondling his chest. She then stepped back, pulled her scrub top quickly over her head and with one movement, undid her bra hooks. The white lace bra fell to the floor. She pressed her breasts against Lester's chest and guided him to lie down on the stretcher. Due to the narrow width of the stretcher, she was on top of Lester, and he could smell the sweet fragrance radiating from RC's hair.

RC reached down and undid the tie to Lester's scrub pants while their lips were locked together, and he helped kick them off his body. She then undid her own scrubs and pulled them off. Lester was wearing K-Mart white boxers, and RC was left in a tiny white thong which she'd always referred to as a "T-back." Lester removed the thong with a tug, and then took off his K-Mart specials.

"I've never done this before," reminded Lester as he massaged RC's firm breasts.

"You're doing great so far," replied RC. "If we're going to go, we might as well go out happy."

They heard wails of anguish coming from the break room, but they didn't stop.

Lester got on top of RC and she felt his penis. "You were never circumcised?" she asked.

"I'm untouched," answered Lester.

"I've never had sex with an uncircumcised man before, so I guess this will be a new experience for me, too."

RC began massaging Lester's already hard penis and then guided it into her vagina. Lester straightened his arms out to give himself leverage and began thrusting his penis in and out of RC's wetness. He held himself back from coming, and he relaxed his arms and kissed and hugged her again with his penis still inside her.

"Here, let me get on top," said RC after a few minutes of passionate kissing. They rolled over and RC sat on top of Lester.

"Wow," said Lester, "if I'd known how great sex was, I wouldn't have waited until the world was about to end to get laid."

They both laughed. "You're an awesome lover," RC said and she began rocking back and forth on top of Lester, using her right hand to massage her clitoris. She could feel herself climaxing and a rush went through her entire body as she orgasmed simultaneously with Lester.

Meanwhile Mrs. Traylor had woken up and was looking around the procedure room wondering what was happening. Gabriel was sitting in a chair next to her stretcher, and he had put the railings of the stretcher up to keep her from falling out but left the scope in her mid-transverse colon in case there was a chance of completing the colonoscopy. The television was still on and showed a picture of the colon wall.

"What's going on?" asked Mrs. Traylor, "where did everyone else go? Is my procedure over? Am I still asleep and dreaming?"

"You're now awake and all of our worst nightmares have come true," answered Gabriel. "The world is going to end in the next few hours due to nuclear and biological weapons."

"What?" asked Mrs. Traylor. "How can that be? We're the United States of America. We have the means to halt any terrorist attack."

"All the electricity is gone and all the cities are gone. We have light and a television working in here because our generator is running. The terrorists hacked into the three major nuclear powers' computers and activated their weapons and sent them to their destinations. Somehow, they were also able to detonate chemical weapons throughout the world."

"This is ridiculous! Give me my cell phone!" demanded Mrs. Traylor. "It's underneath the stretcher in my bag."

Gabriel reached down into her Hermes bag and pulled out her phone and gave it to her. She called her husband's number, but there was no response. "Oh God," she whimpered, "the line is dead. If the world is ending, why don't you get this fucking tube out of my butt? Is that my colon up there on TV?"

"I didn't know if you wanted to find out if there was cancer or not," answered Gabriel, "and yes, that is your colon up there on the television screen."

"Why does it matter if we're all going to die?"

Gabriel paused and stood up. "It matters to me and I hoped it would matter to you. It matters to the way I've lived my life. I want to know if I missed anything last year because it has driven me crazy this past week and will probably drive me crazy for eternity."

Mrs. Traylor shook her head. "Just in case there's any chance at all that I live through this, I want to know, too," she said. "Because I never want to go through that mother-fucking—pardon my French—prep again. Where's the rest of your team? The young black man with the muscles, the beautiful red-headed nurse, and the suave anesthesiologist. Where did they go?"

"They've all left to try and contact their loved ones. Bet they'll be back soon, or they're dead."

"No reason for me to leave," said Mrs. Traylor. "Blaze is in Austin campaigning. I'd imagine Austin got hit hard being the state capital. He's probably gone. He was a wonderful man and the best husband. He knew I never quite got over my first love, Tom, but he didn't let that keep him from loving me with his whole being. We were inseparable for over forty years and were not only husband and wife, but best friends."

She paused for a moment. "You know that scope up my ass is kind of uncomfortable," she said.

"I can give you some more Propofol to make you sleep until I decide if we're going to complete the exam," said Gabriel.

"That would be great," she replied, "that way if the world ends today I'll just drift from sleep to death. That might be the easiest way to go."

"I'm not sure how much of this to give," said Gabriel, "since I usually have an anesthesiologist give it."

He took the syringe and gave her fifteen cc of Propofol. Mrs. Traylor talked for another few seconds and then closed her eyes and went to sleep. The steady beeping of her pulse assured him that he hadn't given her too much Propofol.

Meanwhile Adonis had finished crying. There was no hope left. All he had control over was how he'd spend his last few minutes or hours on earth. He thought about how he'd spent his life training to become a physician, and then practicing anesthesiology for over twenty years. The best thing for him to do as he died, he decided, was to work as a doctor. He rushed back into the endoscopy room.

"Hey, I'm back," he announced as he walked through the door. "Do you want to finish the case? I know it means a lot to you, and it's not like I have a lot of other pressing engagements."

"It does mean a lot to me," replied Gabriel. "It's weird; I lost my son a year ago, now I'm losing the rest of my family and the world is coming to an end. But I'm a doctor and I still want to know what's going on with this patient."

"As I was passing by the recovery room I saw our nurse and tech having sex on a stretcher. Do you want me to get them?"

"No, we've got time. Let them enjoy their short time together. When they're ready they'll come back."

Five minutes later the door opened and in walked RC holding Lester's hand. Her hair was a mess and her make-up was gone but, somehow, she looked better than she ever had before. Even though the world was ending, Lester had a big smile on his face. His scrub shirt was inside out but he didn't notice.

"So, what are we going to do?" asked Lester. "Are we going to finish this case or at least die trying?" He laughed.

"Yeah," added RC, "there's really nothing else for us to do. Being a nurse and helping people was the greatest part of my life, along with being a mother. I can't be a mother anymore, but I can certainly work with you to help diagnose this one last person. Hell, we may be the last health care providers working to help a patient on this entire planet. We'll die doing what we loved and doing what gave our lives a kind of meaning that no one outside the health care profession could ever understand."

"If it's my vote," said Gabriel, "I'd really like to know what's going on with this patient. I'd like to push on until we get to the end of her colon and see what's happening."

"We all agree," said Lester, "RC, Doctor Gonzalez, let's get back to work."

CHAPTER FIFTEEN

There were five of them in their usual positions in the endoscopy room. Mrs. Traylor lay on the stretcher in the left lateral decubitus position with her buttocks facing Dr. Gold and her head facing the television screen. Dr. Gonzalez was at the head of the bed, where he could monitor the patient's breathing and degree of anesthesia as well as view the screen constantly displaying Mrs. Traylor's pulse, blood pressure, and oxygen saturation. Mrs. Traylor was sleeping, but he had the syringe in the bottle of Propofol and the cap to the needle between his teeth, drawing up more "milk of amnesia" for when she began to wake up. Dr. Gold was right next to her, holding the scope with his left hand and working the controls to the scope with his right hand. Standing next to him was Lester, who had his hands over Mrs. Traylor's side and was touching her abdomen without any force. Directly opposite Lester on the other side of the stretcher was RC. She was looking at Dr. Gold, awaiting the order to give abdominal pressure when the procedure restarted.

Dr. Gonzalez's face showed evidence of tears, his cheeks were flushed, his eyes swollen and just slits. He broke out laughing, breaking the silence in the room and said, "What in the hell are we all doing here? Isn't the world ending?"

"We're here because this is what we do as health care professionals," answered Dr. Gold. His tone was the tone he used when answering a child's question at the Passover Seder. *Why is this night different from all other nights?* "On what other day do we face oblivion and get to decide how we'll travel there?" He continued, "I don't mean to be preachy, but Hippocrates said, 'Wherever the art of Medicine is loved, there is also a love of Humanity.' In this room we all love the art of medicine, the art of healing sick people. In this small room there still exists a love of humanity. It may not exist anywhere else in the world now."

Dr. Gold looked at RC who seemed to have a glow. Was it from crying? Then he looked at Lester who also had a contented glow. "Okay, go ahead and give me pressure. Let's see if we can get around to her cecum."

They began to give abdominal pressure and because Mrs. Traylor moaned a little bit and then yelled out the name, "Tom," Dr. Gonzalez injected more Propofol into her IV. They advanced the scope a few inches, but then it stopped, and no matter how hard they pushed on the abdomen it would go no further.

"Let's take a quick break and reassess," said Dr. Gold.

Lester looked across the stretcher at RC. "Do you want to switch places, RC, so you can hold her on the stretcher and I'll give the pressure from that side?"

"Sure," answered RC. But before Lester could remove his hands from Mrs. Traylor's abdomen, RC grabbed both hands and squeezed them. "I love you, Lester. I love you and I love the man you are. I'm sorry you won't have the time to make something more of yourself. You were destined for greatness. I can sense that. I'm so sorry for you."

"I am, too," said Lester, "but at least I got to experience what sex was like. Something wonderful, incredible, and indescribable when you have it with the right person."

Lester squeezed RC tightly as they passed each other, changing places around the stretcher. "I always thought that the meaning of life was making something of yourself. I worked so hard, day after day to improve myself. Someone that I would be proud of, someone that others would be proud of. Someone that my mom would be proud of."

"You did make something of yourself," said Dr. Gonzalez. "Look how hard you've worked. You took care of your grandfather for years. You went out and found your mother and took care of her. You've applied to nursing school…"

"But how could making something of yourself be the meaning to life?" challenged Lester. "There I was right at the door about to kick it down and walk in and now my chances for making something of myself have gone up in flames. I was on the verge of starting to fulfill my greatest dreams and it's all been taken away without me even having the chance to fight for it. That can't be the meaning to life. What is the true meaning to life?"

"That's a very good question," answered Dr. Gold. "The meaning of life. The five of us are left to ponder it. Let's see if we can get the scope around. I've got to know whether Mrs. Traylor has colon cancer."

Lester and RC assumed their new positions, and Lester began giving pressure.

"Hold back up here," said Dr. Gold to RC.

"Give me pressure lower on her abdomen, Lester," Dr. Gold instructed.

Lester pressed as hard as he could lower on Mrs. Traylor's abdomen. His arms began to quiver.

Explosions going off around the building sounded like firecrackers exploding in the endoscopy room. The lights and television again flickered on and off, but then stayed on.

"You know Lester," said Dr. Gonzalez, "you've had tremendous adversity to overcome, and you never gave up. Maybe that was the meaning of your life, that you would be faced with one obstacle after another to stop you, to keep you from advancing, and you never let it."

"I've had some hard times," agreed Lester. "It's been tough with no father or mother. But I never ever considered giving up. I'd never give other people the satisfaction of knowing that I gave up. I went to school with boys who are now doctors and lawyers and investment bankers. Well, I guess you could say they *were* until the world came to an end. I never wanted to feel that I was less than them. I competed against them in sports and I excelled. I competed against them in the classroom and excelled. Now here I am on the very last day of the world, still overcoming the adversity, still trying to help people. Boy, this lady has got a tough colon and a large belly to push on."

"I know," answered Dr. Gold, "you guys are a great team. You know, I always thought that the meaning of life was having children. It took us so long to have Ray. We had such problems getting pregnant. Then once we were pregnant, my wife had two miscarriages. Finally, there was Ray. My perfect little boy that I could help nurture and mold into a great man. All life revolved around Ray, all meaning was attached to him. Everything I could do I did for him. He was my reason for waking up in the morning and going to bed at night. He was the reason the sun came up and then, when it sank in the west, the stars came out. For me, he was my entire life. And then, he died. I loved him so much and taught him so much and did so much for him, but how could he have been the meaning of life when he was no longer around? How could I be expected to go on?"

"Maybe experiencing life is the meaning. We all die sometime," said RC. "Look at my son, Joshua. Severe autism. Yet, somehow, he and I communicated. Somehow, his being alive gave meaning to my life. He made me want to go on, made me want to go on for him. I always wanted to have a stable, safe home for him, just like other children get to experience."

"I think we're close to the hepatic flexure of her colon," said Dr. Gold. "Let's stop for a minute."

Mrs. Traylor woke up a little bit and started to mumble. "Should I put her back to sleep now?" asked Dr. Gonzalez.

"No, you can let her stay awake for a minute while everyone rests. I think we're close to the hepatic flexure. Soon we'll be making the turn into the ascending colon and then we'll be able to see her cecum."

Suddenly Mrs. Traylor tried to sit up. Lester was in position to hold her down, to keep her from falling off the stretcher. "You're okay, you're okay!" Lester shouted at her. "Just relax. You're having your colonoscopy. We're just taking a little break."

Mrs. Traylor smiled as she lay back down. "I was just thinking that I heard conversation about the meaning of life. Was that what you were discussing?" she asked.

"Yes, it was," answered Dr. Gold. "The world is ending but we're going to find out what is wrong with you before it does. While we're at it, we started discussing the meaning of life."

"I think the meaning of life is moving from hatred to love," said Mrs. Traylor. "I think that we're all born as a blank slate, but the world is so full of hatred. One group hates another. Whites hate the blacks, blacks hate the whites. Christians hate the Muslims and the Muslims hate the Christians. The Jews hate the Muslims and everyone hates the Jews. We're all born with equal parts hatred and love. We need to nurture and grow the love in each of us and let the hatred wither away so that we can all live proudly and without fear. We can only build a better world together. I think that's been the meaning of life since the world started. It's never been accomplished, but I hope and pray that someday it will be."

"Since the world is ending now, it's not going to happen for us," interjected RC.

Mrs. Traylor started to cry. "I know that someday it will happen," she choked out the words. "Someday, somewhere there will be a world without hate."

"You're so right," said Dr. Gonzalez. "Love brings meaning to life. If you hate and destroy, you take the meaning out of life, just like taking the air out of a balloon and letting it deflate to nothing. Part of the meaning of life," he continued, "is being true to yourself. That's something I just learned today. My life really didn't start until today. I was living a lie. I think that the meaning of life is not only to love, but to always be true to yourself. To love yourself, to love who you are. Only after you love yourself can you truly love another human being."

"In the central Jewish prayer, the Shema, we declare, 'You shall love,'" Gabriel observed.

"Not to love yourself if you're a murderer or a terrorist," said Mrs. Traylor.

"Oh, no, of course not," replied Dr. Gonzalez. "Loving yourself as a good person, a person of substance. Being true to yourself, knowing that you are someone of worth whether you're gay, transsexual, bisexual. Until you're true to yourself and admit who you are you can't truly experience love and have meaning in your life."

"Being able to empathize with your fellow man is also important," said Mrs. Traylor. "Here I am, sixty-one years old. So many people who work for me are poor. But did I really care about them? This may be my anesthesia talking. But I was never able to understand them. I think they all looked at me as though we were back in the Old South and I was the plantation owner's wife. I never tried to put myself in their position and understand their problems. If I had, I think I would have been more generous to them. I think that being able to empathize with your fellow man is part of the meaning to life."

Dr. Gold said, "Okay, try and give me abdominal pressure again. Put Mrs. Traylor back to sleep, Adonis."

"Will do," said Adonis, "but before I put you back to sleep, I'll agree with you. Being able to empathize with your fellow man is essential to leading a meaningful life."

"Yes, it is," said Lester, "I've always felt that whether people were rich or poor, white or black, I could get along with them and understand them. I really thought that ability enriched my life immensely. Going to a private all-boys school that was pretty much all white taught me how to understand others from a completely different background than mine."

"I disagree," said Dr. Gold in an authoritarian voice. "There really is no meaning to life. Life is a series of random events." By now, Mrs. Traylor was back asleep. "Life just occurs arbitrarily," Dr. Gold continued. "There's really no meaning to life. We're all put on this earth and we go through experiences, some similar and some different. We respond to them either by changing the situation or letting the situation change us. It's all so random. If I hadn't gone to one Jewish Singles' Event I never would have met Sarah. I'd never gone to one of their events before and I made the decision to go to that one at the last minute. If I hadn't lost Ray a year ago, I'd be in New York with Sarah and dead now, holding her in my arms, instead of here, holding this colonoscope. It's all chance, all accident. No rhyme or reason."

"I disagree," said RC. "I think there has to be some order to this life. We human beings wouldn't be made in the image of God unless we were meant to do something. There is some randomness—that's where free will comes into play. By making choices, we influence our course in life. But there is meaning to our existence."

"You know, I was brought up in a small town where there weren't a lot of Jewish people," said Dr. Gold. "I used to go to Sabbath services every week with my father and mother. High holiday services, usually just with my father since they ran too long for my mother to sit. I remember the rabbi's sermon would always include something about Tikkun Olam. That's Hebrew for repairing the world or making the world a better place. A way of being God's partners in repairing a broken world. Tikkun Olam. Yes, that's what I thought as a youngster was the meaning of life. Our meaning, the reason we were here, was to bring light into the darkness... to fix the world which is damaged."

"That sounds good," said Dr. Gonzalez. "That sounds like a very personal meaning to life. Tikkun Olam. I even like the way that sounds. I think the world is fractured and broken. Every part of the world is broken and wounded and needs repair and every human being does, also."

Lester nodded his head as he pushed hard on Mrs. Traylor's abdomen. "Tikkun Olam," he repeated, "it sounds like something from *The Lion King* when they hold up Simba and sing about the circle of life."

"No," disagreed RC, "it sounds like Hakuna Matata from *The Lion King* which means no worries for the rest of your days."

"You're right about life being a circle, Lester," said Dr. Gold as he pushed on the scope and maneuvered the controls to try and get it around the corner. "It's common sense to recognize the circle of life. We're born, we age, we have children, we die, and then our children repeat the process and then their children do and on and on. Tikkun Olam means we live in a broken world and the meaning of our lives is to work with God to fix that world. Even if the job is immense, each person should feel the obligation to try. And each person should feel that their single action can alone bring a new reality. A life where our questions have real answers."

RC was writing down Mrs. Traylor's vital signs. She put down her pen and picked up a big black Sharpie that was on the desk. She wrote in large capital letters on the sheet covering the vital signs:

WHAT IS THE MEANING OF LIFE?

She nodded and tucked the sheet back into the folder.

"I like the idea of Tikkun Olam," RC said. "I like the idea of fixing the broken world I live in. My world has been broken from the time I was a child. A drunk abusive father who beat my mother nightly, and a mother who ran off and never came back or tried to get in touch with me. Maybe I was trying to fix the world by having a relationship with my son who was so damaged."

"Yet how could that be the meaning to life?" asked Dr. Gold. "Because now there's no world left for us to fix. Or maybe I should say there's not going to be any of us left to fix the world. Even for those of us who believed it, who thought that we were contributing something positive, something of value? Now there's no way to say that Tikkun Olam was the meaning because there is nothing to fix. All the work we did was for naught."

"It wasn't for naught," said Lester, "it meant something. Helping others, empathizing with those less fortunate, loving your neighbor as yourself, those are all Judeo-Christian-Muslim beliefs and values. They all helped to change the world into a better place. The world ending doesn't mean that fixing or improving it was not meaningful. It just means that life as we know it's going to be gone. Maybe someday there will be people inhabiting this world who will recognize that the meaning of their lives was to fix our mistakes and never let the world be destroyed again. Kind of like Noah and the flood. After the flood, God made a rainbow as a symbol that the world would never again be destroyed by his hand. Unfortunately, now man has taken the destruction into his own hands. What kind of person steals our meaning? What twisted belief gets meaning from destroying ours?"

"You know what Oscar Wilde said?" asked Adonis.

"Hold that thought," interrupted Gabriel, "let's turn her back onto her back and see if we can get the scope to go around."

The three of them maneuvered Mrs. Traylor onto her back as Gabriel held the scope in place.

"Not to sound stupid, but who was Oscar Wilde and what did he say?" RC asked Adonis.

"Oscar Wilde was a famous English writer and a flamboyant character who actually was imprisoned for being gay. He said that the meaning of life was to create something that outlives your life. Whether it's a book, a painting, a political movement, something that lives on beyond your time on earth. That's what Oscar Wilde said is the meaning of life. He was a homosexual like me, and he wrote books like *The Picture of Dorian Gray*, one of my favorite books in college. His books and stories and witticisms outlived him."

"I wish I could say that I did something to outlive this life," said Gabriel. "I thought it was to have a child and properly raise that child."

"You did a great job," said Adonis. "Don't go back and torture yourself over Ray's death. No one would imagine someone dying of colon cancer at the age of twenty-four."

"Ray was a good man," said RC. "Did you know that he and I once had an affair?"

Gabriel looked away from the television screen at RC with a startled expression on his face. "I never even knew that Ray knew you," Gabriel said.

"Oh, yes," RC replied. "Once he came around here looking for you and we started talking. He was cooler and more self-assured than any man I'd ever met. For a while after I got off work, he and I would meet at a grungy old Motel Six down the street. We'd have sex, sometimes more than once, and then go our separate ways. He was quite a lover. Pardon me, Lester, but I've never been with a man endowed like Ray."

"I'm glad he made you happy," said Gabriel to RC, "but I'm sorry if you feel like Ray used you in any way."

"I don't feel he used me. I feel like we had a sexual relationship between two consenting adults. I could tell he never loved me. I could tell he was in it just for the sex. But he never promised more. He never even brought me flowers or a piece of jewelry. He never took me out to dinner. He told me he had a girlfriend in New York but they had an open relationship. The day I came to his funeral was the first time I really regretted not having had a fuller relationship with him. I listened to all the eulogies and learned more about him than I had in our time together. I watched them lower his casket into the ground and I watched as you first took the shovel and shoveled dirt onto his casket with the shovel upside down. I sat and cried and for some reason I said out loud, 'I forgive you, Ray.'

"Forgive me," interrupted Adonis, "do you think that might be the meaning to life? We're all so beaten up and bruised daily by the outside world. But even more painfully, the ones we love, our spouses, siblings, parents, friends do terrible things to us. Maybe the meaning to life is to be able to find forgiveness, to move beyond the point where we have hatred or dislike or distrust for someone because of what they've done to us."

"I think in a lot of ways forgiveness *is* the meaning to life," said Gabriel. "Forgiving one's family and friends and enemies, but most importantly, being able to forgive one's self." He thought for a moment and then said, "And of course, being able to forgive God who has done so much for us all. Not everything turns out the way we want, but we need to try to keep our relationship with God strong, and not let our anger at life's circumstances ruin that relationship. I regret that so deeply. I've been calling on God for help since we started this case, after saying that I was going to completely ignore him on this holy day celebrating the birthday of our world."

The scope pushed a little further around the colon, then stopped at the area of the liver, the hepatic flexure. They were within an inch of being able to see the right colon, the ascending colon, the Promised Land. Just then the power from the generator went out for a second and the screen blinked off, but then came back on. For some reason, RC made the sign of the cross on her chest.

Dr. Gold said, "For a moment there I thought it was all over. I thought I'd be like Moses and be able to glimpse the Promised Land of Israel, but never set foot in it."

"I have to think that having Jesus Christ as your savior and being saved is the meaning to life," said RC, staring blindly straight ahead. "But I have to admit, in my whole life I've been to church less than five times. I always heard and always thought that if you had Jesus Christ in your life and trusted him to be your savior, then that belief gave meaning to this life. After this life you would move on to Heaven and be with Him forever. I accepted Jesus Christ as my savior at a very young age when I was baptized, so I have hope for myself when the world ends. When Joshua was a baby I had him baptized also, so he'd go to Heaven when he died."

"How are you so sure of Jesus?' asked Dr. Gold. "We know science. Death means decay. We live and then die. That's it!"

"I'm sure of Jesus and Heaven," responded RC, "but that life never interested me. Sitting around thinking sweet thoughts isn't my idea of having fun. I'd much rather be smoking a cigarette or a joint, getting drunk, having sex or doing something wild. But I think if I had this life to do over again I would have at least tried to have a personal relationship with Jesus Christ. Like that Depeche Mode song, *Your Own Personal Jesus*. I would have tried to understand what his words meant and what he taught. I would have tried to understand more about why he died for me on the cross. I would have tried to be more like Lester. Lester, you always seemed to have a relationship with Jesus. It affected the way you acted and treated people."

Lester stood up straight and took his hands of Mrs. Traylor's abdomen. He laughed heartily. "Yes," he said, "for years of my life I did have a relationship with Jesus. Mainly when I was growing up, living with uncles and aunts, grandparents... All of them believed in Jesus and all of them thought that the church was the center of our world. Sundays all day and Wednesday nights were times we always spent at the church. We would sing about Jesus, talk about Jesus. It seemed that no matter how bad things got, we still had Jesus Christ as our savior. But, you all are going to be the first to hear this, and probably the only ones who will ever know this. I converted and became a Muslim in the last few hours."

"You've got to be joking!" snapped RC. "You had such a strong relationship with Jesus. Now you're joining them?"

"I know," replied Lester. "Maybe it's all just a matter of names. And maybe I never had the time to sit down and read about and sort it all out. Now I feel that the meaning of life is trusting Allah to take care of you. To trust in one God, whose name is Allah. I've talked to someone whose belief in Allah is so strong that he convinced me of this. This man, Abraham, has talked to me about his religion daily for four years. I believe him and his convictions and his way of living. He served the same purpose for me that Saint Paul did for the Romans in converting them to Christianity. He constantly preached the Muslim faith and its virtues and rewards. I have done a little reading on my own about Islam, certainly not enough, but enough that I look at death without fear or trepidation, but with hope of being united with my Muslim brethren."

"You realize, of course," interrupted Gabriel, "the world is ending now because of people who think they are serving Allah. They justify this horrible attack by saying it is the word of Allah."

"They're not serving Allah," answered Lester. "They're serving hatred. They never were able to get beyond that hatred to see the love that there is in Allah. I truly believe if I'd had more time to learn that I would have wrapped up my faith in Allah and lived my life praying five times a day, making the pilgrimage to Mecca, and doing all the things that a true believer does. That would have been the meaning of life for me."

"I think that you can live a just life no matter what religion you are," said Gabriel. "I personally think that the meaning of life is living a good, just life and following the Ten Commandments. The Ten Commandments serve as a foundation for life. They provide a system of justice and separate right from wrong." He began to recite the Ten Commandments: "You shall have no other gods before Me. You shall not make idols. Remember the Sabbath day, to keep it holy. Honor your father and your mother. Don't murder, don't steal, don't covet."

"I think more importantly," interrupted Adonis, "is what Lester said. You need to have a daily relationship with God. Every single day you wake up and thank God for this wonderful world that we live in. Jew, Christian, Muslim; again, it doesn't matter. I don't know how atheists can survive without a belief In God. But I think that when you have a relationship with something greater than yourself you feel blessed to be in this world. To know there's something else here, something else to work for, to achieve, to try and rise to a higher level of existence."

"You can only do that," said RC, "by working to conquer evil. There's so much evil in the world. So much hatred. Working to conquer that has got to be part of the meaning to life."

"Maybe we've been asking the wrong question," said Gabriel. "Maybe there really was no meaning to life. Maybe all this talk about the meaning to life should be replaced by the question, what gives meaning to *your* life? For me and RC that was our connection to our sons. For Lester it's making something of himself and trusting Allah. For Adonis, it's being true to yourself and not living a lie. For Mrs. Traynor it's feeling empathy for others. It makes no sense to ask what life's single meaning is. There are many answers to the question. It seems to me that for each of us, our answer is right. If it gives us meaning it must be right. There must be multiple questions and multiple answers that lead to you finding meaning in your life."

"You're right," said Adonis, "each of us has a different answer to the question and nobody can be wrong. Especially now, with the world ending. So much of the meaning to my life right now came from being true to myself. I never felt comfortable living but now I feel comfortable dying."

"RC, would you mind pushing on her abdomen a little lower," Gabriel continued, completely changing his focus.

RC adjusted her hands.

"Something that was said before reminded me of the reason that I used to love to be with my father alone at Rosh Hashanah and Yom Kippur, at our synagogue in a small town in Kansas," said Gabriel. " During the break in the services we'd walk around the block and my father would be silent, deep in thought. Then he'd say something to me. It was something that always made me want to be with him. This is going to sound corny because I know you've heard it before, but he said that every day is a gift from God. Just being alive for a day is a tremendous gift that God has given you. Then he'd smile and say that's why they call it the present. It's a present to you. You know something, he was right.

"When I was young I tried to approach life like that. I would wake up in the morning, open my eyes and be happy. But as my life progressed, I forgot about what my father said. Some days were such drudgery, some days were so anxiety-provoking, some days were full of anguish, and some days almost seemed like torture. I think that the meaning to life is to see every day that we are here on earth as a gift. Now that the world is ending and none of us will exist anymore, I mourn this terrible loss. I wish that I had taken my dad's advice and treated each day as a gift from God."

Just then, miraculously, the scope advanced another half-inch around the corner and suddenly they were in Mrs. Traylor's ascending colon and could see down to the end of her colon.

"Oh my God," gasped Gabriel.

"Jesus, sweet Jesus," shouted RC.

"Allah be praised," said Lester looking at the ceiling as it began to shake.

Amidst the shadows on the television screen there emerged an enormous, ulcerated, bleeding cancer that started at the level of the colonoscope and went down to the end of the colon.

"She would have died within a month or two with her metastases," Gabriel said sadly. Something that was obscured from his vision a year before was now vivid and real and enormous.

Suddenly, there was a huge explosion in the room. As if by instinct, the four of them gathered closely around the stretcher and put their bodies over the patient to protect Mrs. Traylor from harm. Each grabbed a different part of her body to steady themselves. Instinctively, RC grabbed her nursing folder containing her notes off the table and took her place protecting Mrs. Traylor. Being the smallest, RC was underneath the three men as she grasped Mrs. Traylor's right arm. She felt the floor weaken and then heard a roar as the floor disintegrated under her feet. She lost her grip on Mrs. Traylor's arm but held firmly to her red folder. Darkness engulfed her as she fell backward on top of Adonis who was struggling to maintain his grip as he fell backwards. She heard the others crying out, but she couldn't manage a scream. She was falling backwards and unseen rocklike objects hit her face and body as she fell. An image of Joshua appeared in her mind, and she clung to it until everything was gone.

BOOK FOUR

IN THE END

SHADOWS
There is no darkness,
There is no light.
Truth behind lies does hide.

There is no good,
There is no bad.
Life remains a perilous ride.

Look for the answer in the shadows,
Everything else will lead you astray.

Look for the answer in the shadows, but don't
be surprised if there is no right way.

CHAPTER SIXTEEN

Barry Grant hurried through the streets to get to NASA headquarters in Houston, Texas on the planet Htrae. He was covering the big press conference on the Htrae Space Trek for his newspaper, the *Dallas Morning News*. He was so excited that he crossed the street with the teslalight red and had to quickly step back to keep from getting hit by the low flying autoplane. As he retreated to the curb, he saw his roommate from college and now reporter for the *Huntington Herald Dispatch*, Doug Foss.

"Doug, great to see you! It's been quite a few years. You haven't changed much, just a little gray hair. You cover the science and technology beat, too?"

Doug shook Barry's hand enthusiastically and then hugged him. "It's been too long! I still remember our days at the University of Missouri writing for the school paper. What a rag! They'd let us write whatever we wanted, especially after you became editor. We crushed it! I'm not the science and technology writer. We don't have one. We're a staff of ten humans and 20 recording robots. They were going to send one of the robots and at the last minute they told me to pack and teleport to Houston. They wanted someone live to cover the news conference and the biggest story of our lifetimes."

Barry and Doug crossed the street together as the light turned green and the auto-planes stopped on either side of them.

"I still find the concept of parallel universes amazing," said Barry. "That alone blows me away and I've written stories on it for the last fifteen years. But now, to think that after a two thousand-year journey, a rocket ship with our best and brightest has reached the planet Earth is incomprehensible. Earth, a planet exactly like ours with identical land masses and water, identical countries and people speaking our languages. My kids think I'm old fashioned. They act like parallel universes are an ordinary occurrence."

"I just hope that all the planning and expense was worth it," said Doug. "They had that nuclear explosion on Earth two thousand-years ago, and we haven't received a transmission since then. I hope there are still people to talk to. All of the cooperation with all of the other countries here on Htrae will have been for nothing if there's no life on Earth."

Barry held the door and the two of them walked in. It was Doug's first-time inside NASA headquarters, and he was overwhelmed by the sheer enormity of the building. He took his pencil-camera out of his pocket and took some photographs of the long entrance hallway they walked through. The ceiling was thirty feet high, and the entrance hallway extended a mile in both directions. Thousands of people and robots were scurrying around, most headed to the auditorium where the news conference would take place.

"Pretty amazing even by our standards," said Barry. "You know the whole building is made of an alloy material that absorbs sunlight and uses that to power everything. That alloy, named FreJo, is unbreakable and not subject to the forces of nature, so most of this building has been here for over two thousand-years. Frejo stores enough energy to power this place for one hundred years even if there is no sunlight. And it's equally amazing that Frejo is noncombustible. Of course, they're always adding on to the building when they need more room for new projects. I have a source who told me that after our successful exploration of Earth, another mission to the other planets in earth's galaxy will be undertaken to see if life may have existed on those planets millions of years ago."

The two men walked into NASA's main auditorium which seated thirty thousand people and had a large platform in front for the recording robots to stand. The auditorium was already almost full. They heard Russian and Chinese being spoken as they looked for seats close to the stage. There were television cameras the size of wallets mounted on thin tripods throughout the room. The cameras were controlled by a man or woman who stood behind the camera with a joystick in their hands and thick goggles on their eyes. These goggles not only showed them the picture their camera was taking, but also allowed them to see whatever was going on in a radius of 20 feet outside of their current picture.

"There are reporters here from all over the world," said Barry. "So many different countries worked together, sharing technologies, to complete this project. Let's sit here." At every seat there were headphones listing two hundred languages, and both men dialed in English as they put the headphones on. On the other side of Doug sat a reporter whose press credentials hanging around his neck said that he was from Mexico. He shook Doug's hand as Doug sat down and enthusiastically greeted him with, "Hola, amigo."

Before Doug could reply, the lights in the auditorium blinked twice, the universal sign on the planet for silence. The auditorium went from roaring loud to complete silence in a second. A man walked up the stairs to the podium on stage. Barry immediately recognized him as Malcolm Meyer, the chief of NASA.

"Ladies and gentlemen of the press," he began, "welcome to Houston, Texas and to NASA headquarters. You're here for a monumental occasion. What we are going to witness in the next few days on this screen was a long time in the making. It came about in large part due to the intelligence of the president of the United States of America over two thousand years ago, Blaze Traylor, and his brilliant wife, Charlotte. Blaze died at age one hundred and twenty-six, one-thousand nine hundred and fifty years ago, but while he was president he recorded the following speech to be broadcast today to the entire world. It is with great honor and extreme privilege that I give you President Blaze Traylor."

Malcolm Meyer walked off the stage and then the entire auditorium went dark. Suddenly, right behind the podium a three-dimensional hologram of Blaze Traylor appeared and began speaking. His essence was the only light in the vast room.

"Welcome to America, foreign visitors and media members, and welcome to my fellow Americans. If you are hearing me now, it means that our two-thousand-year mission has come to fruition and we are about to land on the planet Earth which is two hundred million light-years away from us."

He paused and then started speaking again. "Once we found out that the cosmos was comprised of parallel universes, we began to explore the closest planets and tried to establish contact. We had been receiving transmitter frequencies from Earth in a variety of languages, and my wife, Charlotte, was able to decode them by using equipment that she invented and perfected. She was helped in her quest to build and maintain the equipment mainly by the countries of Russia and China here on Htrae, and their interpreters helped her understand much of what was said. Of course, a lot of the transmissions were useless and devoid of meaning, and Charlotte figured out that these transmissions came from television shows on Earth."

The auditorium erupted in laughter. It was well-known on Htrae that most of the television shows on Earth were mindless drivel, and they all wondered what had attracted their species on an identical planet to waste their time watching such nonsense.

Using Artificial Intelligence, Blaze's hologram paused until the laughter died down.

"Two thousand years ago an epic event took place on Earth, just as we were getting ready to cryo-freeze our brave explorers for their two thousand-year trip to Earth. We think there was a nuclear holocaust. All transmissions from Earth ceased and the images of Earth we received from our satellites showed huge explosions and then a massive change in the pattern of gases, chemicals, and elements emitted from the planet. What happened, my wife Charlotte believed, was a series of nuclear explosions perpetrated by a group that spoke Arabic and had seized control of the entire arsenal of nuclear and chemical weapons on Earth."

There were press representatives and dignitaries from Arab nations in the auditorium, and many of them gasped when they heard this news. Saudi Arabia had been one of the biggest financial backers of NASA in all its missions, and astronauts from Saudi Arabia and Egypt had manned some of the space missions to explore the other seven planets in their galaxy as well as the planetoid, Pluto. Several Iranian scientists occupied high-level positions in NASA and helped with the details of the current mission.

Blaze continued. "The five astronauts you will see and hear were frozen by a complex cryo-therapy process which we devised in conjunction with Israel, Egypt, Japan, and Mexico. My wife, Charlotte, is one of our astronauts, and she and I agreed to let her go on this historic voyage while I lived out my life on Htrae. I am now long gone, but my legacy lives on in the Htrae Space Trek. Charlotte is the originator and lead scientist of the mission, and she is accompanied by Lester Jones, the leader of the mission as well as the head pilot. Also on the mission are R.C. Jones, Lester's wife and an expert pilot and nurse, Doctor Gabriel Gold, our medical expert, and Doctor Adonis Gonzalez, our backup medical expert, bodyguard, and assistant to my wife. I hope that their journey is safe and successful, and I congratulate all of you for sharing in this historic event.

"Before I finish, if this message is replayed for Charlotte, I want you to know, my love, that I never stopped loving you or thinking about you until the day I died. I missed you terribly, but I knew that our separation was for the good of humankind. I now leave you as our cameras take you into the spaceship as it approaches Earth. Peace, love, and happiness to every universe everywhere."

The hologram of Blaze Traylor slowly faded away and the audience erupted in applause. They all stood, giving the hologram of Blaze Traylor a tremendous ovation. As they were cheering, an enormous screen one hundred yards wide came down from the ceiling and reached the floor. On the screen images from inside the space ship appeared. No human movement was seen.

"I think we're in for the ride of a lifetime," said Barry, and Doug nodded in agreement.

CHAPTER SEVENTEEN

Alarms went off inside the spaceship. Slowly each of the lids of the five cryo-unit opened. Within the last three weeks each of these units had gone from the process of maintaining the bodies in a frozen state to slowly warming them to normal temperature. The spaceship was one hundred thousand miles from reaching the earth's atmosphere. Each of the occupants of the five cryo-chambers slowly woke up and began moving around. The occupants were fully dressed, and the cryo-chambers were positioned in a line, one behind the next. In the front cryo-chamber was the captain and leader of the mission, Lester Jones. Due to the freezing, the aging process had been halted and they remained the same age as when they began the journey.

Lester was not tall, but he was a very muscular young black man. He was the ship's commander as well as the leader of the mission. It was his job to fly the spaceship to its designated landing site on Earth and then lead the mission exploring Earth. Of course, he was also responsible for piloting the spaceship safely back to their planet, Htrae. Lester had been a brilliant student on the planet Htrae (H is silent). He was chosen to establish contact with Earth because he had the highest rank of any rocket pilot on the planet and because of his leadership abilities. He'd already led missions to other planets in their own solar system. He had graduated first in his class from Harvard University, the most prestigious university on Htrae, with a degree in Universal Studies. After graduating from Harvard, he completed a two-year training course at the Space Force Academy which taught him how to pilot the most sophisticated rocket ship of all, the one now barreling towards Earth.

Lester crawled out of his cryochamber and walked to the pilot's chair and sat down. Lester was a legend on the planet Htrae. He'd grown up in the care of relatives. No one ever knew who his father was, and his mother had died of a medical accident when he was only four years old. Lester was a one-in-a-generation dynamo. He'd gotten himself through college on a football scholarship and then the government had recognized his talent and paid for him to go to space exploration school.

Lester turned on the radio that transmitted over two hundred million light years to Mission Control on Htrae. He saw the red light and heard a buzzer signaling that he had established contact with Mission Control. Years of research done by the Japanese on Htrae had developed technology that enabled the rocket ship to speak with NASA in real time.

"Good morning, Lester," came a booming male voice from the speaker that Lester recognized as Malcolm Meyer. "Did you have a good sleep? Was two thousand years of cryo enough rest for you? Hope you had good dreams. Two thousand years of nightmares would be difficult to take. The coffee brewing on the console to your left should be ready shortly. We turned it on for you ten minutes ago by remote activation. Get yourself a cup. We know how much you loved your morning coffee when you were here with us. Over the two thousand years that you've been frozen coffee has been replaced here on Htrae by a wafer known as Constant Energy. The wafer contains Rebrecar, a stimulant twice as strong as caffeine and much better tasting. It also has rejuvenating chemicals. One places the wafer under the tongue and within seconds you feel like you've drunk two cups of coffee and are five to ten years younger. The only coffee that exists on our planet now can be found in our natural history museums. Enough idle talk about how things have changed here in two thousand years. Are you ready to direct the ship to its designated landing point on Earth?"

"Sure," replied Lester, as a map of Earth popped up on the console in front of him. The glowing red dot showed where the spaceship was located. "I think I'll help myself to a cup of joe. Old habits are hard to break, even two thousand years later and two hundred million light years from Htrae. Can't wait to get back to Htrae and try that wafer, though. Are these donuts edible?"

"They've undergone a freezing process that we designed for food. Like you, it's been thawing out for the past three weeks. Not only are they edible, but they should be delicious. The chocolate cream with coconut sprinkles is my personal favorite. Yes, that's right, we haven't replaced donuts here yet, although there are some very tasty low-calorie donuts that most of us over the age of ninety prefer."

Lester poured himself a cup of coffee, took a giant gulp, and then grabbed a donut. He walked back to his command post carrying his coffee and donut and set them down on the console in front of him. There was a special hole designed to put the coffee cup in to stabilize it when they hit the Earth's atmosphere.

A beautiful red-headed white woman with gorgeous green eyes dressed in a single-piece tight white jumpsuit brushed against Lester's arm and then leaned over and gave him a deep kiss.

"Two thousand years is a long time to go without one of your kisses," said Lester to his wife, Rachel Carly or RC as she was known to all. RC sat down in the co-pilot's chair after giving Lester a hug and then kissing the back of his neck.

RC was a few years older than Lester and the two of them had met when she was in nursing training at a humble community college. They'd fallen in love immediately and had been married within a year. RC had also come from a home with essentially no parenting; her mother had left when she was eleven due to her abusive, alcoholic father. Neither had paid attention to RC as she grew up. She'd had some bumps along the way; an unexpected pregnancy which led to an autistic child who was institutionalized in a sanitarium on Htrae where the latest technologies were available to help him progress to his fullest capacity. Like Lester, RC had overcome tremendous odds to get her nursing degree and then her space pilot certification. She was the same height as Lester and both were in perfect physical condition. They had enjoyed their years together, and both agreed that their marriage had enabled them to withstand the most strenuous pilot training program ever executed on their planet. The goal of the training program: a two hundred million light-year trek to the planet Earth that would take two thousand years and require freezing their bodies and then thawing them when the time was right. They knew it would mean never seeing their contemporaries again, including RC's autistic son, Joshua. But to both the experience of seeing the planet Earth, and securing information that could help their own planet, was too great to turn down. Scientists from Htrae had been receiving and interpreting all types of communications from Earth for years. So much was known but so many questions remained. This made the opportunity irresistible for both Lester and RC. Both were tough and determined throughout their training. They had become expert pilots able to foresee and deal with any danger. They'd also taken courses on what had been learned about the history of earth, and courses on archeology.

Lester turned away from the screens which detailed everything about their location, velocity, fuel availability, and exact landing spot on Earth. "Morning, hon," he said to RC, "feeling okay? Any problem with that gorgeous body after two thousand years of chilling?"

"The neighbor's rock and roll music was a little loud... just kidding. I'm well-rested and ready to go. That coffee sure smells good. I'm going to get a cup."

"Are the others up yet?" asked Lester.

"I'll go back and check on them, Captain," replied RC as she unbuckled her seat belt and got out of the co-pilot's seat. She poured herself a cup of coffee, took a bite out of a donut, and walked back to the sleeping part of the rocket ship.

A green light flashed across Lester's screen telling him that it was time to deploy the heat shields.

"Mission Control, we should be at our touchdown location in fifteen minutes and twenty-three, twenty-two, twenty-one, twenty seconds—marked at fifteen minutes and twenty seconds. At this marking we have the touchdown location on our map right on target. Not seeing as much resistance and heat in my databank from the Earth's atmosphere as we had anticipated. Those terrorists really blew a hole in the atmosphere when they detonated their nuclear weapons."

RC was back in the cabins of the spaceship and saw that all three of the other cryochambers were open and their occupants were moving around. The first cryochamber was occupied by Mrs. Charlotte Traylor.

Mrs. Traylor was a sixty-one-year old white woman who was the mission specialist. She was widely regarded as having one of the most brilliant and analytical minds on the planet. She had a background in linguistics, language, and the study of Earth. Her forty years of research had enabled Htrae to understand the signals it was getting from Earth. These signals were picked up by satellites deployed by Htrae in Earth's solar system, and then relayed by thousands of satellites arrayed at various distances from Htrae. Finally, there was a bank of satellites in Washington, D.C. that received the transmission. She'd tried for twenty years to send signals back to Earth telling them they were not alone in the universe. But this was in vain since Earth did not have the advancements necessary to receive her signals. She picked up a signal from a short-wave radio from the terrorists detailing their plans a few hours before the bombs exploded, and she felt helpless as the number of trans-missions from Earth quickly diminished and then ended completely. She'd sent transmission after transmission to Washington, D.C. in the United States of America, warning them of their imminent demise, but to no avail.

Charlotte was also known by another title. Her husband, Blaze, was the President of the United States of America on Htrae, making her the First Mate. Both had come from extremely wealthy families so they never had to work for living credits (the currency on Htrae). While Blaze had devoted his life to politics and had reached the pinnacle of his field, Charlotte's incredibly detail-oriented mind allowed her to be fluent in eight languages and to lead the Department of Communications with Earth. They'd never had children due to a miscarriage leading to a hysterectomy when Charlotte was in her twenties. This led her to develop her career and to pursue as much education as possible.

Htrae had been receiving random signals from Earth for hundreds of years, but no one could organize them and understand their significance until Charlotte took over and revolutionized the Department of Communications with Earth. Charlotte's ambition, genius, and ability to work non-stop were a marvel to the people throughout her planet. They expected rich women like her, with successful husbands, to lead lives of luxury and pleasure. But, this wasn't the life Charlotte wanted and she had dedicated her life to her achievements. The only decision she still debated in her heart was leaving Blaze to go on this mission. Many a sleepless night had plagued them both before they decided it would be for the best for the human species for her to go.

Just before the mission was about to take off, Charlotte had received and decoded the signal that Arab terrorists were at work to destroy Earth. She'd tried to send signals back in eight different languages including Arabic, begging the jihadists not to destroy their planet. She included information about their far-away neighbor, two hundred million light years away, who would be coming to help them resolve any issues they couldn't settle. She tried to tell them that there was nothing important enough to end even a single life.

Unfortunately, Earth did not have the satellites in place nor the technology to receive these messages, so it was like screaming in a deserted forest. Just before the spaceship was about to take off, their synchronized satellites detected levels of radiation coming from Earth that were incompatible with life. Charlotte continued to receive broken transmissions from Earth for approximately two hours after the intense radiation was detected. The last transmission came from a television screen in Plano, Texas and contained images of a cavernous tunnel thought to be the inside of the human colon.

Because this was the location of the last transmission, it was decided that Plano, Texas was to be their landing site and first stop on their exploration of earth.

"Good morning," said Charlotte. "You look well-rested. I bet every woman wishes she could sleep for two thousand years and wake up looking like you."

"Good morning, First Mate," replied RC. "Thanks for the compliment. Feeling okay?"

"I feel great for a two thousand and sixty-one-year old woman," laughed Charlotte. "And cut out the first mate shit. I told you to call me Charlotte and I meant it, RC. I'll be up in my station in a minute. Just dictating my first entry into my log about what it feels like to sleep for two millennia."

RC laughed. Directly behind Charlotte the next cryochamber was opening and out popped the mission's doctor, Doctor Gabriel Gold. Doctor Gold was both an internist and a gastroenterologist. He'd devoted much of his life to learning more about the primitive medicine being practiced on Earth and how to teach the doctors on Earth the advanced technology present on Htrae. He never thought that he, himself, would join the journey, but had trained with several other doctors for this amazing experience. However, a year before the mission was to take place his only child, Ray, had tragically died. Then, it appeared that Earth had been destroyed, and the last transmission received had been from inside a human colon. This made Gabriel the most logical doctor who had completed training to go to Earth.

After Gabriel decided to join the mission he tried to talk his wife, Sarah, into going, too, since there could be an extra cryochamber loaded onto the space ship. Sarah was known as one of the premier artists on Htrae, and the government was willing to let her go to capture in paintings and sculpture what Earth was like. In the end, Sarah decided not to go, but to live the remaining years of her life on Htrae as the planet's most accomplished artist. She and Gabriel had spent their last few weeks on Htrae on a second honeymoon to Bali, where all they wore were bathing suits and all they did was make love, swim in the sparkling waters of the Pacific Ocean, and eat and drink the finest cuisine. Their love was true and honest and deep, and they celebrated the life they had lived together. Each was uncertain if it was the right decision for Gabriel, but when the First Mate and President had personally visited them and pleaded their cases, Gabriel and Sarah agreed that Gabriel must go.

Doctor Gold knew how to take care of any medical problem that could arise, whether it was related to radiation, infection, or injury. He'd taken courses over the last two years before leaving Htrae on treating these conditions and many others and was ready to assist in any way needed.

"Good morning," he said to RC as he stepped out of his cryochamber. "It's time to get going, huh? Feel pretty-rested after two thousand years of sleep. I think I dreamed about my son, Ray, as I was thawing out. Felt like I was with him again. It seemed so real. I wish he could have come, although if he were alive, I never would have gone on this mission. Maybe when we leave Earth and head back to Htrae, I'll see him again when I'm re-frozen."

Charlotte joined them.

"Let's get to our stations and get ready for the landing," said RC. "There will be some amazing views. I'll go to the back cabin and make sure Adonis is up."

"No need to do that," said Adonis as he walked into the hallway. "Looks like they did a great job programming all of our cryo-chambers to defrost us and then open at the same time. I had a great dream about being in Paris with my lover and sitting in the Jules Verne restaurant overlooking the city just before I woke up."

Adonis was the chief of security for the mission and back-up for both Gabriel as a doctor and to Charlotte for information gathering. He'd gone to West Point after graduating from high school and then had gone on to medical school and served several years as an army anesthesiologist. Then he was accepted into the space program and had specialized in utilizing weapons of all kinds and in hand-to-hand combat. He was chosen by the space program for this mission not only for his combat capabilities but also because of his medical expertise. Plus, in the two years before the rocket was launched, he spent a considerable amount of time with Charlotte learning much of what she knew about the planet Earth.

Adonis was six feet tall and two hundred pounds of solid muscle. He was gay, which wasn't thought of negatively on Htrae. No one cared if an individual was straight, gay or transgender; all that mattered was whether you could perform your job and live in harmony with your community. Adonis also was leaving a partner on Htrae, and the two of them had had a tearful good-bye. Both decided, though, that this mission to discover what had happened to the only other known planet with humans occupying it was so important that Adonis had to go.

Of the three astronauts without accompanying spouses, Charlotte Traylor had the hardest time leaving her husband. They had known each other since college and had married shortly after her first boyfriend, Tom, was killed in an airplane crash. Blaze had worked his way up from mayor to governor to president and Charlotte had campaigned for him each step of the way, while excelling in her own work. They loved each other dearly and had been best friends for over forty years. Again, though, the enormity of their mission outweighed all other considerations, and Charlotte agreed to be frozen for two thousand years while Blaze lived out his normal life expectancy of one hundred and forty years on Htrae.

All five of them climbed into their chairs located in the main cabin and buckled themselves in. There were separate straps that went across their legs, abdomen, and torso, and then one enormous sheath that covered the entire body after being buckled. Their heads were held in place by a separate series of self-activating straps which held them firmly against the cushioned headrest. Within five minutes of getting settled, they hit the Earth's atmosphere and there was a constant rocking, jolting, and an up and down side to side motion not unlike a roller coaster. Still, it was less than they had planned for as the atmosphere had been destroyed to an alarming degree. No life could survive this environment, Lester thought as he maneuvered the controls to keep the space ship on target.

Lester was extremely confident at the controls. He used the speed adjusters and directional controls expertly to slow the speed of the ship and to start it flying in a horizontal direction when they got twenty miles over the North Pole. He and RC constantly spoke with Mission Control as they passed along the Earth's surface. They tracked their trajectory on the screen in front of each of them, and were perfectly on course. Lester had been amazed when he found out that Earth was an identical replica of Htrae, with the land masses and water in the same locations. Not only were the planets identical in topography, they were also identical in size and shape. It had been easy to train for navigating around the Earth to their landing site, and Lester and RC had done it multiple times on Htrae.

They descended over the North Pole until they were five miles above it. Everything below was black, no white ice or blue water to break the monotony. Black and scorched and still. It reminded Lester of the topography of the country Iceland on Htrae where they had done some of their training and which was covered by black volcanic rock. Due to its desolate and otherworldly appearance and natural wonders, Iceland had become a popular vacation spot on Htrae. However, with its rough terrain and unmatched volcanoes, mountains, and glaciers it was also the perfect spot for them to train before heading to Earth.

They passed across Greenland which was also black with nothing resembling life. No trees or grass or houses or cars could be seen from their space ship. Over Canada, they were low enough to see barren and dry landscape, with vestiges of the dried-out rivers and lakes. They passed over what had been Niagara Falls and Lester pointed it out to the rest of the crew members. There was no water flowing and the rocks that formed the falls were black. Many had crumbled, leaving wide gaps in the formation. Lester had vacationed with RC at Niagara Falls on their planet, and he could sharply contrast the power of the water and crushing sound it made with the collection of rock piles he was seeing now. There was absolutely no vegetation and again, no signs of life. The Earth had been burned and then scorched and then burned again by waves of nuclear weapons and then by the penetrating rays of the sun which poured in through gaps in the atmosphere.

They were over the United States, their home country on their planet of Htrae, and the leading country on their planet in space exploration. The five sat in front of a wall of unbreakable windows. Each of them gasped but remained silent as they looked out, unable to comprehend the desolation that lay before them. They knew that it was all an act of human destruction, but what could have led humanity down such a pathway? New York City had no skyline. All the buildings were rubble. The Statue of Liberty lay on her side, her right arm and torch broken off, lying next to her decapitated body.

RC had tears in her eyes as the spaceship turned south and sped over the United States. They passed over West Virginia where Charlotte had grown up on Htrae. Charlotte remembered the beautiful mountains and luscious valleys of her home state, but none were visible now. Everything she saw reminded her of the desolation to land left by strip mining. Charlotte was openly crying, using tissues to wipe her eyes so she could see what was left of West Virginia. Even Lester was choked up, but he calmed himself down and radioed back to Mission Control. "We're now making the turn that will take us to Texas."

CHAPTER EIGHTEEN

Thirty thousand people sat motionless in the auditorium in NASA headquarters, unable to take their eyes off the screen that relayed Earth's appearance. There were occasional profound gasps, and passionate sobbing broke out spontaneously as various landmarks were passed. The reporters would quickly say words into their headset microphones detailing the horrors they were viewing, and their words would appear on the computer screens on their laps. Their stories had to be dictated and published for the next edition of their publication, but no one sitting there felt that words were adequate to describe the devastation they witnessed. They were thankful that the robot cameras were recording the trip and that billions of their brethren around Htrae were watching the event live.

"You're right on target," came the immediate reply to Lester. "According to our radar you are within one thousand miles from where we received the last transmission from Earth. The pictures we are seeing of Earth are amazing. Total wipeout. Total devastation. No life. No vegetation, no water, and no people. Just the monotony of burned wasteland after two thousand years and some dust blowing around. Very hard to understand and to maintain focus with such devastation."

Lester brought the spaceship down to five hundred feet over the earth's surface. They occasionally saw decayed collections of connected bricks or stones where a building had once stood. As they got closer to Plano, Lester put the space ship down to fifty feet above the surface, and they began to see thousands of skeletons below them on the ground. They could make out intact skeletons as well as scattered skulls and unattached bones. Nothing moved. The lack of oxygen slowed the process of decomposition and made the scene eerily unchanged in two millennia. The appearance reminded Gabriel of the time he and Sarah had descended far below ground to see the catacombs in Paris, France. It had been one of the most unusual and riveting experiences of his life. He'd seen skeleton after skeleton stacked one on top of the other. He had read that over six million people's remains were in this narrow system of tunnels.

"I think this is the landing point," Lester said as a large red arrow started blinking in front of him and the Mission Control voice said, "You're there!"

They had picked a field for landing across the street from where the last transmission had come. Charlotte

Traylor had determined that the transmission came from a medical facility since there were pictures from inside the colon. She'd done extensive research on what such facilities might have looked like on Earth and was eager to explore whatever remained underground of this one. One of the last cell phone transmissions they'd received was also from this same facility, but something in the Earth's atmosphere had damaged it and it was not decipherable except for the words "love" and "good-bye."

The spaceship landed with a soft thud on the open field next to the area they would investigate first. The only things that kept the landing from being completely smooth were the piles of skeletons they ran over and the crunching sound it made. Some of the skeletons RC recognized as being from dogs, and she felt herself shiver when she recognized them. It reminded her of the sweet mutt, Mustard, she had bought for her son, Joshua, when the people in charge of the sanitarium suggested that having a dog would help his condition. Joshua had bonded with the dog, until one-day Mustard ran away from them into the street and had been crushed by a speeding auto-plane.

Lester landed the spacecraft perfectly, right on the coordinates that appeared on the screen in front of him. The land around them looked uniform; if he hadn't had the complex guidance system from Htrae, he would never have known where the landing point was. The wheels on the spacecraft had deployed perfectly and the braking mechanism, which included four enormous parachutes at the rear, went into precise position at the optimal time. Lester took off his many protective belts and stood up, facing the others. "Everyone put on your space suits now. Complete radiation protection with both radiation level detectors in place. Also, make sure your helmet's oxygen is working at full capacity and is set for the maximal time limit of twenty-four hours. We don't want any exposure to radioactive or chemically dangerous gases."

Each of them returned to their cabin and put on their gear. They wore several layers which had been tested intensively on Htrae to protect them from radiation and all known toxic gases which their satellites had detected swirling around the Earth and into its atmosphere. Their satellites had detected ricin, mustard gas, lewisite, phosgene, and chloropicrin in various parts of the Earth. Each space suit had its own oxygen system sufficient for twenty-four hours and an emergency tank good for eight hours in case the main one failed. All together they were each wearing over sixty pounds of gear all of which had been produced to fit the exact size of its occupant.

Adonis put his various weapons in different places in his space suit and took out his laser shovel to dig with. Not only was he the crew's security chief, but he was also the strongest and had experience at excavation sites on the planet Htrae. He'd undergone extensive training in archeology at the space academy, and when Htrae received signals that the Earth was subjected to a nuclear holocaust, he was added onto the crew as its fifth member. Besides his weapons, his backpack carried enough explosives to level an area four miles square. Doctor Gold carried smaller weapons but carried all the medical equipment necessary for an emergency on Earth. He had the necessary equipment in his backpack to reproduce an emergency room. They all carried laser shovels, and picks that used diamond heads on rotary blades to cut through the hardest surfaces.

All of them went through checklists to make sure that their equipment was working properly. They tested the equipment themselves and then used a computer scanner which went over their entire bodies and beamed data back to Htrae. They got confirmation from Mission Control that their gear was working properly and was impenetrable by any gas or radiation. The lasers were turned on at the ends of their shovels and they kept the lasers in light-only mode, waiting to turn to cut mode when they reached their destination. The diamond rotary blades were of different sizes, with RC carrying the smallest one that could easily cut through an area the diameter of a human hair. Only Charlotte carried no weapons, digging devices, or medical equipment. Her backpack was filled with three-dimensional computers containing information about Earth and what this last area sending transmissions would look like. She hoped to be able to recreate the ambulatory surgical center the way it had been two thousand years ago. She carried a transmission camera that would send the pictures she took to a data system on the spaceship and then on to Mission Control. She also carried very sensitive instruments that would allow her to determine immediately the age and complete chemical composition of any object she shined them on.

They gathered at the spaceship's entrance, all in full gear including space helmets.

"If everyone is ready, I'm going to open the door," said Lester.

"Ready," said RC Jones.

"Ready two," said Adonis Gonzalez.

"Ready three," said Charlotte Traylor.

"Ready four," said Gabriel Gold.

Lester opened the door by pushing a pneumatic lever. They walked into a staging room that would protect the ship from the Earth's atmosphere. Lester pushed the lever down outside the cabin door, and it slowly shut. They walked across the room to the exit door on the opposite side.

"Ready?" asked Lester. "We've waited two thousand years for this and as your commander I feel the need to say something. Let me tell you that I truly love you all, and I know that by working together and utilizing our individual strengths for the collective good, this mission will be a success. Now, are you ready to find out what brought about the destruction of Earth and what intelligence we can take from this planet to our own planet?" he asked.

"I'm ready," said Adonis as he shifted the large shovel from his right to his left arm. The shovel was his heaviest piece of equipment and contained the largest cutting laser they had brought with them. Dr. Gold, Lester, and RC also carried this type of shovel, but were half the size of Adonis'. On his back Adonis had a portable flame thrower, a two-foot long machine gun that could fire up to five hundred rounds a minute, and a no-recoil shoulder held missile launcher, all of which he could access by pushing the appropriate button on his wrist watch. There had been intense debate about the need for weapons on such a mission. It was decided that if there was other life in the cosmos which had reached Earth, that other planet's inhabitants could be violent and destructive and bent on controlling the universe. Certainly, creatures from that other planet would try to kill them or take them prisoner. Therefore, the weapons were carefully selected and taken.

The other three shouted ready, and the five of them joined their hands together and formed a circle.

Lester shouted, "One, two, three, ready?" and all ten hands went up into the air, and they all shouted, "Ready" again.

Lester also had a machine gun and he carried a portable transmission device which looked like a walkie-talkie so they could stay in contact with Mission Control.

Lester opened the door from the staging room and they all stepped out of the space ship and onto what remained of planet Earth. Immediately they were stunned by the intense heat. Temperature gauges registered one hundred- and thirty-degrees Fahrenheit, but to feel the heat was even more oppressive. The tremendous explosions two thousand years before had destroyed much of Earth's atmosphere and the sunlight penetrated through intensely. Lester looked at the thermometer on his watch-it's reading had now climbed to one hundred- and forty-degrees Fahrenheit.

"Turn your space suits' cooling function up," Lester said, "it's even hotter than we planned for."

Each of them turned their cooling devices to maximum and now the only thing that felt even a little warm was their maximally insulated feet. They were equipped with special boots that protected their feet against the burning core heat of the earth, but it still felt a little warm, like bare feet on the sun-soaked sand of a beach.

There was nothing moving around them. There were no colors; everything was black. No trees, sidewalks, human beings. Skeletons and parts of skeletons were strewn about, some with hands still raised towards the sky. On one of the skeletons there appeared to be the remnants of a shirt caught between the clavicle and scapula. They saw that this skeleton was intact from the waist up but had no leg bones visible. There was no wind to blow anything around, so what they saw in every direction remained constant.

"Mission Control, we are out of the space ship and walking in the direction you are showing me on my helmet screen," said Lester. The other four astronauts looked at Lester's helmet and could see a television screen inside it which was showing pictures taken from the camera on top of Lester's helmet. Mission Control, the reporters in the auditorium, and the entire planet of Htrae could now see what the five astronauts saw. Mission Control was mapping out the directions in red lines across the Earth's surface that the crew was to follow. The other four followed Lester. They went several hundred feet and then turned north. They walked a total of a quarter mile and each constantly looked in every direction for any sign of life. Everything was gone. Only the gray-white of the skeleton parts broke the monotony.

They reached the area where the red line on Lester's television screen stopped. There was a loud beep and then a picture of Commander Meyer from Mission Control came on Lester's screen.

"This is Mission Control. You are now standing directly over the area where we received the last television transmission inside the human colon from Earth. We picked this site to start your exploration since it's the last known location of anything living on the planet. Since it is a medical facility, let me remind you to be on the lookout for anything medically related that may advance our knowledge on Htrae. Good luck in your exploration of the site. We are monitoring all five of your helmet cameras, so we will see things as you do. Hopefully you won't step in any shit. Get it, last pictures came from the colon, and shit? Sorry, just a poor excuse for an attempt at humor."

The audience roared with laughter.

Lester looked down at the scorched ground beneath his feet. He kicked off the dust and there was something hard just below the surface. He used his laser shovel to dig out an area about four feet by four feet and found what appeared to be a pile of Formica tables buried just below the surface.

"Should we continue digging here?" Lester asked Charlotte.

"From my re-creations of the endoscopy centers used on earth two thousand years ago, certainly Formica tables would have been utilized to hold computers and other equipment. I think this is where we should start. Do you confirm that Mission Control?"

"Confirmed," came the reply. "Start digging and I'll watch with you along with the seven billion people on our planet who will be watching your every move."

In the auditorium Barry whispered to Doug, "This is the most incredible thing I've ever seen. I'm activating my waste disposal system so I won't have to miss anything by going to the bathroom."

Barry pushed a button on his lapel and then pulled the lever that made up his right arm rest. His seat elevated two feet into the air. There was the sound of the bottom of his pants opening just as a drape came down from inside his jacket to cover his private parts. The sound proof and odor proof disposal system came out of the chair and Barry silently emptied his bladder and rectum of their contents. A blue liquid containing both antibacterial solution and soap washed his anus and then heat radiated against his anus until it was dry. He pulled the lever back and first the disposal system silently disappeared and then the seat went back down to its normal height. The bottom of his pants slid back together and fastened into place.

"Now I'm comfortable and ready for whatever happens next," Barry whispered.

Doug nodded and wiped his brow with his sleeve. "Getting a little hot in here," he said, although he knew he was sweating from watching the intense drama unfolding on the huge screen in front of them. He pulled the left armrest towards him and the portable air-conditioning unit built into the seat in front of him turned on silently and began to envelop him in cool air.

"Just watching the astronauts and hearing the heat they're experiencing makes me hot," Doug explained to Barry. "So glad I chose as my career to report on the news and not make the news. I can't imagine going through what those five have gone through. And who knows what they'll find and what they'll be like in two thousand plus years when they return to our planet."

"Couldn't agree with you more," replied Barry. "Those five are the cream of the crop of humans on our planet and they're risking their lives to try and make our lives better. Great humanity on their parts, but not something I'd want to experience. I hope and pray they make it back to Htrae in one piece. They will all be heroes on this planet, no matter what happens. I've heard that they're already working on a huge mountain sculpture in South Dakota with all five of their faces etched into the stone. Looks like they've started working on excavating that site."

CHAPTER NINETEEN

All of them except Charlotte pulled their laser shovels out of their backpacks and began digging. Within an hour they had created an opening twelve feet in diameter and six feet deep. By the remnants of destroyed equipment they confirmed that it was, indeed, a medical facility. RC found the colonoscope, which was largely intact, at her end of the hole. She dug further, following the course of the colonoscope and could see it was leading to something several feet down in the debris.

They dug deeper and deeper. Lester saw something moving in the corner of their excavation site. He laughed and pointed to where he had seen the movement. He said, "Look, they have cockroaches here, too. They can survive a nuclear holocaust."

Charlotte laughed and said, "I once debated that very point in an advanced biology class at the University of Virginia. I said the cockroaches would outlive us all but the professor took the opposite side. He reasoned that the more complex the organism, the longer it would live and the more catastrophes it would be able to adapt to. To his way of thinking, survival was all a matter of brains and adaptability. I argued that the cockroaches had been around since the dinosaurs and have been able to adapt to any environment, from the cold North Pole to the heat of the tropics. Too bad he's not around two thousand years later to learn how wrong he was."

They dug deeper and now there were cockroaches everywhere in the hole. They had to brush the roaches off their spacesuits, and each of them shuddered as they did so. The radiation had caused the mutation of the DNA of the cockroaches and many were the size of a man's fist. Some had small claws instead of front legs. They paused to watch one of the giant cockroaches have sex with a medium-size cockroach and then eat it in one gulp.

"That must have been the female cockroach doing the eating," Charlotte said. "Good sex drive and good appetite."

"Sounds like me," Adonis joked as he kept working.

After a few hours they took a break and put their laser shovels down.

"This may be all we'll do today," said Lester. "I don't want anyone to get too worn out on the first day of our expedition."

RC replied, "I know we've been working for hours, Lester, but I think we're close to something important.

I'd hate to see something happen to cover this site before we return tomorrow. We've got plenty of oxygen. Let's break for fifteen minutes and then try to dig further."

"All right," said Lester, "if the rest of you agree."

They all nodded in agreement.

"Mission Control, we are taking a fifteen-minute break," Lester said into his head set.

"Roger that, Lester," the voice from Mission Control came back. "Your transmission has been perfect and the pictures amazing. We'll wait for you to resume your excavation."

When they started again, they were about twelve feet below ground level. They had not come across the roof or the outer shell of the building that had been there; they assumed it had disintegrated. But they saw pieces of what appeared to be acoustical tile and the remnants of the outer wall of the room they were seeking. As they resumed digging, Charlotte constantly consulted her notes and the drawings of the building they were excavating.

Suddenly Lester's shovel hit something of a different texture. "Stop, look here!" he said, "I think I'm on top of skeletal remains."

They all switched to their diamond rotary blades and began digging carefully around the skeletons. They used the sharper, more focused diamond rotary blades to carefully separate the skeletons from the immense debris.

Finally, they unearthed five intact skeletons all within five feet of each other including the one that had the colonoscope exiting its buttocks. This was the colonoscope whose controls RC had found higher in the excavation. They kept working until all five skeletons were completely free and lay on the ground next to them. The skeletons' hands were empty except for one. Dr. Gold carefully examined the skeleton holding a folder in its right hand. He could tell from the size and shape of the pelvis that this skeleton had been a female. As they carefully pulled the dirt off her, they could see that somehow the pale red folder she held was completely intact.

Lester tried to take the folder gently out of her hand, but the skeleton's hand held tight, as if it didn't want to let go. He pulled harder and got the hand to release the folder. He handed it to Charlotte Traylor.

"What do you make of this?" he asked. "It looks like the kind of folder school children on Htrae used in ancient times before everything in education was computerized and digitalized."

Mrs. Traylor opened the folder. Inside was a white page with a few lines made by a thick, black pen. "I can't read what it says yet," she said," but it looks like it was written with a powerful marking pen since some of the lines have lasted two thousand years. I brought chemicals along that I can brush the paper with and that may reveal its meaning."

She reached into her bag and took out a box filled with small, labelled bottles and varying sizes of paint brushes. She opened a bottle labelled "Print Restoration Dye" and dipped a brush with medium bristles into it. She swirled the brush around the bottle so that it was completely saturated with the liquid. "This has worked on documents I've found where the writing disappeared over time. Let's see if it will work its magic here on Earth."

She started at the top of the paper and with broad confident strokes covered the entire white page with the resinous goo. "It's in English as I expected," Mrs. Traylor said, "I've almost got it to where I can read it." She pushed a button on her helmet and accessed a bright spotlight that she adjusted to illuminate the paper with ultraviolet light.

The other four gathered around Mrs. Traylor and looked as the words slowly emerged from the brittle page. Billions on the planet Htrae were glued to their television screens as they saw the document framed by Charlotte's helmet camera.

The five astronauts read the paper together. "What Is the Meaning of Life?" they shouted in unison.

Dr. Gold chimed in, "We have found one document in all these ruins. We knew that the people on Earth, destroyed the planet themselves, not an asteroid or comet. Now we may have the answer why: They didn't know the meaning of life."

Lester said, "Maybe that's why our planet has been so successful and so advanced compared to Earth. And why we never reached this point of destruction. We all know the meaning to life. We're taught the meaning to life at a young age and reminded of it throughout our lifetimes. Like on planet Earth, it has been debated since the beginning of time, but the consensus has held for the last ten thousand years."

"That's right," agreed Adonis, "that's what makes our planet so loving and that's how we've been able to advance so far in every field of endeavor. We're all taught the meaning to life and we adhere to it."

"We have one religion," said Mrs. Traylor, "and I know from my interpretation of data we received from the planet Earth that they had many religions which often fought with each other. As you already know, our one religion is named 'The Religion' and it's a combination of their Judaism, Christianity, Islam, Buddhism, and Hinduism. 'The Religion' helps us work together to improve ourselves and our world. It's led to great advances in science, medicine, art, architecture and every other discipline. It's why we live to an average life expectancy of one hundred and forty years while my data suggests people on this planet died in their seventies and eighties. That's right, they had only half of our life expectancy. It's the reason we were able to develop the technology necessary to receive and interpret messages from Earth and now why we're able to complete a mission over two thousand years in the making covering over two hundred million light years in distance."

"By the way," piped in Mission Control, "Our average life expectancy is now well over two hundred years and many have lived to three hundred years on Htrae."

"The meaning to life," said Lester, "is that we are all family. Each of us on our planet, whether we are black, yellow, white, or brown, all come from the same place. We treat one another like loving siblings, children, or parents. The meaning to life is that we are all equally in this experience together. We are all one family."

Adonis continued. "We had our great prophets: Moses, Jesus, Muhammad, Buddha. They all preached the same message—we are all one family and one people. They preached we should never enslave or cause harm to our fellow human beings. Jesus, my personal favorite, preached about the importance of loving everyone as a brother and turning the other cheek when wronged. He said that we must all follow 'The Religion.' Then Muhammad added to this and spoke of how we could create a world that welcomed everyone and helped everyone. They all preached the importance of living life to the fullest, enjoying each moment, and creating an environment of peace and love. Certainly, each of the great prophets could have left 'The Religion' and sought to develop their own teachings and their own following.

Instead, they chose to bring new ideas and laws to better 'The Religion' and not to divide it into competing ideologies."

"My favorite, or course, is Buddha," said Mrs. Traylor. "His advice, 'Do not dwell in the past, do not dream of the future, concentrate the mind on the present moment,' has been one of the cornerstones of my life. He also said, 'All that we are is the result of what we have thought,' which I think is so important since anyone can rise above their circumstances and accomplish greatness."

"We have different countries on our planet which correspond exactly to the countries on Earth," said RC, "but we all get along together and treat one another with respect and dignity. Even though we speak different languages and have different cultures, we all choose to communicate in a peaceful and harmonious fashion with each other."

"Just like Muhammad preached, wealth accumulation isn't a goal for us," said Mrs. Traylor. "Helping each other to achieve, to excel, to live a full and happy life, that's what all the great prophets told us is our goal. I could never have children of my own, but I wanted our planet to be better and stronger because I'm a strict follower of 'The Religion.' I truly believe that we are all one family and there is no time or place for bigotry or hatred, but only for love. In fact, although I loved my husband for forty years, I have double that amount of love left over for him."

"Moses is a personal favorite of mine," said Dr. Gold. "Among all the great prophets I think he trusted God implicitly and believed In God's great power to help us all. He taught me that no odds are too great to overcome and that there is always light at the end of the darkest day. He showed that a plain man with a stutter could act as God's messenger. Plus, he preached that although we all believe in one God or a supreme being that watches over us all, there is a little bit of God in each of us. We can never forget that we are made in God's image and that He trusts us to carry on his righteousness and goodness on Htrae."

They stood silently for a moment, taking in a scene that had been frozen for two thousand years. All of them shook their heads at what they beheld and then bowed their heads in silent prayer. They prayed to God and each also prayed to the prophets who had influenced them the most and who had brought the most meaning to their lives.

CHAPTER TWENTY

They raised their heads and looked lovingly at one another. Clumsily they hugged one another through their space suits and then had a group hug. They shared their deepest thoughts and emotions with each other. After this communing of minds, Lester spoke to Htrae.

"Mission Control, I think we found out why Earth was destroyed. Certain groups used religion as an excuse to hate and as an excuse to destroy the entire planet. The years that we followed Earth we received these messages of hatred, violence, and destruction, and now we know why. They never knew the meaning to life. They never understood that we are all the same. They utilized the teachings of the greatest and most pure human beings in the most destructive of ways. If they had understood that we're all one family, this never would have happened and we would be rejoicing now with our family on another planet instead of looking at their bones scattered everywhere."

The five of them stood in their space suits looking down at the five poor skeletons buried so close together.

Charlotte said, "The fact that these skeletons are so close together is intriguing. Almost like they were huddled over something trying to protect it. That one skeleton with the colonoscope hanging out its ass, I wonder if she was the patient and they were trying to protect her in the end. Maybe they were doing the procedure on her, tried to protect her, but somehow the explosion caused the controls of the colonoscope to land in a higher part of this excavation. The four of them appear to have been performing a noble act at the end, by trying to save their patient's life. I'm amazed that the procedure was continued even though they had to know their world was ending," she added as she knocked a large cockroach off her face shield.

Gabriel laughed, "Maybe she was higher-born so her pelvis with the attached colonoscope ended up higher in the ground. By higher-born I mean richer. Poor joke, sorry. But in my readings about Earth there was so much information about the importance of wealth and how that was prized above everything, including intelligence and empathy. Being rich was the one common goal for the people of Earth, and in the end, that was truly useless. The rich died just like the poor and their graves are the open dust which is all that is left of this planet. If you were rich on Earth, I read, you were treated with tremendous respect and reverence. If you were poor, you were often ignored and treated horribly. They even allowed the poor to live on the street without any shelter. An abomination!

"I also found tremendous variation in how the different doctors on Earth perceived their jobs and their responsibilities. I was given a phone communication from a gastroenterologist on Earth arguing with a pathologist about the results of biopsies that the gastroenterologist had done. The pathologist said the biopsies wouldn't be back for a couple of weeks since they were concerned about diagnosing lymphoma of the colon which requires special stains. The pathologist added that since it was a holiday weekend and they were also closed on Monday the wait would be even longer than usual. The gastroenterologist yelled at the pathologist and asked him how he'd like it if he were the patient waiting for results that could be life-altering. Certainly, the pathologist would want to know his diagnosis as soon as possible. The pathologist took it all in stride, never raised his voice, and said, 'we're the only game in town so you'll just have to wait,' and hung up. They really had a sharp distinction in where their loyalties lay depending on what field of medicine they practiced."

RC removed the colonoscope from the female skeleton and said, "Wonder what they could have been looking for that kept them looking at her colon so long after their fate had been sealed? Did they hope to find something in there that would allow them to survive this holocaust?"

Dr. Gold said, "I expect they were medical professionals like me who were unwilling to leave a patient until they knew their diagnosis. Mission control was still uploading the last pictures from the colonoscopy when we left. Nothing that I saw up to that point seemed deadly. We'll contact Mission Control when we get back to our space ship and have them send the last images from the colonoscopy to us so that I can interpret them. Then we'll at least know the answer to the last mystery that these five humans pursued."

CHAPTER TWENTY-ONE

"I think our oxygen is getting low," said RC as she photographed the entire hole they had dug. She took picture after picture of the five skeletons. The four were draped over the fifth, who was the patient and whose lower body had been thrown above the group with the explosion. Then she turned her attention to the walls surrounding them. They were obviously in a procedure room, and some of the walls still contained medical equipment and paraphernalia.

She turned to Mrs. Traylor and asked," What do you think this room looked like before it imploded?"

Mrs. Traylor looked around the hole they were in, and then reached into her bag and pulled out her computer with some notes. It was strange how this whole scene seemed so new and yet, weirdly familiar. She walked over to where she felt the door must have been and looked in the room the way Charlotte Traylor had done from her stretcher two thousand years before.

She pointed to the wall on the right. "There's nothing hanging there now and just rubble below it, but those shards of hardened plastic most likely came from an x-ray screen that was mounted on that wall. A lot of times when they weren't using it to examine x-rays, they'd post important signs on the screen like how to do CPR or how to press on the abdomen to advance the colonoscope. They had a whole science dedicated to maneuvering the scope around the colon. It involved a series of pushing the scope forward and pulling back, placing pressure on different parts of the abdomen and then releasing that pressure. There was always a crash cart in each room fully loaded and ready to go, and I think that might be a broken paddle off the crash cart lying with the shards of plastic from the X-Ray screen."

Doctor Gold patted his backpack. "That looks a heck of a lot different than the crash cart I have in here," he said.

Charlotte looked to her left. "This side probably contained a desk since there's still a broken desk top here. I wouldn't be surprised if the wires coming out of the wall were from a telephone. They still used copper wires to transmit signals on Earth, not ultrasonic waves like on Htrae."

"Now, on that back wall you can still see another Formica table top. Those things are indestructible. The upside-down, broken stool with wheels suggests to me that this area was where the gastroenterologist sat as the patient was being sedated for the procedure. There's a corroded computer tower in the mess over there which the doctor could use to bring up records on the patient. They still used computers on earth to access records and hadn't advanced to our level of flexible, easily replaceable silicon chips implanted in the body. As you know, our doctors can just scan the chips and immediately bring up a hologram which contains all the information regarding a patient's health and past medical history. The hologram can immediately deliver all the patient's current blood test results as well as revealing information like how much alcohol the patient has consumed in the last hour, week, or even in their lifetime. The hologram scans the patient's body in milliseconds to reveal what surgeries were done and how successfully. Within seconds, our holograms deliver everything that needs to be known about a patient's health and they have a great accuracy rate in diagnosing what is wrong with the patient."

She walked over to the side of the room. "There are scraps of latex lying on top of the Formica. They used gloves made of latex for their procedures, so this is where they were stored. They also used latex to manufacture condoms, sheaths that went over the male penis for birth control. The sperm couldn't penetrate the latex. They didn't have chip birth control perfected to the level that we do. They relied on less reliable means, which often led to unwanted pregnancies if the condom malfunctioned. Since their birth control system wasn't perfect and often no birth control was used, they practiced abortion on this planet where unwanted fetuses were destroyed before birth. Anyway, I digress. The doctor could read about the patient on the computer, and then put on his gloves and if he chose, a gown, right here. On Earth, like on our planet, the computer was a big deal and revolutionized the treatment of patients and the practice of medicine. I think overall computers were a good thing, although I constantly received messages from nurses in the hospitals saying that their jobs no longer involved taking care of the patient, but, rather, filling out the required information on the computer. Many nurses would spend up to four hours of their eight-hour shifts sitting over the computer filling out screen after screen of information that was useless to anyone except the hospital administrators. The administrators could point to the nurses' prolific output on the computer and report to the insurance companies that their patients were being well taken care of, when only the computer screen was well taken care of."

"I learned in nursing school how important it is to interact with the patient," said RC. "So much of getting a patient well involves talking to them and finding out their expectations and needs. On Earth the nurses wanted to do that, I'm sure, but they were limited by the responsibility of typing useless forms into their computer. Believe it or not, while training for this expedition I came across a nursing note from Earth that contained ten pencil-drawn human faces containing eyes, noses, ears, and mouths in various expressions depending on the degree of pain the patient was in during their shift. The nurse actually had to pick one of the faces to describe the patient and then detail why her choice wasn't the happiest face if she hadn't chosen that one."

Mrs. Traylor nodded at RC and then walked over to the far side of the room from the entrance. "If you look here, you see a broken platform and crushed machinery." She took a moment to pull another of her computers out of her bag. She scrolled to a page containing drawings and studied them carefully. "Almost certainly, this was the power source for the scope and was what the scope plugged into to enable it to examine the intestinal tract. Most likely there were also controls for suction, water, and air on this wall. The suction container probably hung on the wall, and the air probably came from that large tank we've uncovered here."

She took a rag from her bag and started cleaning off the large gas tank which was lying on its side. "I beg your pardon," she said, "it says CO_2. They must have used carbon dioxide instead of just air to inflate the bowel. Would you agree?" she asked Dr. Gold.

Dr. Gold laughed and said, "I've practiced gastroenterology for close to thirty years, and scopes like this that fed to a high-definition television screen went out approximately one hundred and fifty years before I started practice. This is all like a museum to me. From what I've read, though, I think your depiction of this room is accurate. The television that they viewed the intestine on probably sat here," he pointed to a place in the room across from where the scope plugged in, "and the patient's stretcher sat in between the doctor and the television with the business end of the patient facing the doctor. We all know that CO_2 is more easily absorbed into the tissues than air, so using CO_2 left the patient with less distention of the bowel and less discomfort after the colonoscopy was performed. This signifies a great advance on Earth."

"How long has it been since we used scopes like this on Htrae?" asked Lester.

"Nano-technology and robotic controls replaced scopes like this before I started to practice," answered Dr. Gold. "I can use a nanorobot and send him up into the colon. Not only does he find the polyp or precancerous growth, but he also instantly determines if it is cancerous, pre-cancerous, or benign by reading its histology. If it's pre-cancerous or cancerous, the nanorobot immediately calculates the amount and trajectory of laser needed to remove the growth. It then lasers off the growth and brings it back out of the anus in a matter of seconds. I can do five to ten colonoscopies at once by standing at a control station and monitoring my nanorobots. If someone is bleeding internally I can send up nanorobots from the anus for a lower gastrointestinal bleed or from the mouth for an upper intestinal bleed. The robots are equipped with all the tools necessary to stop internal bleeding anywhere. They even have laser vision that can penetrate through puddles of blood, find the bleeding source, and then fix it. And don't forget, this was the technology present on our planet two thousand years ago. Who knows what amazing advances have been made since then."

"That's about everything that I can tell you about this room, now," said Mrs. Traylor. "Their technology was far behind ours, but it was rapidly improving. Medicine was a big business, especially in the United States. They used a significant portion of their country's wealth on medical care, most of it in the last six months of a patient's life when such costly treatments should never have been used. The lawyers in the United States also ratcheted up the cost of health care by suing doctors for malpractice when there were bad outcomes. The doctors covered their asses by ordering way too many tests including x-rays and invasive studies. The other big driver of the cost of medicine here on Earth was what they called the health insurance companies but which I like to call the 'unhealthy insurance companies.' Unlike on Htrae where everyone gets insurance that is paid for out of their taxes and so is affordable to all, here in America a group of companies gained control of the health care system and ran it into the ground. These health insurance companies' sole mission was to enrich themselves. Their executives made millions of dollars that should have been spent on the patient or distributed to all the health care providers. These insurance companies even interfered with the practice of medicine by dictating what drugs the doctors could prescribe or how often particular tests could be done. In America, the dynamic was health care providers and patients versus health insurance companies.

On the positive side, many internet posts that I received said that their amount of knowledge in medicine doubled every five years here on Earth. There were dedicated scientists and researchers who wanted to make a difference and wanted to improve the human condition. They would have fit in well on our planet."

"Do you think where I'm standing now," asked Adonis, walking to a place in the room where the head of the stretcher would have been, "is where the anesthesiologist would have stood?"

"I do," answered Mrs. Traylor. "They would have had monitoring devices to monitor the blood pressure, pulse, oxygen saturation, and carbon dioxide output all situated in a place where they could easily read them. They did everything possible to make the procedures as safe as possible for their patients."

"Except for preventing a nuclear holocaust," said Dr. Gold off-handedly. "Sorry, wasn't thinking about what I was saying. Of course, with our nanorobots, we don't need anesthesiologists present to monitor the patients while they undergo endoscopic procedures. The patients just watch television or listen to the radio while the bots do their thing as I monitor them. I've seen college students write papers, lawyers write briefs, detectives review their evidence, and teachers develop their lesson plans all while undergoing colonoscopy on Htrae."

They all grew silent and looked around the room, taking in the details that Charlotte had just pointed out and imagining what life would have been like here two thousand years before. Dr. Gold thought it was ironic that they had unearthed five skeletons in the endoscopy room and there were five of them on this mission. The breakdown by sex, two women and three men, was also identical to their crew.

Breaking the silence, Lester said, "I bet the radiation content of these bones is astronomical." He pulled out a portable Geiger counter and quickly confirmed what he had just said. "It's time to go back to our spaceship. It would be dangerous to our health to bring these five skeletons back on board. We'll return here tomorrow before we head off to visit other sites on Earth. Hopefully a storm won't come up and ruin the work that we've done. We've got a busy schedule ahead of us: New York City, Los Angeles, Chicago in the United States and then off to Mexico, Central America, and South America. After that we'll go to Antarctica, London, Paris, and Russia before heading to Africa and Japan, China, and Korea. We'll finish in Australia. We want to see all seven continents and learn as much as possible about Earth."

"I need their teeth," said Mrs. Traylor, "for a DNA study. The pulp will have the most intact DNA. I brought along special dental devices to extract a few teeth from each of the skeletons. The teeth are very radioactive but are small enough that they'll fit into the special safe containers I brought along. When we get back to Htrae, I'll analyze the DNA from the subjects we find and see how it differs from ours. I'll also be able to tell if there are any genetic diseases that they still had floating around that we were able to cure in the distant past with gene therapy. I'll look for mutations and will be able to accurately predict from their genetic profile what each of their life expectancies would have been on Earth. If it's agreeable to our government and to the governments of our world, we could use this DNA to clone these humans and allow them to live on our planet. However, this is probably far-fetched since this DNA has been in the presence of intense radiation for two thousand years and may be badly damaged."

"That sounds a little creepy," said Gabriel Gold. "That part about cloning them. Bringing one of these Earth skeletons back to life sounds risky to me. The government will only let us use cloning to replace body parts or organs of our people. As a scientist and a doctor, I would favor it, but as an inhabitant on a planet that has done so well for so long, I think it could be dangerous. Do we really want to mix our DNA with the DNA of a civilization so far behind us in every way and so destructive? A civilization that was around for thousands of years but never understood the true meaning of life?"

"You're probably right," nodded Mrs. Traylor. "But those decisions aren't for us to decide tonight." She handed each of them a pair of pliers and showed them how to grip a tooth with the pliers and then extract it along with its pulp by pushing a button on the handle of the pliers.

Each of them took one of the skeletons and began extracting its teeth and placing them in a special DNA preservative bag which was impenetrable by radiation. They didn't know it, but by chance each of them was working on the skeleton who shared their name and appearance when they were alive two thousand years before. Each of them cradled the head of their skeleton carefully as they worked on extracting the few teeth. They took the teeth but avoided harming the skeletons or doing anything to disrupt their burial site.

Dr. Gold said to the group, "I wonder if this skeleton was the gastroenterologist? His neck is so arthritic, I wonder if he trained on scopes like we have in our science museums. You know, the ones that are like a microscope and have a lens at the top that you strain your neck to look through. I have read history books that many of the doctors on our planet who practiced gastroenterology with these scopes had to retire early due to neck issues. Many suffered from chronic neck pain and even had to get their neck vertebrae fused."

Dr. Gonzalez said, "My skeleton was middle-aged and had dental implants. There may not be as much pulp to extract. He must have really cared about his looks. Judging by the condition of his skeleton, he took good care of himself."

RC laughed. "Well my skeleton is smaller and has the pelvis of a female. I wonder if she was a nurse like me since a higher percentage of the doctors on Earth were men. Plus, she was holding the folder containing the paper asking for the meaning to life. That suggests that she may not have been as actively involved in the procedure but was monitoring the procedure and the patient from a desk."

Lester looked at his skeleton as he removed the teeth. "Don't know what to say about my skeleton other than he looks about the same size as me. He may have been a doctor also, or possibly a technician helping the doctor. He has a relatively large cranium; probably was brilliant like me."

They all laughed.

"And I'm left to remove the patient's teeth," said Charlotte. "Hard to deduce much about her other than she must have been very important for them to work on her so diligently when they knew their time was up. She may have been rich, since that's the one thing we know the people of Earth cherished above all else. She may have died while under anesthesia and never known what her fate was to be. Probably never had the chance to say good-bye to her loved ones, her husband and children."

Just then they heard a scratching noise from behind the wall nearest Charlotte. Charlotte jumped forward as a long, black rod pushed her in the back.

"Must be a limb of a tree we unearthed" Charlotte started, but then she screamed. The rod began wrapping itself around Charlotte's body.

"It's an enormous insect antenna," shouted Lester.

Charlotte screamed, "Help me!" just as a gigantic claw pushed down the rest of the wall and an enormous cockroach entered the room. It was at least twenty feet in size and had two ten-foot lobster-like claws. The left claw suddenly rose up from the ground and reached out and clenched Charlotte by the neck.

Adonis pushed a button on his wrist watch and immediately held a missile launcher in his hands. He fired at the yellow band that outlined the area behind the head of the mutated cockroach, and it reared back on four of its six legs, releasing Charlotte's neck from its claw and pulling its antenna from her body. Charlotte was bleeding massively from a gash in her neck, and her helmet and upper space suit was ripped off by the withdrawing claw as she fell to the ground unconscious. The cockroach reached out for Adonis with its other claw, but Adonis hit the claw repeatedly with the back of the missile launcher, causing the cockroach to move back for an instant. At the same time, Lester sprayed the cockroach's body with machine gun fire.

As the cockroach reached out, trying to locate Adonis with its antenna, Adonis launched a missile that landed directly on the cockroach's enormous head. The head flew off and hit the wall, spraying the cockroach's brain all over the wall. The headless cockroach slumped to the ground. Even with their protective space suits, the repulsive smell of cockroach brain soon permeated the room.

"Holy shit!" cried RC. "It could have killed us all. We need to help Charlotte immediately."

Gabriel got out his medical equipment and used his hands to examine the gaping opening into Charlotte's neck. The bleeding was coming from a punctured carotid artery. The hole was small enough that the blood just came out in slight gushes, but he could already tell the amount of blood loss had been staggering.

Gabriel took a vascular repair kit, which had been invented to repair defects like this one, from his supplies. "Hold her neck's skin apart," he shouted to RC, as he began to work. He placed the sheathed stent from the kit inside the defect and then used the controls to maneuver the sheath up and down until the stent was in position to cover the entire defect. He pushed a button on the control unit he held in his hand and the stent was deployed. The bleeding stopped. The sheath over the stent retracted into his control kit.

"Got it," Gabriel announced.

Adonis quickly made his way over to where Charlotte was lying. "Can you feel a pulse. Is she breathing?" he gasped.

"Very weak, thready pulse. Breathing is now agonal. Can you intubate her, Adonis, and start a line so we can pump blood into her?" asked Gabriel.

Gabriel handed Adonis the intubation equipment out of the medical backpack and Adonis quickly got an endotracheal tube into Charlotte's trachea. He began squeezing the Ambu bag. RC and Lester joined them looking down in horror at Charlotte.

"I've got the carotid closed. No more bleeding. RC take over the Ambu bag and Adonis get a line in her so we can start giving her blood. We've got eight units of O negative in my backpack cooler in compression bags. She'll need them all," finished Gabriel.

Charlotte's helmet was now off her head and its camera was turned in the direction where the giant cockroach had been. The coverage being beamed back to Htrae was now coming from Charlotte's head camera.

Back in the NASA auditorium, Doug almost jumped out of his seat. "Fucking hell on Earth!" he yelled, "that monster is still heading towards them! Somebody do something to help them! Please alert them," he screamed.

Just then RC looked up as she was squeezing the Ambu bag and let out a piercing shriek. "It's coming towards us!"

The headless giant cockroach was standing up now and using its antennas to guide itself towards them.

"Fuck," said Lester, "I forgot that cockroaches can live a week without their heads. Give me your flame-thrower, Adonis. I can blast it while you work on Charlotte."

An antenna circled over Lester's head, and then a claw reached out and grabbed Lester around the waist. He could feel the claw tightening and tightening as he shot it with his laser gun. His legs were going numb, just as Adonis handed him the flamethrower. He fired the flamethrower into the body of the cockroach and smoke began to fill the hole. The cockroach's claw released Lester's body, and he could feel his legs again. The cockroach began flailing around madly with its claws and knocked RC and the Ambu bag ten feet into the air. RC landed on the other side of the hole, stunned and momentarily confused. She regained her bearings and crawled back through the smoke to where Charlotte was and resumed bagging her.

Lester turned the flamethrower up to its highest setting, even though he knew of the danger the larger diameter of fire meant. He was afraid to burn one of his colleagues. He fired into the cockroach's body, and after several seconds, putrid black smoke started pouring out of the cockroach's side. It moved back and flattened itself. Massive wings came out of its sides. It started flapping the wings furiously, blowing fetid smoke into Lester's face and temporarily blinding him.

"I can't stop," shouted Lester as he regained his vision and again fired the flamethrower into the body. "I think it's trying to fly above us and then land on top of us and crush us. I've got to separate the body into pieces and kill it."

Lester continue to fire the flamethrower as the wings flapped madly but the cockroach stayed on the ground. RC picked up Adonis's machine gun with one hand while she bagged Charlotte with the other hand. She fired the gun into the opening where the head had been. They saw the cockroach's wings spasmodically slow down and then stop fluttering and then retract into its body. The cockroach swiped in front of itself one more time with each claw and then quit moving. Tissue in the middle of the body was now burned through completely, and the cockroach's body split in two as it rolled over on its side, dead.

Lester used the largest laser shovel to cut the cockroach into pieces and then joined the other three who were working on Charlotte. Adonis had gotten an IV into Charlotte's right subclavian vein using the ultrasound IV placement system which found the vein and then automatically fired a sheath into it through which fluid and blood could be pumped. Gabriel squeezed the bag of blood as hard as he could to get it to go into Charlotte as quickly as possible. RC was still ventilating her with the Ambu bag, and Adonis had attached a central monitor over her heart to monitor her heart rate, blood pressure, and oxygen saturation. Suddenly the screen showing her heart rate went into ventricular fibrillation, and the blood pressure read "unable to obtain."

"She's in V-Fib," shouted Adonis. "Stand back and I'll shock her."

Adonis removed the black, pencil-sized instrument from the resuscitation kit and placed it over Charlotte's heart. The instrument began to beep at a low frequency as he moved it over her chest, and then beeped slower and louder when it found the SA node, the pacemaker of the heart.

"Clear!" he shouted and everyone stepped back. RC stopped bagging Charlotte. Adonis pushed a tiny red button at the top of the black shaft, and Charlotte's body shot up in the air from the electrical burst. Adonis watched the monitor, which still showed ventricular fibrillation.

"Attach the automatic chest compression device to her and activate it," Adonis shouted to Gabriel, "while I give her antiarrhythmics through her IV."

Gabriel attached the compression device and immediately turned it on. He watched as Charlotte's chest moved up and down. Adonis pushed two antiarrhythmics into the IV. The monitor still showed ventricular fibrillation.

"Everyone back off," shouted Adonis. "I'm going to shock her again."

Adonis put the pencil on Charlotte's chest and waited until the beeping slowed and became louder. "Clear," Adonis shouted as he pushed the red button, defibrillating her again.

Adonis looked at the monitor and Gabriel joined him, having just finished giving her the sixth unit of blood. The monitor now showed asystole, no electrical activity from the heart.

"Let's keep going," said Adonis. "We've got to bring her back. Keep giving her the blood, Gabriel, and put the chest compression device back on her. You keep bagging her, R.C., and I'll give her the code drugs."

"I've already given her six units of blood," said Gabriel. "We may be fighting a losing battle."

Back at Mission Control the auditorium was silent except for the occasional whirring noise of a recording robot moving its head. Crying could be heard throughout the room, and then across the entire planet of seven billion.

Doug Foss was crying and started choking on the snot running down his nose into his mouth. He turned to Barry Grant and choked out, "They've got to save her. They've just got to. She means so much to this mission. It doesn't happen without her. Please let her live."

Barry Grant hugged his friend and colleague to comfort him. His eyes were also red from crying. "They're doing the best they can, and they're both top notch doctors. But the blood loss and now radiation exposure may just be too much to overcome."

On Earth, the crew kept working on Charlotte for an hour, but she never regained a heart rhythm or blood pressure. On the large screen in the NASA auditorium it was painfully apparent that Charlotte's head hung at an unusual angle from the rest of her body. It was obvious that the cockroach's claws had cut through the neck muscles on that side. After an hour, Adonis stopped the chest compression machine and pronounced her dead.

The four of them were in shock. Lester and RC were in significant pain from their encounters with the cockroach, but their spacesuits and protective equipment were intact. No one said a word as they repacked their weapons, digging devices, and medical equipment.

It was dark in the hole now. The only light came from their headlamps. A voice from Lester's radio broke the silence. "Lester, this is Mission Control. We and billions of people on our planet watched your valiant fight against the mutated American cockroach, and your efforts to save Charlotte Traylor. She was a great woman. She devoted her life to this mission, and now she's dead."

Lester was still breathing heavily. "She was amazing," he said. "What a tragedy for her and for all of us. She was willing to leave her life as First Mate and leave the man she loved to accomplish something that would benefit all mankind, and now she's gone."

"Lester, unfortunately with her injuries and loss of protective gear, she's suffered tremendous radiation exposure. She needs to be left there with the skeletons you unearthed. If you brought her back to the space-craft, her radiation would kill all of you."

"How can we leave her here?" cried RC. "She's one of us. I love her." RC put her gloved hands on Charlotte's head and massaged her blood-soaked hair.

"We've got to," answered Adonis. "She'd want us to live and finish the mission. We need to get out of here and go back to the space ship." Adonis gently pulled RC away from Charlotte.

"About that," Mr. Meyer at Mission Control said. "We're going to have to cancel the mission and bring you four back here. It's too dangerous to continue to explore Earth. There are probably mutated giant cock-roaches underground all over, and we can't risk your lives. It's like on Htrae sixty to two hundred and fifty million years ago when the dinosaurs ruled our planet and no human beings existed. It may take millions of years for Earth to become habitable again by humans. Now Earth is controlled by the most repugnant creeping thing that God ever produced, the cockroach. Get back to the spaceship and we'll start working on bringing you home.

CHAPTER TWENTY-TWO

They finished packing their equipment and took one last look at the skeletons, Charlotte, and the pieces of cockroach. The stench from the cockroach parts was overwhelming. Charlotte lay next to the skeleton who had lived on Earth as Charlotte Traylor. By now it was so dark that only the forms outlined by their headlamps could be seen. This was all that was left of the highest form of life on Earth and of their mission's director. They were sure that each of the skeletons had a story to tell, but the further details would have to be gleaned from their DNA. They would leave this burial site like they found it. Before the mission they had met with some of the leading clergy of 'The Religion' who had instructed them to do nothing that would desecrate any part of Earth or its dead.

They'd also been instructed on the elaborate burial practices on Earth and the value that people on Earth placed on the afterlife. On Htrae 'The Religion' said that nothing was known about the afterlife. Although they all hoped for a next phase after death, they were more concerned with enjoying their lives and working to make their planet into a place where all could live good lives. The afterlife was talked about and debated by some of the most brilliant minds, but they had been taught by the great prophets that since the afterlife would forever be unknown, all effort should be spent enjoying and improving their daily lives.

The four astronauts climbed out of the giant hole and began using their shovels to put dirt back into the hole and cover it entirely. RC and Lester cried as they saw the dirt cover Charlotte. It took over an hour, but when they were done, no trace of the endoscopy center remained in view and the burial site was as close to its original condition as possible. The skeletons were back in the positions in which they had been found, missing only a few of their teeth, and Charlotte's skeleton no longer contained the colonoscope.

They silently began the long walk back to their spaceship. A line of dead cockroaches extended from where the hole had been almost all the way to the spaceship. At first, they saw the small cockroaches, but as they got nearer to the spaceship they found some as large as a basketball. All had lobster claws and all had died from exposure to the aboveground radiation and chemicals.

They looked up at the sky and saw the millions of stars and knew that somewhere beyond those stars was their planet. They helped each other clean the dirt off their space suits and continued to walk back to their spaceship. They were hungry and tired and mournful. Each recited a silent prayer thanking God for letting them live through their battle. Each prayed for Charlotte and remembered her brilliance and kindness. Lester and RC joined hands, and then RC took Adonis's hand and he grabbed Gabriel's hand. The four of them walked back to their spaceship linked by their hands. The only light was provided by the headlamps on their helmets and the Earth's moon, which was full on this night.

In the end
only three things
matter: how much
you loved
how gently you
lived, and how
gracefully you let
go of things not
meant for you.

—Buddha

ACKNOWLEDGEMENTS

There are several people I must acknowledge for their help in making this book a reality. First, I need to thank the world's greatest PR person, Diane Feffer, for all of her help. Diane helped from start to finish, from trying to retrieve a lost copy of the manuscript on the computer to finding a publishing company. Diane, your knowledge of so many things in this world constantly amazes me. I would also like to thank Amy Rogers for doing the first edit of this book and for all of her ideas and corrections. I want to thank Kim Downes, the world's wittiest nurse anesthetist, for coming up with the title for the book. My medical assistant and computer genius, Kerri Buffington deserves thanks for constantly helping me solve computer issues as I wrote and re-wrote and re-wrote this manuscript. A round of applause to Wendy Thornton and Sarah Spencer at Gatekeeper Press for the final editing and publication expertise. Finally, I'd like to thank artist and friend Marion Wilner for allowing me to use the description of one of her paintings in this book.

Please share your thoughts about IN THE END. You can do this by scanning the QR code (below) with your smartphone. This will take you directly to Dr. Weisberg's Amazon page where you can post a review.

Made in the USA
Coppell, TX
16 April 2022

76695511R00203